Red Snow Bride

(Wolf Brides Series, Book 2)

By T. S. Joyce

Red Snow Bride
ISBN-13: 978-1503136908
ISBN-10: 1503136906
Copyright © 2014, T. S. Joyce
First electronic publication: November 2014

T. S. Joyce
www.tsjoycewrites.wordpress.com

All Rights Are Reserved. No part of this book may be used or reproduced in any manner whatsoever without written permission, except in the case of brief quotations embodied in critical articles and reviews. The unauthorized reproduction or distribution of this copyrighted work is illegal. No part of this book may be scanned, uploaded or distributed via the Internet or any other means, electronic or print, without the author's permission.

NOTE FROM THE AUTHOR:
This book is a work of fiction. The names, characters, places, and incidents are products of the writer's imagination or have been used fictitiously and are not to be construed as real. Any resemblance to persons, living or dead, actual events, locale or organizations is entirely coincidental. The author does not have any control over and does not assume any responsibility for third-party websites or their content.

Published in the United States of America

First digital publication: November 2014
First print publication: November 2014

Other Books by T. S. Joyce

Wolf Brides
Wolf Bride
Dawson Bride

Bear Valley Shifters
The Witness and the Bear
Devoted to the Bear
Return to the Bear
Betray the Bear
Redeem the Bear

Hells Canyon Shifters
Call of the Bear
Fealty of the Bear
Avenge the Bear

Chapter One
Lorelei

"Are you all right, my love?" I asked Daniel. He'd been quiet all evening which was very uncharacteristic of my usually boisterous spouse.

His blond hair threw threads of golden color under the extravagant crystal chandelier, and his blue eyes were like ice frozen into his pale skin. A fine sheen of sweat dusted his brow, and I frowned as his gaze settled on me without really seeing me. Maybe he was ill or perhaps he was having a vision of his time in the war again. Those came frequently in recent months. Or maybe it was just more of the same, ignoring me because he found me useless in some way or another.

The Countess Delecroix d'Maine sat next to me and touched me lightly on the arm with her gloved hand. "And so I said, 'Well get them to the ships then. Get them all to the ships!'"

The dining room exploded with delighted laughter and some small applause, but I still couldn't manage to take my eyes away from Daniel. Something cold moved within my center, like some long buried instinct that told me to run.

The clamor quieted down as my husband rose with a toasting glass and spoon in his hand. "I have an announcement to make to you, all of our dearest friends."

Twelve sets of dancing eyes settled on him as he made a tinkling sound against his crystal glass. The delicate noise was quite beautiful.

Richard Pratter, who sat at the end of the table with his fiancé, lifted his glass. "After a year of marriage, have you finally an announcement of the next heir to the Delaney fortune?"

The crowd burst into a happy murmur, and I wrenched my hands under the table. Giving Daniel a son would be wonderful, but he hadn't visited my bed in months, and even when he'd done so before that, I was quite convinced we were doing everything wrong. No, there was no child growing in my belly to announce.

Daniel laughed but it sounded forced with an edge of cruelty. "No, something much better is happening."

Richard's deep-set eyebrows turned down. "Well, tell us, Delaney. What could be better than an heir?"

He looked down at me and smiled vacantly. "Right now, at this very moment, I have a team of lawyers working on a divorce between my wife and I."

A few of the ladies at the table laughed. "Oh, Daniel's just putting us all on again," one of them mumbled behind a gloved hand.

The Count said, "Here, what's this about divorce, Delaney? It's hardly a joking matter to utter that word in mixed company."

Something had grown cold and dark within me at the shame he'd brought by joking about it in front of me. In front of anybody, really. Divorce wasn't talked about in society. It just wasn't done.

"The law clearly states a divorce can be granted in the presence of impotence in the marriage. And if a man can be divorced for impotence, then Lorelei can be divorced for leaving my bed cold and wanting. She'll never grant me an heir as is her wifely duty, and so the proceedings have begun long before now."

Different flavors of horror sat upon everyone's face. The only sound was the kitchen door opening, but the servant holding a tray of food froze when she laid eyes upon the table of silent high-born. Heat, burning and telling, crept up my neck and landed in the very tips of my ears until I had to stifle the urge to cover them with my cold, clammy hands for comfort.

"What is this?" The Countess whispered. Under the table she clasped my hand in a steely grip. "The disrespect you've shown your good wife in this joke is insurmountable. I've never witnessed anything so crass in my life. Give us the punch line and be done with this conversation, sir."

Daniel's mouth set in a grim and somber line. "No punch line, I'm afraid. I deserve better than the person I married."

The Whitten's and Ash's stood as one, throwing their embroidered napkins onto their dinner plates with fire in their eyes. Without a word they left the room, quickly followed by Richard and his betrothed.

I couldn't move. Every angry glare was a lance across my heart.

My friends stood and left one by one until only a few endured to witness the remainder of my plummet from society. The Count waited by the door for his wife, and the Countess stood over me with a poisonous glare for Daniel.

Her delicate nostrils flared as she said, "You've ruined her with what you said here tonight. News of her cold bed will reach even the darkest crevices of Boston by morning."

"That's the plan. It's the only way my lawyers will be able to win my case. It has to be common knowledge that she is an undeserving wife," he said dryly before he downed his champagne.

"She's a McGregor," the Countess fumed. "You've just spat on generations of good breeding for the chance to elope with one of your whores." She turned and with a whoosh of deep, red silk skirts, she disappeared through the door after her husband.

"Why?" I asked in a small, trembling voice.

"I've already told you. You don't please me in bed. You bore me, like the flavor vanilla or the sight of yet another brown horse."

The tears that built in my eyes made dual rivers of warm water down my burning cheeks. "I want my dowry back."

He sat heavily in the chair beside me and poured more champagne until his glass was filled to the brim. "Your dowry was spent in the first few months of our marriage, I'm afraid. You'll have nothing, and no one from society will call on you after this scandal. Your best bet is to borrow money from your family and move away. The farther the better."

White hot anger boiled inside of me until surely I'd explode into a million broken pieces. "I hadn't any idea you hated me so much, Daniel."

He made a clucking sound with his mouth. "Poor naive Lorelei. Your problem has always been that you're too sweet for your own good. I don't hate you. I just never loved you. We married because my family line benefited by being tied to the McGregors, but now, I don't care about all of that so much. I'll remarry and this scandal will be old news by next season. At least for me it will be." His eyes were cool and emotionless, like some slithering serpent. "I've arranged for a carriage to take you to an inn. You may gather your most personal possessions, but I'm afraid I'll have to ask you to leave the valuables here in my care. Go now. I'd like to eat my dinner in peace."

The palm of my hand itched to slap him across his smirking face, and if I were lower born and able to get away with such behavior, I would've. Instead, I covered my mouth to hide my treacherous sobs and ran from the room. He didn't deserve to see how much he'd hurt me.

Divorce! That was the foulest word you could dare to utter, and he'd thrown me under a carriage in front of the most prominent members of society with it. The Countess was right. I was ruined—utterly, unerringly, and devastatingly ruined.

No man would ever touch me after such a scandal. I'd die cold in my bed, alone and without the comfort of a husband, or of children. He'd cursed me to an existence beneath everything I knew.

Mariel Loche flitted across my mind and my heart sank in terror. I didn't know anyone else in the living world who'd weathered divorce except for Mariel Loche. Her husband divorced her and left her nothing but a meager living to eat on. When that had been spent, she'd fallen further and further and last I'd heard, she was working in a brothel in the worst part of town. Whoring and making coins by selling her body to survive.

That would be my fate.

No. I was still a McGregor. I could borrow money, surely, and eventually some man would overlook my scandal and marry me. I shook my head in devastation. What man would ever want a woman who'd been so cold in bed, she'd pushed her husband into *divorce*?

Shame filled my veins until I was filled to bursting. I hadn't known how to fix that part of my relationship, so I just let it go. How could every other woman manage to please their man but me? I'd bare this humiliation like a heavy metal chain around my neck for the rest of my life. My fists clenched until my nails dug into the skin and the smell of moist iron hung faintly in the air. I'd never marry a man for anything but necessity ever again. I'd loved Daniel and look where that got me. Men were harsh and unfeeling creatures, incapable of receiving love, incapable of giving love.

As long as I breathed, I vowed my heart would never be touched by another again.

Up the stairs I ran and no sooner than I'd entered our chamber did I slam the door behind me. My wooden jewelry box stood on the stone surface of the mirror I brushed my hair in front of before I went to bed every night. In a flash of fury, I emptied its contents into the bottom of a large, floral-printed bag. On top of the miniature pile of gold necklaces and sapphire rings, I thrust two of my plainer dresses that fit inside because of the thinner skirts. Stockings, shifts, hair ribbons, a silver embroidered brush set, and a nightdress, as well as a few toiletries that I managed to shove in the sides. I threw my coin purse into the pocket of my dress and forced my knee against the bulk of the bag and fastened it as best I could. When I pulled it off the bed, it pulled me right down to the floor with it.

Right. Much too heavy for me to lift.

With a pitied look at the gleaming surface of the perfectly polished wood floors, I dragged the bag, leaving a scuff trail behind me. Good riddance. I hope it reminded Daniel of me every time it annoyed him.

The bag clacked down the stairs like the burst of gunfire as I flew toward an escape. Hesitating at the door, I spared a glance for the dining room. Daniel's polished black shoes rested on top of the fine fabric of the table cloth.

Wrenching the bag over the door frame, I didn't say goodbye. His smirking face was the last thing I wanted to see as I headed off for my new wanton life. The luggage skidded noisily behind me as Jacob, our groom, tipped his hat. He jumped down and hefted my luggage on top of the fine, black carriage with the golden embroidered D for my soon-to-be previous last name. Jacob was usually the friendly sort, but he didn't say a word to me. Daniel must've talked to him before the announcement. Apparently it was against the rules to show me any kindness in my last moments in society.

Further and further the clopping two horse team led us until Jacob pulled to a stop in front of an old, dilapidated building a long way from home. *Hell's Tavern*, a sign that hung from rusted chains said.

"Jacob? Are you sure this is the right place?"

He dropped my baggage from the top of the roof and opened the door. "Afraid so, mum. Mr. Delaney said specifically to take you here." His eyes swam with the reflection of the oil lantern light and something more. Pity? "Have a nice life, mum." He tipped his hat and jumped spryly back onto the carriage bench. "Hup!" he said with a smack of the reins, then he was off down the cobbled street.

Three rough and heavily bearded men stood under the high post of the street lantern. They whistled and sneered as I put all of my strength into dragging my luggage across the layer of grime that decorated the walkway to the inn. Upon opening the splintered front door, it was abundantly clear that Daniel had sent me to the most unsavory place in all of Boston. The wooden floorboards were covered with liquor and spit and I screamed as a couple of men flew through the window right beside me as they fought each other violently. A portly woman behind the bar smiled widely, but was missing most of her front teeth and I was all but certain she hadn't bathed or brushed her hair in a truly long time.

"You must be Mrs. Delaney," she said. She gave my bag a hungry look before she pointed up the stairs. "First room on the right is the one for you, deary."

"Thank you," I said.

She put her hand around her ear and yelled, "Huh?"

"Thank you," I said louder to be heard over the crowd cheering on the fight that was still raging in the street outside.

She'd already gone back to talking to a group of raucous men who were drinking heavily at the bar. I weaved my way through the smog of cigar smoke that seemed to fill every crevice of the small inn. More than a few terrifying men watched me with unsettling smiles as I bumped and bounced my bag up the stairs and when I was finally to my room, I leaned my back against the closed door and sighed in relief. That was, until I opened my eyes. The room stank of unwashed linens, dirty men, and wood rot. I dragged my luggage around a large hole in the floor boards and was horrified to find I could see straight to the bar below through it. The bed was lumpy and before I even sat upon it, something crawled across the covers. I placed the back of my hand across the mouth and clenched my nauseated stomach with the other.

I wished tonight had never happened. I wished I was back in my own bed, sleeping at this very moment with all of the comforts of home, surrounded by the things I loved and the knowledge of my secure place in the world.

Instead I was in my own personal purgatory sitting uncomfortably atop my luggage because it was the cleanest area to sit in the entire filthy room.

Bang! The door flew open and hit the side of the wall so hard, the room shook. Two men with black handkerchiefs over their mouths strode in, their boots making clomping sounds against the moist wood floors. Their hats were lowered and all I could see were their eyes—cold and empty eyes to match my husband's.

I clutched my chest as my heart jumped straight into my throat. "What do you want?"

"A peek inside your fancy bag there," said the one with green eyes.

"You can't. It's mine." I lifted my chin bravely while my insides turned in on themselves. These were bad men who stank of alcohol and bad decisions. I pulled my skirts farther down my ankles.

The other man chuckled a sound that chilled the air in the room. "Oh, well if the bag is yourn, I guess we ought to be on our way."

I gave a prim nod. "I think that's best."

The other advanced on me and before I could scream, he yanked me off of the luggage so hard my head banged into the harsh-cornered foot of the bed. My vision doubled but I kicked frantically at the man hoisting my bag onto the filthy bed. "Get out of here," I screeched as I flew at the man's face with my fingers clawed. That bag was necessary for survival. I scratched him down the neck but strong hands grabbed me from behind and wrenched my wrist behind my back until I gasped in pain. Surely it was being snapped in two!

Carelessly, the man threw my only belongings on this earth to the ground until he reached the bottom of the bag.

"Well, Syrus, what do we have here?" He pulled out the small handful of treasures I'd smuggled from my old life and his eyes squinted happily from above the handkerchief.

"Please, I haven't got anything else. Please don't take those," I begged. "They were gifts from my family."

"Well," the man who held me rasped against my neck. "Tell your family, thank ya kindly from your friends at Hell's Tavern."

He shoved my back and I went flying across the room, lucky to have missed the hole in the floor by just inches before they left my room laughing. Something warm trickled down my face and the dizzy, throbbing pain in my head was disconcerting but I hadn't time to worry about such things. I had to get out of here before something worse happened.

Wracked with the sobs of my misfortunes, I shoved my belongings back into the bag and hauled it back down the stairs as fast as my clunking high-button shoes could take me. Out on the street, I searched in vain for a carriage that could take me away from this horrid place. With nary a one in sight, I hobbled at top speed down the walkway in hopes of finding one eventually.

A small buggy sat a few streets up, and sweating freely and chugging breath, I asked if he would give me a ride.

The man wore thin cotton clothes and a drooping cowboy hat. He took his time looking me up and down and then spat onto the ground near my feet. "Pay first."

I pulled a few coins out of my purse and tried unsuccessfully to haul my bag up with me. By the third try, the driver exhaled a put-upon sigh and helped. "Don't have all night," he said. "Where to?"

The Count Delecroix d'Maine's house, if you please."

"Where the hell is that?"

Oh, right. The drivers on the other side of town knew where all of the high-born ladies and gentlemen lived, but down here was a different world. Horribly different. I gave him the address and hoisted myself into the buggy before he took off at a clipped pace.

I couldn't burden my parents with this scandal. If I sought sanctuary in their house while all of the turmoil of my failure enveloped the whole of Boston society, they'd be dragged down on this sinking ship right along with me. Unlike Daniel, I couldn't hurt good people for my own comfort.

If anyone could help me in my desperate moment of need, it was the Countess.

Chapter Two
Lorelei

The driver didn't wait long after he'd dumped my bag, upside down I might add, onto the clean cobbled street beneath the buggy. The smelly man said he, "wasted half the night driving all the way across town."

The time of night was atrocious and I hesitated for a moment before I knocked. The clenched knuckles of my fist froze in midair just inches away from the polished burgundy door. My options were to sleep on the stoop or let her know I was here though, so knock I did. One of the Countess's servants opened the door and ushered me into the parlor while she went to fetch my friend. The Countess came down minutes later, tightening a silk night robe around herself and glancing with the startled eyes of a deer from side to side. She sent all of her servants to their quarters and commanded that they not usher a word about my late arrival.

"You can't be here," she whispered, sitting directly across from me with a worried expression knitted into her perfectly groomed eyebrows. "This thing you and Daniel are going through will pass, but until then, we can't be caught up in the firestorm."

"It won't pass. He sent me to an inn in the darkest corner in Boston," I rushed in desperation. "Please, I don't want to ever put your reputation up to question, but I've been mistreated and all of my valuable possessions lifted from me."

She frowned at my temple. "You poor thing. Is that what's

happened to your face?"

I lifted my fingers to my head, but only dried, crackled flakes of crimson came back. "I have nowhere to go."

She shook her head slowly. "You married an evil man, Mrs. Delaney."

"Don't call me that. It'll be Ms. McGregor again now."

Her silk robe billowed behind her as she disappeared into the library, only to return moments later with a small wad of money in her hand. "Swear to me you won't tell anyone of my help, least of all the Count. He's forbidden me to become involved in the scandal."

"I swear."

The money crinkled into the palm of my hand and I pressed it firmly into my coin purse. Begging for money like some commoner put a sadness on my heart I couldn't quite swallow. "Look how far I've fallen in one night." Even I could hear the devastation in my voice.

Pity pooled in her hazel eyes. "I daresay it's going to get much worse, Lorelei."

"Where will I go? I can't go back to Hell's Tavern. I'll be killed or worse there."

She inhaled deeply and adopted a faraway look. "One of my servants stays at a small hostel not far from here. It's mostly women and children and terribly simple, but the rent is cheap and men leave it alone for the most part. I'll send her with you so she can show you the way. You must go before my husband returns from the ale house."

Nothing in me wanted to get her in trouble. I knew the risk she'd already taken by giving me money and advising on shelter. I squeezed her hand. "Thank you, Countess."

"I wish I could do more. Take your bag to the back entrance near the servant's quarters and I'll send for Analise. She's the one who'll make sure you get safely into a room."

Analise was a small and frightened looking sort of girl. Her eyes were overly big and it gave the impression that she found everything with suspicion. "Evenin' Ms," she said with a small curtsey before she opened the back door for me to follow her out. "It's a bit of a walk from here. Are you sure you're up for it?"

"No choice for it, I'm afraid." I had no choices at all in my life at the moment. What a horribly depressing situation I'd found myself in.

"You can't go the whole way dragging that bag noisily down the street like that. Heft it up, will you?"

I grimaced and tried, but failed. I'd been toting it all night and my arms shook as if they were branches in the wind.

"Here let me," she said. She boosted it up onto her tiny hip and hobbled toward a back alleyway at a fast clip. It was amazing how her tiny body could shoulder that kind of weight. "Hurry up, then," she snapped.

I bustled after her. "Pardon me but I don't appreciate you talking to me in such a manner."

"I can talk to you however I please now. You're just like me."

Shocked, my legs locked into place and I skidded to an ungraceful stop. So the horrid truth of my scandal had already reached some of the help. I wasn't just like her though. High breeding laced my veins with noble blood. I was a McGregor with family and lineage and money. Well, my family had money at least.

"Hurry up before all the rooms are taken," Analise called over her shoulder.

Familiar streets passed into streets I'd never paid attention to from the cab of a fine carriage. Blistered and dismayed after what felt like hours of hobbling across the entirety of the city, exhaustion was my closest companion by the time I talked to the mistress at the hostel and secured a room. Room was a subjective term when referring to the closet I was renting. Analise grunted as she threw the bag onto the screeching, miniature bed.

"There's a poultry house two doors down. You'll be pluckin' chickens all day, but by the end of the month you'll have enough to rent your room." She shrugged. "It's better than doing nothing at all with yourself."

"Thank you," I breathed as she tried to shut the door. It was cut at an odd angle and creaked back open. Perfect.

I pressed my body weight against the wooden structure to no avail. It wouldn't be shoved into its frame tonight. Half the room was taken up with the tiny bed, and the other with a small writing table and waiting lantern. A fractured mirror hung on a cracked plaster wall that had been painted an atrocious shade of pink at some time in the building's history. Now, long strips of the stuff hung down like the walls were shedding their skins. At least it didn't smell of dirty men and cigar smoke though, so there was the upside. A washbasin sat atop the table beside the lantern and semi clean water graced the crude stone dish.

I dared a glance in the spider web mirror. Blood had trickled down the side of my face and dried. It looked like some winding river eking out an escape through canyon country. Lovely. I must have looked a fool showing up to the Countess's manor in such a state. My dark hair had come out of its pins and instead of looking perfectly coifed like it had earlier this evening, it looked like the nest of some wild animal. My amber eyes looked sunken, tired, and scared and I turned away from my reflection before shame could overwhelm me. Who was that weak woman who'd stared hollowly back at me?

I dressed for sleep behind the door where passersby in the hallway wouldn't be able to see me. If my husband hadn't been able to bear the sight of my body, I sure wasn't sharing it with complete strangers. The walls were thin, and the sounds of crying children and harried mothers could be heard through the night, but somewhere in the darkest hours, I found sleep.

****

"Do you know how difficult it was for us to track you down, Mrs. Delaney?"

"Ahh!" I screamed at the man whose face was much too close to mine for comfort. I threw the covers over my night dressed body and sat up. "Who are you and what do you want?" My quaking voice didn't sound quite as brave as it had last night.

"We are Mr. Delaney's lawyers. I'm Michael Fitz and this here," he said gesturing to a stout, balding man by the door, "Is Mr. Gerald Herbert."

"Why are you in my room at such an early hour, sirs?"

"Why, Mrs. Delaney, it's nearly nine." He pulled a stack of papers out of a leather handled folder and tossed them upon my lap. "You were supposed to be at Hell's Tavern where your husband had arranged," he said in a tone that rivaled Father's when he was disappointed.

"That place was dreadful," I said as I lifted the top page. "No honorable man would send his wife to such a dangerous place."

"An honorable man wouldn't be charging you with divorce either, my dear. Honor has nothing to do with any of this, I'm afraid."

"Then why are you representing him?"

"Because he's paying us handsomely," he said with an air that suggested the answer should've been obvious. Indeed honor did not play a part in my downfall. "You'll need to sign all the places I've marked and then you'll be done with this trying matter."

"I won't be done, sir. I'll be ruined."

His slack face didn't seem too impressed with my claim to destitution. "As it stands, it's going to happen whether you like it or not. You left his bed cold and without a way to provide an heir."

"But that wasn't my choice," I argued. "I want to give him a child but he won't come to my chambers."

His thin lip pouted out. "Maybe so, but that's not what it'll look like to the masses. You're the talk of the town this morning, dear—the butt of many a joke. Now sign this and be done with it. Mr. Herbert and I have more appointments to make today and you've already put us far behind schedule."

My glaring at Mr. Fitz wouldn't save me from the scandal. It only drew out the time these horrible men cluttered up my room. I snatched the pen from his outstretched hand and signed the papers as fast as I could.

I wouldn't cry, I wouldn't cry, I wouldn't cry. That horrible man I thought I'd loved didn't deserve my tears. He didn't deserve for me to mourn the decimation of a marriage that consumed every important corner of my life. Remorselessly, I prayed one of his many mistresses would give him the pox.

I tried to slam my door after those horrible lawyers left, but it only bounced back and almost struck me in the face.

Last night, I'd somehow managed to undo all of the pearl buttons that fastened the back of my prim gray dress, but putting it back together was a different matter. A soft knock on the door stopped my grunting and growling, and I faced it so my visitor wouldn't see my half done up outfit.

Analise peeked her head in. "The Countess has sent me."

"Oh. Well, come in and shut the door. I'm changing."

She stood awkwardly in the tiny space of the room not taken up by me and the furniture and watched my undulations with an arched eyebrow. "You need to be wearing simpler dresses now, Ms. No one's going to be helping you dress anymore."

"Yes, well I wasn't thinking about that when I was fleeing my house in the dead of night." My arms were tired and I flung them to my sides.

Analise sighed heavily. "Let me, but just this once and just because I can't stand to watch you flounder around when I have a message to deliver." She started buttoning up the top half of my exposed back. "I have a dinner party to prepare tonight and you're wasting both of our time. Best you get to a dressmaker and trade these fine garments in right away before you get robbed."

Too late. Analise didn't need to hear any more embarrassing tales of my woes though. Her head was likely plenty full already.

When the high neck was adjusted to hide all of the creamy skin beneath it, I asked, "What news do you bring?"

"I told the Countess something absent-mindedly this morning while I was dressing her and she seemed to think it relevant to your situation. She's asked me to come right away and tell you what I told her." She handed me a cream colored piece of folded paper.

"What's this?" I asked, unfolding the fragile newsprint.

"You know old widow Flemming? Before she died, did you know of her?"

I nodded slowly. Everyone knew of that old bat. She was awful to converse with and if it hadn't been for her profound wealth, no one in society would've ever given her another blink. If I was a betting woman, which I wasn't, I'd bet that was one sparse funeral.

"Well she had a ward, her niece, do you remember her?"

"Yes I think I met her once. She had red hair and was very pretty. Funny too, if I'm thinking of the same girl. The widow Flemming kept her locked up in her mansion because she was a bastard child and shamed their family. Had the same name as her aunt too. Margaret Flemming."

"That's the one, except she don't go by Margaret Flemming anymore. She goes by Maggie Shaw. She ran off to Texas and married a man she barely knew."

"That's awful," I interrupted. "How did she know his worth if she didn't know him before she married him?"

Analise gripped her hips and canted her head. "Did you know the worth of that rat Mr. Delaney before you married him?"

Touché, little hand maiden.

"Now Maggie, she blossomed after she left the city. She's happily married, her man's devoted to her, and she's expecting her first child this June."

"How do you know all of this?"

"I'm friends with one of the servants who used to serve the Flemmings. Berta keeps me updated because it's a terribly romantic story, if you ask me."

"What does this story have to do with me, Analise?"

She jabbed a finger at the advertisement. "There's your Texas, Mrs. Delaney."

"McGregor," I corrected. "And this isn't from Texas. It's from a man in Colorado Springs, Colorado."

Analise rolled her giant eyes heavenward. "Just read the danged thing already."

Honorable man seeks wife with good breeding and manners. Must be accomplished. Must like dogs. In return will provide shelter, provisions, and safety. Whores need not apply. Contact Jeremiah Dawson of Colorado Springs.

Whores need not apply? How very country. "So the Countess thinks I should answer an advertisement for a mail order wife and move to the wilderness to marry a man I've never met?"

"She does, and if you ask my opinion, I think you should too."

"Well, I didn't ask your opinion."

"Suit yourself." Analise opened the door. "I've done my duty, now good luck in your endeavors, Ms. McGregor." A whoosh of tepid air blasted against my face as she slammed the door.

A mail order wife? Was that what the Countess really thought my life had come to? I'd only been scandalized last night. Surely everything would calm down and I'd move on with my life. I wasn't getting pushed out of my city that easily.

Determined, I stomped down the street to the poultry house. The smell assaulted me long before I saw it, and a sign on the door had a picture of a chicken with x's for eyes. Even if the smell wasn't nausea inducing, I supposed the illiterate could guess what it was. My knuckles wrapped against the thin wood of the door but no one answered. Just as well, I wouldn't be easily deterred. "Hello?" I called as I swung it open.

The building seemed to be one giant room with rows of women seated and plucking white feathers from deceased chickens. Up in a loft, a group of freely sweating ladies pulled a line of poultry from a giant, steaming pot. Rows of hooks held featherless birds hung upside down and crates of clucking chickens donned the back wall. The only light in the musty room was the rays of brave sun that burst through the waves of cheap paned glass, and tiny down feathers dusted the air like swirling snowflakes.

"You're late for a job today," a sneering man said through a discolored smile. Tresses of greasy hair hung down the sides of his face and the short man was filthy from head to toe. Even the whites of his eyes were more of a yellow color.

I swallowed the lump in my throat as he approached, dragging a bad leg behind. "Please, Sir. I'll do any job you have. I need the money."

Tilting his chin, bottomless gray eyes raked across the length of my body. The breath froze in my throat, like it simply refused to inhale the odor this man no doubt emanated. "Maybe I have something for a lady pretty as you. You'll only get paid for half the day for being so late. Follow me."

He led me to a row of plucking women and stopped in front of a portly lass whose nose was too big for her face but whose eyes were kind enough. "You, up to the steamer."

She froze with a fingerful of feathers. "I'm sorry sir? Have I done something wrong?"

"Off with you, you little gobshite! I said I wanted you steaming those damned birds and I meant it. If you have questions, you can leave."

"Yes, sir," she whispered and dropped her chicken into a bucket.

I watched her hustle up the stairs with wide eyes. "I didn't mean to steal her spot."

"You want the job or not?" he asked.

"Yes, but I—"

"Sit down!" he roared.

My hands flew to my ears like it could protect them from the man's angry bellow. I sank into the woman's seat and absorbed the looks of disdain from the ladies around me. Each downturned mouth smirked its own practiced flavor of bitter, and each wave of the women's animosity hurt in a different way.

The foreman stomped away and I picked up the half-plucked chicken by the stiffened foot.

"Not like that," the dark haired woman next to me said. "Like this." She gestured a quick ripping motion and feathers flew from the bird into the bucket in front of her.

Wiping an already moist forehead with the back of my sleeve, I leveled that poor bird with a look of rampant determination.

I, Lorelei McGregor, was going to prove I could make my own way in the world.

Chapter Three
Lorelei

Boston had defeated me in two days. It had to be some sort of record. My fingers were clawed and stiff and didn't want to move after two almost full days of backbreaking chicken plucking. I stank of dead animal and I'd never get all of the white feathers out of my hair. The pidley amount I'd been paid for all those tedious hours of work had turned my stomach. At this rate, I'd be able to pay rent but only if I never ate again for the rest of my life.

For the tenth time I unfolded the advertisement kept safely in my pocket. Jeremiah Dawson did sound like a fine name. It rolled off the tongue in an attractive way. Even if he was some horrid looking man, or dwarf, or cripple, who was I to be picky? I'd married a beautiful man with a heart of black. Maybe the other way would work in my favor this time around. And more importantly, I would be far away from all of the horrid things people whispered as I walked by.

I'd made the decision today, as it became apparent the foreman was more interested in me than the other girls who sat around me. He'd whispered foul things into my ear as his rank breath brushed my face and lifted the dark tendrils of hair that had fallen in front of my eyes. The man gave me chills and not just because of his odor. It was because behind his emotionless gaze was something that terrified me. He was a man who'd do anything to get what he wanted. My rebuffs were only proving a delightful challenge for him—a piece of red meat added to the hunt.

Decidedly, I scribbled across the last piece of fine paper in my possession before I could change my mind.

Dearest Mr. Dawson,
I write to inform you of my interest in an advertisement you placed in a paper some months ago. For reasons I can't quite sort through right now, I have a mind to consider your offer. You have written of your want for a proper wife, and I assure you my high bred pedigree stretches for generations. As I've fallen on misfortune, I don't have any dowry to offer or material possessions to give if that is what you are looking for, but I'll be easily companionable and diligent in my wifely duties. I have to admit, as I would feel terrible for pursuing you under false pretense, that I have been a victim of a serious scandal here in Boston recently and won't bring any prestige to your lineage. However, if you are willing to overlook all of that and still would consider me a candidate for your arrangement, please contact me in Boston.
Yours,
Lorelei McGregor

I scurried to the post office as fast as I could dodge the rank mud puddles in hopes of making it before the post man flipped the handwritten sign to 'closed.' Just in time, I swished in through the door, smearing muddy water over the wooden planks beneath my feet. "I need this mailed to Jeremiah Dawson of Colorado Springs, Colorado," I said breathlessly.

He took the letter from my outstretched hand and with a grumpy frown said, "It'll go out with tomorrow's post."

A sense of relief I didn't quite understand flooded me as I left my letter there in the care of the post man. Maybe it was because it was out there in the world now and out of my hands, or maybe because the stranger, Jeremiah's, answer would be a chance to feel something other than rejection. Whatever it was, I sat in my tiny room and read his advertisement over again, and this time I felt a sense hopeful fear.

My path in life had been altered by the cruelty of my husband, and now Mr. Dawson's answer would be my destiny.

****

Jeremiah

The sting in my cheeks attested to how bitterly cold it was. The snow had finally stopped falling last month, but the wind remained to remind a man winter wasn't done with him yet. The black horse under me snorted, and steam blew out of his nostrils in front of us like the Denver train as we picked our way through the woods. In the next month, my brother and I would have to prepare the land, as we did every year, to plant the crops but for now, the weather was too volatile to do anything other than survive. I wasn't even to the clearing our cabin had been housed in before it was burned by Hell Hunters a couple of months ago but still, my sensitive ears picked up the sound of my brother and his wife talking. Arguing was maybe a better word.

Shrugging through the last tree line defense that separated our home from the wilderness, my horse snickered out a greeting to the winter coated mare in the corral. The view of the clearing after a long day always stirred a feeling of sadness. Hell Hunters intent on burning my brother's wife, Kristina, and hanging Luke and I from the big tree out front had tainted this place. The old house stood in a pile of burned rubble, dilapidated and abandoned. With it, the fire had taken everything we owned and now we were forced to live in the barn or in a rough camp in the woods.

Usually the clearing made me sad, but today it stopped me short. Piles and piles of fresh cut lumber cluttered the ground and Luke stood in the middle of the chaos with a letter clenched in his white knuckled grip.

"What's all this?" I asked as I steered my horse through the maze of different sized wooden planks.

Kristina stood with her fists clenched at her sides and her cheeks so red they could rival the tomatoes in our summer garden. "Apparently," she snarled, "your brother became great friends with the man who ruined me!"

A wise man stayed out of marital affairs but this bait was too tempting. "You met with Barron French while you were in Chicago?"

Luke threw his hands up in the air. "You too? Look, I had to do something in order to get close to his mother, and meeting him was my move. I wasn't drinking buddies with the guy or anything. The man was a cockchafer and I threatened him within an inch of his life until he gave me the information I needed!"

I narrowed my eyes at his use of curses in front of a woman, but his foul language only managed to inch a tiny smile from Kristina. Luke often forgot the manners Ma had instilled in us. Luckily, he'd found him a woman as crass as him. "What does Kristina's ex-lover have to do with the wagon loads of lumber on our land?"

Luke handed the letter to me.

Mr. Dawson,
I heard of the misfortune that befell you as a direct result of the unfortunate situation born between Ms. Yeaton and myself. In thanks for fixing the little problem I was having while you were in Chicago, I've delivered enough lumber to rebuild your home. Give my regards to

Kristina. Tell her I'm sorry—for everything.
Barron French

What the devil? "The bastard thanked you for killing his mother?"

Luke's green eyes held steady on the distant horizon. "City folks are a different breed. That's for sure and for certain," he muttered.

Kristina crossed her arms and from what I remembered with my late wife Anna, that little gesture told a wise man to run. "When were you planning on telling me?"

"Never," he said remorselessly.

The sound of her smacking his arm echoed through the clearing and I did the smart thing—walk away. That much lumber wasn't just enough to rebuild our small home. It would provide enough cut lumber to build two small houses and if I was going to bring a wife out here, a house separate from those two rutting newlyweds would probably be a good idea.

In the barn, I pulled my horse into a stall and slid the saddle from his back. The faintest brush of air and a slight movement of straw gave her away. If that didn't, her smell would've done the trick. I liked to let Kristina think she was getting closer to sneaking up on me though.

"What do you want?" I asked, pulling the saddle blanket from the back of the horse.

A frustrated groan came from the vicinity of the barn door and she moped toward the stall I was shutting. "I come here to say my piece and then I won't bother you no more."

Uh oh. I eyed an escape route to the door but thought better of it. If she was determined, and the steel in her voice said she was, she'd track me down to the ends of the Colorado territory to talk at me. Stubborn as a boar, that woman was. "Go on," I said gruffly.

"I know for a fact you haven't responded to that woman in Boston and it ain't right. She might be waiting on that answer, Jeremiah Dawson. She might be hard up and needing an escape and you're keeping her waiting. For all your fancy manners, you'd think you at least would have the decency to tell her yes or no."

Damn her insight, she was actually right. She fiddled with her sandy blond braid and set her blue-eyed gaze on me. It wouldn't work as well as on my brother, but we'd been through enough that it'd work just fine on me too. Her whoring days had taught her many a thing, including getting what she wanted.

"You been waiting a mighty long time for a response to that advertisement to just sit on it. What's going through that head of yours?"

"For one, where am I gonna put a city slickin' lady? You and Luke live in the barn and I live in a tent out in the wilderness. I have no house to give her."

"Not yet," she piped up.

"It still takes time to build a house, Kristina. And what if she reacts to what I am like you did with Luke when he changed in front of you that first time? What if she goes running for the hills?"

"There was always the risk of that. That's nothing new, now what is the real problem?"

I narrowed my eyes and clenched my teeth. "I don't want to bring no woman up here to marry and share the secret if she ain't the right woman."

Kristina's eyes flashed with anger. "Are you talking about me? You're scared because you mail ordered me and I ain't what you thought you were getting?"

"I advertised for a lady, which you wrote you were, and you showed up in the dress you were whorin' in not the week before. My concerns are valid."

"I ain't a whore no more, Jeremiah! And you're never going to know if Lorelei McGregor is right for you or not if you never respond. Coward," she spat before she threw the barn door open to leave.

It was obnoxious that she was right the majority of the time. Educated or no, she had a good head on her. "Wait," I drawled.

She turned with a furious swish of skirts, but what I'd say next would warm her up to me again fast enough. "I said I didn't want to bring her out here until I was sure, not that I wasn't going to respond. We don't have to put the seeds in the ground for a while yet, and if you and Luke are okay with holding off on building the houses, I was thinking of paying Ma and Da a visit."

"We're going to Boston?" she breathed with a look of such hope I couldn't help the smile that cracked my face.

"We'll leave tomorrow for Denver and take the train and everything."

I hunched in on myself and covered my sensitive ears at the shrill shriek of excitement that burst out of my sister-in-law. She was off running and yelling for Luke before I even got a 'thank you kindly for the invite.'

Chapter Four
Jeremiah

The looks we received in town as we waited for the carriage would be downright humorous if my sensitive ears didn't pick up all of the despicable things the town's people were saying about Kristina.

"It's scandalous, her living up there with those two men. Look how they hover around her! You can't even tell which one she's married to," Martha Pricket said as she gossiped with the old ladies in front of the cabinetry shop.

I sighed and hefted Kristina's baggage for her anyway. No matter what any of them said, Kristina was a lady and shouldn't be carryin' her own bag. And Luke was too busy talking to the driver of the coach to do it himself. With a subtle glance to make sure the women were watching, I pressed my hand on Kristina's back and helped her into the carriage. They puffed up like angered hens, and I hid my satisfied smile.

Kristina wouldn't ever think anything of it. She and I had bonded over the winter Luke had left her alone in my care. There'd never been any physical attraction between us, but she was special to me. I'd die along with Luke to keep my sister-in-law safe. It was my wolf that loathed her for reasons I couldn't fathom other than the assumption that the animal side of me had snapped the day Anna had died.

Plain and simple, my wolf was insane. The human side of me, however, cared for Kristina like she was my own flesh and blood sister. Actual flesh and blood sisters didn't exist for werewolves because they withered and died straight after birth, but I wasn't taking Kristina for granted on a technicality.

"Kristina! Wait!" Trudy called from the stairs in front of Cotton's. She was a freedwoman, making her home in Colorado Springs after the Emancipation, and though she was frowned upon by many for the caramel color of her skin and choice in a white husband, she was the best damned cook in town and everybody came to eat her recipes at Cotton's. She was also Kristina's friend. Her swollen belly led the way, and I jogged over to help her across the bustling street. In her hand was clutched a white cloth with a weight in it that smelled suspiciously and deliciously like cornmeal and butter.

"Thank you kindly, Mr. Dawson," she said behind a brilliant white smile. "I thought for sure I'd miss my farewell."

"No ma'am, we're just loading up."

She stood on her tiptoes and peered through the window of the carriage. "I packed you some of your favorite cornbread, and I put a few extra pieces in there for you Dawson boys."

Kristina leaned out the window, flashing her cleavage for the whole town to see and Trudy laughed as she kissed her lightly on the cheek and took the sack.

"Trudy, I'm going to miss you somethin' fierce! Don't you have that baby without me, you hear?"

"We have a few months still. So long as these boys bring you back soon, we'll be all right."

"We'll get her back long before you're due," Luke promised. "This'll be a short trip." He hopped into the carriage with Kristina. "You tell Elias he better brush up on his poker face while we're gone. We're playing when we get back."

Trudy groaned as I scaled the carriage to take the seat next to the driver. "That man doesn't need to learn a poker face. I like bein' able to tell when he's fibbing to me."

"Fine," Luke called. "Tell him our animals need to be fed every two days then."

"Don't worry about your livestock. They're in capable hands. Bye!" She waved until we turned the corner and couldn't see her anymore.

I settled into the rickety seat and lowered my hat to keep the tips of my ears protected from the whipping cold wind. It was going to be a long trip to Boston with a lot of down time to imagine everything that could go right and wrong with Lorelei McGregor.

Hopefully she liked surprises.

****

After five days on the jouncing carriage I was about ready to explode like a short-fused stick of dynamite. I hadn't had the chance to change in way too long, and that much time spent in one form left me edgy and sore to my very bones. From Luke's foul mood, I could only assume he was feeling the same. Normally we changed every two to three days. We could go longer if we had to, but to keep a good balance, we had to let the wolf out pretty often.

I would've felt sorry for Kristina being trapped in a small carriage with a testy werewolf, but that clever woman had somehow figured out a way to tame Luke's darker side with minimal effort. These days, just a touch of her hand soothed the ice in his eyes.

I wasn't so lucky and there wasn't anywhere safe to change. Oh, we were surrounded by wild woods that would suit my needs just fine. The problem lay with Kristina. Every time I changed, my wolf tried his very best to get to her and what he had in mind were some unsavory deeds. I'd seen the horrors of his dark imagination. He'd kill her given half a chance. *I'd* kill her, and her death would be forever on my conscience. My brother's happiness depended on me not changing until his wife was safe in a hotel somewhere.

Denver was a sight for sore eyes by the time the first buildings showed over the horizon of the tree lined dirt road. From where I sat, the sounds of the city bustle, bellowing cattle, and the whistle and chug-chug of the train were as easy to hear as the birds chirping in the trees we passed.

Tonight would be my only chance for a while and the urgency to transform hummed through my blood at the nearness of it. A second, but less serious problem was that I didn't trust my wolf to run with Luke's. He needed to change just as bad as me and because his animal was in control and still harbored human logic even when completely furred and fanged, he was the one to jump first. He'd hopped out of the carriage, announcing to the driver he wanted to walk the rest of the way miles ago. With a little luck, we'd stagger our changes enough that his monster would stay clear of mine.

Kristina's breathing was deep and rhythmic and I tapped on the hood gently. "Wake up. We're here."

Her head popped out the window and she rubbed bleary eyes. "Where's Luke?"

"Said he wanted to walk a while," I said with a wink.

A knowing look washed over her face. "Will you see me to a hotel?"

"Of course. I already have one in mind."

The Railhead Saloon was one of the finer establishments our modest pocketbooks could afford, and though it housed working saloon girls, Kristina had once been one and had, on multiple occasions, enlightened my brother and I she was fine around them. Of course the first time we'd listened to her, she'd pulled the wig off of the best whore in Colorado Springs for putting her claws a little too deep into my ramblin' brother, but that was then, and she'd probably grown from the experience.

Really, as much as I hated to admit it, she was downright entertaining when pieces of her old life shined through the polish of her new dresses and monogamous ways. I'd never tell her that in a hundred years because I had a reputation in our pack for being the mannerly sort and I aimed to keep it, but that was the secret truth.

With the carriage paid for and the luggage sitting in a neat pile in front of the Railhead, the shocked look on Kristina's face was priceless when she realized I meant to put her up there.

"I never thought you'd be taking me to a saloon after the tantrum you threw last time," she said through a wicked grin.

"This is where we usually stay when we drive the cattle into Denver, so some of the girls may know Luke, if you catch my meaning."

"I'm perfectly capable of handling myself in a whore house," she said primly and tried to heft her bag. It stayed right where it was.

"I don't know what you put in here," I said, lifting it and the two smaller bags easily, "because you only own two dresses and everything else burned in the fire."

Kristina lifted her chin. "A lady has to keep some of her secrets."

I cocked my head to the side and squinted at her. "You usually say that about weaponry. Did you bring your guns?"

She shoved the swinging saloon doors open and took a noisy draw of whiskey soaked air like she was sniffing at a rose garden. "A lady can never be too careful."

"That's a yes," I mumbled.

After our bags were dropped in the room, I offered an arm and escorted my sister-in-law to the dining area below. She was the only lady in the room besides the whores but she managed to look right at home. There really was no point in wasting good money on a meal for me since I'd be ripping into a bunny in a matter of hours, so patiently, I waited for her to finish her shepard's pie while I sipped a shot glass of whiskey. The amber liquid scorched my throat the entire way down and reminded me of how long it had been since I'd had a drink.

A table full of poker players argued and laughed loudly beside us and a couple of them shot considering looks at an uninterested Kristina. When their eyes fell on me, something about my expression had them ignoring us for the remainder of her meal. Luke sauntered in with eyes only for her, and Kristina lit up like a shooting star in a black sky at the sight of her husband.

"You're up," he told me through a relaxed smile as he pulled Kristina toward their waiting room. "Don't come into town looking for her, Jeremiah," he said from the stairs without looking back. "They'll shoot you."

The creature caged inside of me scrabbled and clawed at me to hurry up, and when I'd hiked miles from town, I dropped to my knees and lifted my head to the eyelash moon. Half-moon, full moon, harvest moon, or blue moon—the moon didn't matter overmuch to a werewolf as legend suggested, so long as it gave off enough light to hunt by.

The hunt was what mattered. It's what sated the beast and coerced him to give the human skin more time. The hunt made us able to adapt to the changing times by compromising with the monster.

My brother had always hated what he was before Kristina came along to soothe him, but I'd always accepted it. There was no dread about the pain. I could flip the switch and turn my apprehension off completely. Fear made you tense up when you transformed from one animal to another. Fear made it last longer and hurt more. There was no use for fear when it came to the change. That was something I'd understood since Da told me what would happen on my sixteenth birthday half a lifetime ago.

Accept the beast, and he'll hurt you less as he rips out of you.

The ritual was short and always the same: fold my clothes and leave them nestled onto a low lying branch where I'd be able to find them later, but where ants and scorpions wouldn't bother them. Propped on my knees and two clenched fists, I let the first wave of pain tear through me to the sound of my crunching, snapping, reshaping bones. My mutating muscles were quieter but they hurt just as much. What would Lorelei think of me if she saw my neck snap back, or all my fingers break and reform into a wolf's paw?

Stop it. The change was no place to think of the woman. Thinking only slowed the pain down. *Focus, Jeremiah.*

I groaned as my ribs imploded in on themselves one by one, and in the last blinding moment as needle sharp fur blasted through my sensitive skin, the noise in my throat turned into a savage growl. The last of my humanity slipped away as the snarling beast pushed me out of my head.

"Please," I whispered in the final wisps of consciousness. "Don't let me kill anyone tonight."

Chapter Five
Jeremiah

We boarded the train the next morning. It would be a six day ride with all of the stops but surely it would be smoother than a carriage bouncing through all of the winter divots in the pot-holed dirt roads. The passenger car was made of short, red cushioned benches and the walls around the ample windows were painted a deep forest green. As I took my seat by Luke, the door handle at the back of our car caught my attention. It had a lock on it, which in my book meant a car that carried valuables, like the payroll for the railroad workers. It was located directly behind ours.

A shiver of something instinctual ran through me and I nudged Luke. He frowned at the locked door too but shrugged and draped his arm around Kristina, who was staring excitedly out the window at the huge puffs of steam coming from beneath the train. There wasn't anything we could do to make the situation less precarious.

The other passengers watched us curiously but seemed nice enough. Blatant stares were understandable. My brother and I stood a head taller than most grown men, and Kristina was on the petit side of a woman and blond and mouthy where we were dark-haired and reserved. She had a small waist but was curvy where it counted and Luke liked her wearing low cut dresses, to which she happily obliged his taste. No doubt, we were a different group of travelers from what people usually encountered.

Luke hung his hat on his knee and ran calloused hands through his long, dark hair, come by honestly from Da. The train jolted forward and blasted a whistle, bending both my brother and I over in startled pain. The train jolted again and gave a little, chugging its wheels below. By the time the ride steadied out completely, we were a quarter mile away from the loading area.

"What if your Ma doesn't like me?" Kristina asked.

"Ma will like you just fine, don't you worry about that," Luke said. "She'll be surprised I settled down is all."

"You haven't told your family we're coming?"

I shook my head while Luke fiddled with his hat.

"Well," she asked, "did you at least let them know you're married?"

"Nope," I said, making a popping sound at the end.

Her face paled so I threw her a bone. "Why're you worried about Ma liking you but not Pa?"

She smiled brightly. "Because all men like me. I got both of you Dawsons to propose to me, didn't I?"

I tried not to roll my eyes to the roof of the train as the young family beside us jerked their heads at our conversation. Kristina hadn't ever been one for subtlety. The young mother cradled her palms over her toddler's ears as Kristina gave her a cheery two fingered wave.

"Don't worry," she said to the mother. "I turned one of them down. Challenge! Can you figure out which one I picked over the next five days?"

I put my cowboy hat over my face and leaned back into the cushioned seat while Luke chuckled away beside me.

Let her have her games.

I didn't have to play along.

****

Lorelei

"Lorelei McGregor, what are you doing in this wretched place like some commoner?" Mother asked from the doorway of my home-sweet-home.

"Mother! What're you doing here?" I rose so fast from the tiny table the lantern rocked dangerously before I steadied it.

"Your father and I want you to come home. You've punished yourself quite enough."

"Has the scandal of my divorce affected your reputation in any way?"

"No," my graying mother said with a stubborn twist to her mouth.

Father stood just outside the door, watching something with interest down the hall. Probably the two whores who lived in three-sixteen.

"You haven't noticed a dip in dinner invites? Have you been hailed to go to dances and political parties?"

Mother didn't answer which meant there had been a drastic change, just as I'd feared. "Think of how it would be if I were living under your roof, Mother. I'm not punishing myself here. I'm trying to make my way in the world without the charity of others."

She snorted. "You're skin and bones, child. This is no place for you. At least let us give you money to rent a proper apartment in the city."

A flash of stubborn anger seized me. "I don't want to be supported by my parents after being on my own and married."

"Daniel is engaged," Mother blurted. Her gray eyebrows knotted with worry and I sat slowly on my croaking, miniature bed.

My voice sounded very small. "To whom?"

"Marigold Remington."

"Marigold? But she's only just come out in society. She's a child!"

"She's woman enough to catch his proposal. He's moved on. It's time you do, too."

"Mother, you know as well as I things are different in society for men and women. No one batted an eyelash when Daniel flaunted his mistresses, but if I'd taken a lover they would've lynched me. His reputation survived. Mine did not. *This* is my place now. It's the only way I can support myself and help you to stay as clear of the scandal as possible."

"Lorelei," Mother said in an agonized whisper.

Tears stung the backs of my eyes with her pleading but couldn't she see? I was doing this for their own good. "I love you, but please leave before someone sees you in this place."

"She's right, Karina," my father said in a gravelly voice. "She's grown now and has to find her own way around what's happened." He looked at me with somber gray eyes. "If it ever gets too hard, come home. Hang the scandal. Your our daughter and our door is always open to you, little wren."

Emotion cracked my voice. "I will, Father."

After he led my crying mother away, I lost it. My bed wasn't much but it could cradle a sobbing woman who had doubled in on herself. It had been easier to be strong and keep trudging forward when I hadn't the vision of my parent's desperation and disappointment to draw from. With a frustrated groan I wiped my puffy eyes in the mirror and counted the change in my coin purse. After a day such as today, I deserved to buy myself a crust of bread. Maybe I'd even spring for some cheese to eat with it.

The coins jangled in my pocket as I pushed open the flimsy front door to the hostel. I turned and ran into a mountain. Or at least, that's what it seemed like, but the mountain was actually a giant man. He towered over the others who hurried along the sidewalk near him and he was leaned against my building, not even at his full height.

"Pardon me," I said, stepping around him and into a puddle of what was likely someone's waste they'd thrown out of an upper window. Lovely.

The man held out a hand to steady me, but I waved off his touch.

His voice was rich and deep. "You wouldn't happen to be Ms. Lorelei McGregor, would you?"

I turned and looked up into coffee colored eyes. He was a well-made man. Upon second look, he was devilishly handsome with dark, slightly slanted eyes, a straight nose and a strong jaw. Short, dark hair peaked out from under a cowboy hat, and the dimples in his cheeks made my heart pound a little harder.

"Excuse me," I said quietly. "I'm just on my way to dinner."

"Is that a yes? Are you Lorelei?"

"Who wants to know?"

He placed large, elegant hands on his chest. "I'm sorry to have surprised you like this, but I'm Jeremiah Dawson."

I don't know what the towering man saw in my face, but he grabbed my elbow like he thought I'd faint. "Jeremiah Dawson," I repeated. "I thought you'd found someone else. You never answered my letter."

He pulled me closer to the wall of the building to get out of the way of the bustling foot traffic around us. "I apologize for that. Things came up—big things and then I wanted to meet you before I made you travel all the way out to Colorado Springs. I should've written you. I see now it was a mistake to spring up on you like this."

It was really hard to concentrate with his dark eyes looking so sincerely into mine and his masculine eyebrows knitted with such concern. I wiped my tearstained face with the back of my hand and tried to straighten my hair. "I must look a mess."

"You look just fine to me. Where're you going to eat?"

"Uh, there's a bakery a couple of streets over."

"Can I accompany you there?" he asked.

Despite the cowboy hat, duster jacket, spurs, tall boots, and thick southern accent, he was being more gentlemanly to me than anyone had been in weeks.

"Okay." I don't know why it sounded like a question.

Jeremiah pulled my hand into the crook of his arm like we'd known each other for ages. It was really hard not to squeeze obviously onto his bicep but his muscles were tensed and strong and despite my deepest desire to remain unaffected by a man, my stomach was filled with a warmth I didn't recognize. His nostrils flared and he smiled down at me before he launched into a story of his travels to find and track me down. His voice was deep and soft and easy to listen to, like some lullaby I didn't want to stop playing. He didn't require me to talk much, just the minimal response to encourage him onward, but I couldn't tell if it was from him being a naturally self-absorbed individual or if he was trying to give me a chance to recover from the shock of his unexpected visit. Thinking of Daniel and every other red-blooded male I knew, it was probably the former.

The bakery was busy with patrons desperate to get bread to their families for dinner. When I reached for my coin purse, Jeremiah pushed it away gently and said, "I'll buy you dinner."

My eyes were likely as big as the other woman's who stood gawking at the strapping gentleman who'd descended upon the poor man's bakery. Was he even real? I pinched myself subtly and the prick of pain definitely proved it. Jeremiah Dawson, who I'd imagined for months looked like some pockmark-faced squat man with a balding scalp and scurvy teeth, had actually turned out to be a man a girl would dream about. I frowned. He should've had no problem procuring himself a wife. Not with a face and body like that, so why was he seeking a wife in a newspaper? What was wrong with him?

"What'll you have? Choose anything you want," he said.

Anything? My stomach rumbled but thankfully it was too loud to hear over the noise of the crowd. A concerned look flitted over Jeremiah's features, but just like it appeared, it was gone in an instant.

"I'll have the baguette with chicken and cheese," I said in a voice much softer than I'd meant.

"What's that?" The baker asked.

"She'll have the baguette with chicken and cheese and I'll have the same," Jeremiah said, his voice oozing command and confidence. Here was a man born to lead people.

"Are you some kind of criminal?" I asked as we left the bakery. I was so hungry my mouth was watering, but answers felt necessary.

"You eat, I'll talk," he said. "I'm not a criminal, though in Colorado Springs ranchers do, on occasion, have to take the law into their own hands."

"So you've killed men?" I asked around a giant bite. "I'm sorry!" Where were my manners? A month out of society and already I spoke like a peasant.

"I've killed men," he said as his eyes held mine. "None who didn't deserve it though."

"Oh." For some reason that made it a little better that he was a murderer. At least he was a murderer with a conscience.

We strolled slowly as I ate my baguette and sifted through which questions ranked most important. "What do you do?"

"I live on a homestead outside of town. My brother and I ranch cattle and drive them to Denver every year. Sometimes twice a year depending on the size of the herd. We also grow crops and sell them to mills, the general store, anyone who needs to store up rations for the winter, that kind of thing. Ranch life leaves us pretty busy but we get downtime during the evenings when it's too dark out to get work done. Can I ask you a question?"

"Sure," I said, resisting the urge to lick my fingers like I'd seen the whores down the hallway do at almost every meal they ate on their doorstep.

"I'm on my way to see my parents. They live here in Boston, you see. I'm supposed to meet my brother and his wife before we head that way and I was wondering, would you like to go with me?"

I stopped chewing and my pulse quickened. "Would I know your family?"

"I don't know but I don't think so. They're a modest family. They moved here only ten years ago."

"I suppose I should meet your parents if you still intend to go through with our business arrangement."

He nodded slowly. "I suppose you're right."

"Then yes. I'll go with you. I just need to stop by my room and change into something more suitable."

"You don't have to fuss over your appearance on my account or theirs. We're a simple lot. You look just fine for dinner."

The hem of my dress was still soggy from the puddle fiasco fifteen minutes ago and my scuffed shoes hadn't managed to keep the water from my socks, which sloshed uncomfortably with every step. "It won't take but a moment."

"As you like," he said with a kind smile, then escorted me back to my room.

What did one wear when they were meeting their future in-laws for the first time? They were strangers just as my escort was. Fiancé? How did this mail order marriage stuff work? I'd have to talk to him about the logistics.

I pulled both dresses up to the window and compared. One was a deep gray color with a cream sash and puff sleeves. The other was a gold color with white lace trim. With Daniel's parents, I'd worn my very finest dress in an attempt to impress them, but both dresses I held up to the light were of plain quality and one of them smelled like dead chicken. That one I threw over the bed. The soiled streets of lower

Boston usually masked the stink of my job, but we would be in a house somewhere and I didn't want people putting delicate handkerchiefs to their offended noses as I passed.

Dressed and ready, I wrapped my threadbare coat as tightly around me as I could manage, then made my way back to the street below. What if I'd imagined him out of my desperation for an escape? A tall, strong, mannerly prince charming riding up in his cowboy boots to save me from destitution? Sounded pretty farfetched—but no. There he stood, waiting for me.

Something about his greeting smile made my heart skitter a little faster. It had been awhile since a man looked at my face without a trace of disdain.

"Where can we get a buggy around here?" he asked.

"Oh." I looked around for inspiration. "There won't be any around here. No one can afford them. Maybe up a few streets, that way." I pointed.

The walkway had become congested with people arriving back to their homes after a long day of labor. The sky was darkening and pink streaks mixed with deep blue of the coming evening. I followed closely behind Jeremiah as he used his imposing size to cut through the crowd. A portly man bumped me soundly in his haste.

"Watch it," he said in a harried tone.

I rubbed my shoulder tenderly and opened my mouth to retort, but Jeremiah spoke up from so close beside me, I jumped.

The man had kept on his way but Jeremiah looked down at me with such a look of tenderness it tugged on my tainted heart strings. "You all right?"

"Yes, of course. Just got a little behind is all."

He grabbed my hand and held it close to his back as he led me out of the chaos. I couldn't quite take my eyes from the sight of his large fingers clasped protectively around mine. I'd never held hands with a man before. There wasn't even a glove to provide a protective barrier between our palms. How very intimate to hold hands with a man I'd just met.

The crowds eventually cleared and he pulled me up next to him. I thought surely he'd let me go so my heart could have a break and not explode from my chest, but no such luck. He held firmly onto my hand as if we'd grown up together.

"Are we engaged?" I asked in a much higher pitch than I'd intended.

"How many men you been with?"

I floundered. I'd expected a yes or no and instead he'd asked the most intimate question I could even name. I puffed up. "How many woman have you been with, sir?"

The corners of his eyes tightened and he looked ahead to a waiting buggy.

"Too many to count?" I asked in a prickly tone.

"Look, I apologize if I've offended you. I'm not used to talking to ladies and my sister-in-law—well, she speaks like a man most of the time and gets me confused on how to converse with your more delicate gender." He growled deep in his throat and pulled me to the side. His voice was low as he stared earnestly into my eyes. "I've been with one woman. My late wife."

My eyes had to be the size of saucers and the silence stretched out like a canyon between us. Well that answer was just about as unexpected as one could get. "You've been with one woman?"

His smile was self-deprecating. "Hard to believe?"

"No. Yes. Are there no women where you come from?"

"There're women enough. I just didn't have the urge to bed them all."

I cleared my throat delicately and answered, "One," so quietly there was no way for him to hear me.

"Is that part of the scandal you wrote me about?" he asked without batting an eyelash.

"I was married and now I'm divorced."

He leaned back and stared at me as if I were making a joke he didn't understand. "Divorced? Your choice?"

I straightened my spine and tipped my chin. "His."

"Did he say why?"

"Yes he did and no I don't want to discuss it." I spun and stalked toward the buggy. *Hello almost stranger-husband, I was abandoned by the man sworn in front of God to take care of me through sickness and health because I was that terrible in bed.* No way was I admitting that to the dashing man behind me.

"Will you marry me?" his deep voice resonated against the skin of my neck.

Startled, I spun. "So we're engaged?"

His smile was slow and simmering and his dimples deepened with the movement. "If you say yes."

I glanced around. A woman screamed colorful curses at the trio of men catcalling her from beneath a window. Another woman threw a wooden bucket of urine that came terribly close to splashing my skirts. One filthy woman stood on the corner with no skirts on and smiling like a lunatic. My hands smelled like dead poultry and that baguette he'd bought me had been the most elegant and filling meal I'd had since that awful night at the dinner party.

I dragged my eyes back to him and the background seemed to blur to unimportance. "Yes," I breathed as my heart hammered like a war drum.

"You aren't a whore, so that's good enough for me."

"Of course I'm not a who—ahh!" I yelped as he scooped me over a water filled crater and set me into a buggy like I was as light as a piece of parchment paper.

"Then I suppose we'll get along just fine is all I'm saying."

Okay. So a matter of weeks ago I was married and living in an extravagant mansion, and today I was engaged to a handsy country stranger and would be moving to the wilderness of Colorado to be his country wife. My life had taken a hard right turn somewhere and I got the distinct feeling the Fates were laughing their teeth off.

Chapter Six
Lorelei

"You're staying in a tavern? I thought you said your sister-in-law was meeting us here."

The establishment in question stood two stories tall and the entrance featured six men drinking amber libations out of atrociously large glasses.

"We live a modest life, Ms. McGregor. This is the best place for us to stay for the money, and Kristina doesn't mind. I wouldn't presume to set you up here though, so you don't have to worry."

"Oh. I didn't mean to imply anything about money." He didn't react to my failed attempt at an apology so I tried again. "What I mean to say is, I live in a hostel much more questionable than this place, I'm sure."

"Hmm," he grunted noncommittally. "It's no place for you, so wait here. I'll bring them out."

"Right," I muttered with a nervous fidget.

A saloon girl ran out of the ale house and I shrieked when she barreled straight for me. I'd be run over and stomped into the walkway! She stopped just shy and threw her arms around me as the force of her forward movement rocked us both backward. Prying her arms from around my neck, I ducked around her and held my hands in front of me like I was soothing a wild dog.

"Lorelei McGregor, right?" the woman asked with a slight frown.

Why did I get the feeling I'd stepped into quicksand all of the sudden? Upon further inspection, her dress wasn't as gaudy as the other whores who were kicking their legs up in unison near a piano inside. It just showed an ample amount of skin in her...chest area. And she didn't wear the thick rouge the others did either. Uh, oh.

"Kristina, I presume?" I said in a small voice.

She cleared her throat and held her hand out in a very masculine gesture. "Pleased to meet you."

Jeremiah stood in the entryway by another tall man with blindingly green eyes who was likely none other than his brother. The matching dark colored hair gave him away. I held my hand out and Kristina shook it until my bones rattled.

"Lorelei McGregor," I said when my teeth had stopped clacking together.

"Let's go meet the in-laws shall we?" she said with a wink before she took off for the nearest buggy.

Her husband, Luke I thought his name was, tipped his hat as he followed his wife. "Good to meet you, Ms. McGregor." His voice was as deep and smooth as his gargantuan brother's. Somewhere in their lineage was herculean blood, of that I was sure.

Jeremiah placed his hand where my spine touched my tailbone and I jumped away from him like I'd been scalded. "Sir, you are far too intimate in a public setting. I'm not used to such audaciousness."

His dark eyes swam with confusion, but before he could argue with me, I helped myself up into the buggy. Maybe I was being too harsh, but I'd only just met the man and already he'd held my hand for all to see and tried to guide me with the intimate touch of his palm. If I didn't draw my line in the dirt now, when would I be able to speak against what I knew to be improper? Scooting as far over as possible in the open buggy, I pulled my skirts in and tried not to touch the other passengers.

The view from the rough areas in Boston to the cleaner streets of the modestly housed would have been quite nice if I could take my astonished gaze from the bouncing, snow-white, bosom of Kristina as she pointed and laughed and talked about the passing city. When she turned her neck, a horrific angry scar peeked out from her hairline and disappeared into the neck of her dress. I'd never seen such an injury and my mouth went as dry as a cottonwood when she caught me staring.

"I don't mind you lookin', Ms. McGregor," she said, but as the words left her lips, her hand drew self-consciously over her marred skin.

Luke pulled her hand away and whispered something into her ear that brought an attractive blush to her fair cheeks.

"Does it hurt?" I asked over the noise of the wheels.

"Yes ma'am, for it's only a couple months healed. I expect it always will, but somewhere along the way I'll get used to it." Her voice was so cheerful and open, that a deep gash of regret took me.

I was making a terrible impression on a woman who'd had a hard time too—on a woman who would be family soon. I'd always wished for a sister, I just hadn't ever imagined she'd be so scantily clad and uneducated. Best not to look a gift horse in the mouth, I supposed.

The buggy pulled in front of a small house on a quiet street. Someone had planted gads of early white daisies out front which made it stand out from the other houses that were perfectly groomed. Kristina was nearly overflowing with excitement and her hum was catching, except for me, it came out as acute nervousness.

Luke helped his wife out of the buggy while Jeremiah jumped over the side in a motion so graceful he looked like some exotic stag. If I'd ever attempted something like that, I'd fall straight on my face with my skirts over my head. He was waiting patiently for me to exit the buggy and while I was tempted to stay right where I was until he gave up on touching me, I didn't want to embarrass him in front of his waiting family. I sighed. There was no help for it. His strong hands wrapped almost all the way around my withered waist and he lifted me down like I weighed nothing at all.

The house had been whitewashed to match the daisies and boasted darker shutters. It was a cheery little home but before I could walk up the front porch, Kristina put her fingers to her lips and held me back.

"Let them have their fun," she mouthed like someone on the empty street would be able to hear a whisper.

A loaded look passed between the Dawson brothers, and quiet as foxes on the hunt, they crept around the back of the house with such agility the fine hairs rose on my arms. Moments later a scream came from inside the house but it was void of fear and filled with surprised delight.

Kristina grabbed my hand and dragged me up the stairs. "Now we can go."

I tried to pry my fingers from hers, but she'd have none of it. Country folk seemed very dependent on physical assurances.

Murmuring grew louder from inside the house, and as the door opened, there Jeremiah stood, saying, "Ma, Da, Luke and I have a couple of ladies we'd like you to meet."

With one hand behind his back and one hand offered to me, I gritted my teeth and placed my ungloved fingers in his while Kristina gave a dainty curtsey to the woman inside the doorway.

She looked absolutely shocked at the appearance of two strangers on her doorstep. She had her arm clasped tightly around Luke and elegant eyebrows knitted together as she asked, "Boy's, are you mated?"

Mated? What a peculiar word to call what Jeremiah and I were. Betrothed strangers sounded much less crass. If I weren't looking directly at Jeremiah, I would've missed the slight shake of his head.

"Married is what I meant to say," Mrs. Dawson backpedaled. "You'll have to forgive an old lady. The right words slip me more and more these days."

From the way her intelligent, moss green eyes seemed to miss nothing, I rather doubted she said anything she didn't mean. The older gentleman who ducked under the frame of the sitting area couldn't be mistaken for anyone other than Jeremiah's father. He was tall and stood straight, as if the strength in his back hadn't weakened at all with age. His dark hair was streaked with an attractive, regal silver, and his dark eyes skipped with humor from Kristina to me.

Jeremiah took his hat off and motioned to me. "This here's my fiancé, Lorelei McGregor."

"McGregor?" Mrs. Dawson said with a tilt of her head. The startled look on her face said she'd heard a whisper or two of me already and my heart sank with despair. For some reason, this woman's acceptance of me suddenly seemed very important.

"Ma, I'd like to introduce you to my woman, Kristina. Dawson," Luke finished with a devilish grin.

Mrs. Dawson's shock over my celebrity faded into oblivion. Her brilliant eyes, so much like Luke's, grew round and the smile that took over her face showed the woman's beauty. "Lucas Dawson, you're married? Well, I never!" she exclaimed, hugging him and shaking his shoulders slowly. "Out of all three of my boys, I'd never in a hundred years pegged you for the one to give me grandsons first!"

The transformation in Luke's face was almost startling. He dropped a concerned look to Kristina, who'd gone still and silent. The moment lasted too long, and silence filled every nook of the small home right down to the crevices between my fingers.

"No grandson's from us, ma'am," Kristina said. "Afraid you'll have to be okay with just a daughter-in-law."

The wrinkles beside Mrs. Dawson's eyes deepened. "Ladies, help me set the table for dinner."

She led us in through a small parlor decorated in fine forest green wallpaper while the men disappeared down a hallway. At a loss as to how to help, I stood awkwardly behind a dining chair as Kristina jumped into action, setting plates and pouring waters like she'd been raised a servant. Maybe she had. I suddenly wished I had some knowledge of such things so I could be of use to the kind family who'd offered to share their food.

"Have you been trying long, Dear?" Mrs. Dawson asked Kristina in a whisper-quiet voice. "Sometimes these things take time."

I didn't mean to eavesdrop but the tinkling of dinnerware didn't quite cover up the conversation. I busied myself with folding and refolding the cloth napkins to make myself look busy.

"Oh no, ma'am. We've only been married a couple of months." She slid a blue-eyed glance my way and lowered her voice as she grabbed the matriarch's hands. "I know." She arched her eyebrows. "It ain't my choice to keep on with my bleedings, but I respect Luke's decisions and I understand why he don't want to."

"Oh. I see." She turned to me. "What about you and Jeremiah? Will you be breeding soon?"

"U-uuh," I stammered, wishing for anything short of a shooting star to come crashing through the living area to interrupt this conversation. "I actually just met Jeremiah today. We haven't had a chance to discuss such things."

"Hmm. Are the rumors about you true?" she asked.

My stomach turned.

"Ma!" Jeremiah warned from the doorway.

"I'm your mother, Jeremiah, and I have a right to make sure you know what you're getting yourself into."

Luke and Mr. Dawson filed in slowly and I swallowed the bile that threatened to escape me.

Five sets of curious eyes held me and my whispered answer sounded strangled even to myself. "Yes."

"All of them?" she asked.

"I don't know which rumors you're referring to, but it's true I'm recently divorced and denounced from society."

Besides the completely inappropriate chuckle that came from behind Luke's clenched fist, the room was as still as a graveyard.

As the moment dragged on, I fought the stinging tears that tried their best to wrench themselves from my downturned eyes. I couldn't bear to look at Jeremiah. Sure he already knew, but my shame could only be shared with him once in a day. It was Kristina and her wide, blue eyes my gaze settled on.

She downed the glass of wine in one long chug and set it down. Gulping, she blurted, "I'm a whore."

A wash of gratefulness and shock washed over me. Her dress and manner made so much sense now. My soon to be sister-in-law was a whore and the insanity of my own situation pulled a giggle from my lips. Luke frowned but I waved him down in apology before another fit of giggles took me.

"I'm so sorry," I wheezed. "It's just I can't imagine what you must be thinking when your sons bring a divorcé and a whore to family dinner."

It was Kristina who cracked the smile first and then snorted a laugh, soon to be joined by Luke and the rest one by one.

A deep, booming laugh sounded from behind me and Jeremiah's dark eyes closed as he threw his head back. He was a beautiful creature in full laughter. Pulling the chair out for me, he leaned into my ear. There was a delicious, lingering smile in his voice when he said, "I don't care about where you come from, Lorelei. I care about where you're going."

That claim loosened something inside of me I'd clenched from the moment I'd been shamed. This giant of a man was willing to marry me despite the scandal that'd curdled my life. His reward was that I didn't flinch away from the brush of his jaw against my neck.

"Thank you," I said shyly as he took the seat beside me.

"I should clarify I don't whore anymore," Kristina said, putting a plate of sliced roast in the middle of the table. "Luke's good enough for me," she said with a wink.

Luke grabbed her waist and pulled her onto his lap. Growling he nipped at her neck and she giggled and leaned into him. I couldn't take my eyes from their scandalous manner. Never in a million years would I have carried on so with Daniel. My gaze collided with Jeremiah's and he shook his head good naturedly at their antics.

Clearly, I was running off to live with a family of heathens.

The smell of dinner was heavenly to my nostrils. If the baguette earlier had been the best food I'd eaten since my fall, the rich roast, potatoes and ham flavored snap beans rivaled for best meal in my existence. The meat was tender enough I didn't even have to use a knife, and I hefted a healthy dollop of gravy where that would've been frowned upon at the lavish dinner parties of my old life. Women were encouraged to keep their figures after all, but no one at this table went sparing with the seconds and thirds.

The women couldn't keep up with the sheer amount of food the men inhaled and I found myself enamored with watching Jeremiah eat out of the corner of my vision. I supposed it was only natural for a man his size to require that much sustenance but good gracious! Was a country wife expected to cook? If so, Jeremiah better enjoy the good food while he could, because the man was about to starve.

"What happened to your neck, dear," Jeremiah's mother asked.

"Well, Mrs. Dawson—"

"Margery, please. Both of you girls are family now. It'll be best if you call me Margery."

Kristina beamed. "Well, Margery, they're burns and those are the best looking ones of the bunch."

"How much of your skin was marred?"

The frank way in which this family conversed had me praying no one asked more questions of me.

"Down this part of my body," she said, pointing to her side.

Luke draped his arm around the back of her chair and traced the injury on her neck absently with the tip of his finger. "She's more beautiful with them," he said in a somber tone. "I don't mind the scars."

"What happened?" Mr. Dawson asked. He was a quiet man, and everyone seemed to sit up a little straighter when he spoke. His bottomless dark eyes had the same catlike slant as Jeremiah's, and he looked at Kristina like he could see into her soul.

"Men came two months back and tried to burn me." Kristina was a very brave woman to hold his gaze like that.

Whatever look passed between them, he leaned across the table and squeezed her hand. "Are you the one to thank for saving my son from that scar on his neck?"

Luke flinched. How hadn't I noticed the mangled flesh that encapsulated the entirety of the front and sides of his throat? I was yet a baby to the dark ways of the world, but I knew a hanging scar when I saw one. Only the worst and most dangerous men were sentenced to hanging. A tiny sliver of fear moved in my gut.

Luke's brilliant gaze landed on his wife. "I thought she'd burned alive, but she came striding out of the night to shoot that rope from my neck not two seconds after the horse had been smacked out from under me."

Mr. Dawson leaned back into his chair with a dark arched eyebrow. "She shot it? That's a mighty big claim to shoot a hanging rope. It's nearly impossible to do."

Kristina leaned forward. "You want to see my weapon of choice?"

Jeremiah groaned beside me. "Say no, Da."

Mr. Dawson's dark eyes swam with humor and he flicked two fingers at her. "Show us."

She bounced up and stuck her foot in the chair beside her before pulling the skirts up to her thigh and exposing a lot of skin and a red and black lace garter that holstered a tiny and intricately carved gun.

As I sat there with my mouth hanging open, Mr. Dawson's laugh was almost as boomingly loud as Jeremiah's had been and Margery stifled a smile behind her napkin.

"A Derringer and you're good enough with it to shoot a hanging rope," Mr. Dawson said. "Luke, I knew it would take a special kind of woman to turn your head."

"I'm getting good at shooting the pistols, too. I've got big plans to teach Lorelei as soon as we get back home."

Mr. Dawson became serious. "It's a useful talent to have when you're the wife of a Dawson."

What did he mean by that? Would I be shooting people? Maybe they were outlaws. That would explain the hanging and even though Jeremiah assured me he wasn't a criminal, how could I trust that the man I just met wasn't a full blown liar? The man I thought I'd known everything about had lied about loving me. From what I was learning the hard way, all men did it to get what they wanted.

What had I got myself into?

Chapter Seven
Jeremiah

The more time I spent with Lorelei, the more I liked her. She was a quiet woman unless she had something important to say. She reminded me of Da, and I respected him more than any other person in the known world. She was well-bred and unsettled by the way our family behaved, but there wasn't any point in trying to stifle their antics. She'd have to get used to them or not. The choice was up to her. She should be aware of the caliber of family she was marrying into, and though they were the best people I knew, they wouldn't ever be a highly mannered lot.

Kristina and Ma were whipping up a desert in the kitchen, and my sensitive ears picked up Luke telling Da all about the Hell Hunter's attack on our home in the drawing room, so I led Lorelei to the front porch. A pair of rocking chairs sat waiting in the cold evening air. Her jacket was too thin for my liking, so I draped mine over her skirts and took the chair beside her.

"What do you think?" I asked. "You still up for this ride?"

She hesitated. "It's a lot to take in with the hanging and the whoring and the burning and today I saw more skin on your sister-in-law than I've ever seen of any woman." Her almond shaped eyes met mine. "When are you planning on leaving?"

"Tomorrow morning. We have to get back to plant the crops and one of Kristina's friends is heavy with child. She aims to be there for the birth and I wouldn't ask her to stay any longer. It's a long trip back.

Do you need more time to think on it?"

She exhaled long and slow and settled into the warmth of my jacket. The wolf inside of me relaxed with her acceptance of the small gift. It was the first positive feeling I'd drawn from him in years and an unfamiliar fear of loss echoed through me at the thought of her turning me down. Lorelei was so beautiful, sitting here on my parent's rocking chair with the moonlight kissing her cheeks. Dark tendrils of hair hung down in her face like the waves of a babbling creek. Her nose was small and elegant and her lips full on the bottom. Perfect for nibbling. I hadn't seen her smile much, but when she'd graced me with the tiny ones, my heart had thundered in ways I hadn't felt since Anna had been alive. She was much too skinny, but from the way her stomach had been rumbling earlier today, it was probably from the lack of funds to eat well.

Her scandal was bad, awful in fact, but she'd survived it and nobody in Colorado Springs would care overly much about the affairs of city society. She'd be safer there, with me. Hell, who was I kidding? I was bringing her to a wolf den without a warm place to sleep. I was a horrible man for doing this to her, but I couldn't drag myself away from her living in that poor house. I'd find a way to keep her comfortable.

"I'll have your answer by tomorrow morning then," she said quietly.

To hide my disappointment, I looked away. Why couldn't she just say yes so I wouldn't have to worry over it all night? Sleep would be unattainable now with the risk of this marriage not working out.

The clomping of horse's hooves sounded from far away. It must be a husband returning late from work or a show to be out this late hour. Or maybe it was someone returning from a drink at one of the nearby taverns. The gently rocking rhythm settled me, but as the carriage stopped in front of Da's house, my spine stiffened again. Instincts were a very serious part of daily life, and a wise werewolf listened when they were blaring like the blast of a steam engine whistle.

A man stepped out of a black carriage with a gold letter D written in fine print over the door. The driver was dressed in black from boot to top hat and when the door opened, a blond haired man in silk suites stepped from it.

The smell of Lorelei's fear was bitter and made me want to kill the man who'd caused her reaction. "Your husband?" I asked.

"Not anymore," she said, standing. "What're you doing here, Daniel?"

My jacket slipped from her legs, but I caught it before it brushed the cold wooden planks beneath us. She hid her quaking fists well but the tiny vibrations in the air had a sound. I reached out and held her hand in mine and it was warm against my skin. She looked up with wide eyes but didn't push me away.

"You have no place here," I said, sliding my gaze to him. "Be on your way."

His icy eyes narrowed. You could tell a lot from a man's eyes and his held nothing. No fear, no feeling. He was a dangerous creature with a wicked soul. I pulled Lorelei behind my back.

He pressed the toe of his polished shoe casually against the bottom step. "My spies told me you came here tonight and I found myself curious about what you were doing with people above your new station."

Lorelei lifted her chin and squeezed my hand gently. "They aren't above my station. They're my new family. You moved on and so have I."

I was family? Well if that wasn't what turned my insides to fire in a bitter winter, I didn't know what did. "Mr., she ain't your wife no more so you keepin' tabs on her stops right here. Tonight. If you come within ten feet of her, I'll know—and then you'll regret it," I promised, swallowing a billowing growl that threatened to rip from me.

"Ah, the threats of a country man. I'm afraid you wouldn't be able to touch me, though. I'm well known around these parts."

"Great for you. Around my parts, we feed stronger men than you to the pigs. Take the hint, sir, and leave before I forget my manners." I stepped forward and the idiot held his ground. Did he have no instincts whatsoever when he was pushing a wild animal too far? City slickers.

All conversation had stopped inside and if I was right, which I often was on occasions such as these, my brother and Da were just on the other side of that door waiting for any hint of trouble. And they'd tear him to pieces just the same as me.

"Are you sure you know what you're getting into with this one?" the man asked. "There's a reason I divorced her. It's quite well known around here, but you being a foreigner to Boston, maybe you aren't up on current events. Has she admitted why she's been shamed?"

"Daniel, stop," she breathed, and the smell of her fear became more potent on the chilly breeze.

"I know she's divorced and it don't bother me none. You're a damned fool for throwing her away."

"Lorelei's in the position she's in now because she is, mmm, how should I say? Lacking in bed? You'll never get your cock sucked with this one."

Red hot fury blasted through my veins and I closed my eyes against the push of the wolf. Every inch of skin on my person tingled with the want to burst into an animal and rip his throat out so he couldn't ever utter her name from his vile lips again. I needed an out. I needed something, anything, to soothe the urge to kill or I'd reveal myself as a monster right here in the middle of the city.

Unable to think over the pounding in my ears, I pulled Lorelei to me. Grasping the back of her hair, I leaned down and pressed my lips to hers. She squeaked and stood rigid for a moment before her lips turned soft and inviting. When I pulled her hips flush against mine, a tiny accidental sound came from her throat that made me want to claim her right here on the porch. I'd give everything I owned to draw that little noise of pleasure from her again. I kissed her once more, softly, then turned my head to her gawking abuser and growled, "She's been nothing but warm to me. It's pretty obvious you weren't doin' it right."

Lorelei was leaning on my arm heavily, her breathing ragged. "Get on inside," I told her.

"Okay," she said in an odd tone. Her boot prints were unsteady across the wooden floorboards and when the door clicked shut behind her, I leapt from the porch and wrapped my hands around his throat.

"It's all become really clear to me now what's happened," I said as I pulled his choking form around the shadowed side of the house. "You've slandered her to get your divorce, am I right? And now you've moved on but you want to keep her impoverished. You get some sick kick out of that, don't you?" Desperate fingers grappled at my hand and his face turned the shade of a saloon girl's made up lips. His body thudded against the side of the house as I slammed him into it. "If you come near my wife again, I'll kill you. I don't care what kind of high falutin' blood you're convinced is runnin' through your veins, trust me when I say a pedigreed man dies just the same as a pauper." I released my grip and he dropped flailing to the ground. "Have a nice life," I said, turning with a bow of my head. "I know I will."

Lorelei sat in Da's favorite chair with a glass of water in her shaking hand. "Is he gone?" she asked.

"You don't have to worry about that man botherin' you again. Are you okay?"

She nodded slowly. "What he said about me—"

"You don't have to say nothin' about that. I told you, I don't care what happened. Did you mean what you said out there? We're family. Does that mean you're coming with us tomorrow?"

Her whiskey colored eyes were big and scared looking when she nodded. I didn't care if she was saying yes to my proposal for the wrong reasons. None of that mattered as my innards loosened with hope for the first time in a long time.

"The hour's late and I should return to my apartment," she said as she set her glass on the table beside her.

"You sure you don't want me to put you up in someplace nicer?"

"Like the tavern? No, I'll spend my last night in Boson in my own room. I need to pack my things and gain some closure."

None of me was okay with her staying in that rat hole. The tavern wasn't the classiest place for a woman, but she'd be safe there with me. I couldn't protect her in a place I hadn't any access to. Pushing her wouldn't get me what I wanted though. That she was scared was apparent, and my crowding her would only make her run. I had to be a patient hunter.

"I'll take you back," I offered.

Ma shooed me away to talk to her alone for a goodbye, but I stayed just on the other side of the wall so I could listen.

"I've heard the reasons your man divorced you," Ma whispered. "If it's true or not isn't any of my business but I must warn you, Dawson men are a needy lot. You'll have to get over your reservations if you're going to keep Jeremiah happy."

I rubbed my hands over my face until the skin was raw as Lorelei gulped on the other side of the wall. "I'll try," she whispered.

When they returned, a glare at Ma only received an unapologetic shrug. She hugged Lorelei and Kristina in turn and told them to take good care of us.

Ma, tiny human Ma, stood up to her full height and hugged me as hard as she could. "You write me the second Gable returns," she said. Our other brother hadn't returned from the War Between the States, and the lack of communication had been an unsettling situation for the entirety of our family.

"I will, Ma. I love you."

"My boy," she cooed happily as she kissed my cheek. "Be patient with your new mate. She'll have a hard time finding her place out there." No one knew that as well as Ma. She'd been a lady mated to a werewolf out in the wilderness and had struggled to adjust. And now the same challenge lay ahead for Lorelei.

Pa clapped Luke and I on the backs and in that silent way of his, passed a million words with a glance before he waved us off. Luke and Kristina walked hand in hand toward the tavern and I led Lorelei toward a waiting buggy up the street. Our journey to her part of town was much farther than my brother had to travel, and Luke was perfectly capable of redirecting any riffraff intent on bothering them on their walk back to the inn.

Across the wagon from Lorelei, I selfishly drank her in while she watched the passing houses and stores. She looked nothing like Anna. They were as different as night and day and I preferred it that way. It didn't feel like a betrayal to Anna's memory because I wasn't replacing her. I was simply trying to fill the void she'd left behind the day she died.

Lorelei touched her lips absently. Was she thinking about when I'd kissed her? If I'd been in my right mind, I would've given her time. The warmth of her body up against mine was a satisfying memory though, and I was glad I'd had the rage and courage enough to touch her.

She was already mine and she didn't even fully know it yet.

Chapter Eight
Lorelei

The range of emotion I'd felt since meeting Jeremiah Dawson swung high and wide, but the tingling in my stomach was so obviously disappointment when he didn't kiss me goodbye. *Wanton woman!* What would mother say if she could take a peek into the scandalous thoughts that had raced through my mind when that man's lips had crashed upon my own on the porch?

It was the God's honest truth that I, Lorelei McGregor, had never been kissed by a man like that before. I waved as Jeremiah disappeared down the street in front of my apartment and stumbled abstractedly up the stairs to my room. The violence and raw power had terrified me in the moment it happened, but as he'd nipped at my lip, all thoughts had washed out of my head until only the most primal and base consciousness existed there. There was no way an honorable man kissed like him, but I was having difficulty caring about such things as that. My, had I changed my tune over the last month of struggle. Murdering? Okay, so long as they deserved it. Holding hands and touching in the midst of the public eye. All right. Kissing a man like some shameless commoner in the street? So long as it's Jeremiah who was doing the kissing.

I had to admit to an acute satisfaction at the sight of Daniel's enraged face when Jeremiah had pulled away from me. What did I care what he told everyone in the morning? My reputation could get no worse, and I wouldn't be around Boston to hear it anyway.

I kicked the door closed with my shoe only to have it fling back open. I pulled my bag out from under the small bed and folded my few belongings neatly inside of it.

"You going somewhere?" Analise said from behind me. We'd become friendlier over my time here.

"I'm following your advice."

She gasped and flung herself onto my screeching bed. "You answered the advertisement? That's so romaaantic," she sang, clutching the lumpy pillow to her chest.

I didn't know about romantic, but it did seem terribly exciting to leave the heartache behind and start fresh in a new place with new people. "I met him today. He surprised me and was waiting outside when I left for dinner tonight. I just met his family."

"And?" she all but squealed.

"They are scandalous people with almost no manners on proper etiquette or conversation." Analise frowned and I pursed my lips to contain the excitement. "And I liked them."

"When are you leaving?"

"In the morning. He wants to leave early. If I pen a letter for the Countess, would you mind delivering it?"

Anilise lay on my bed staring at the ceiling with a dreamy look in her eyes. "Yes, of course."

I'd tell Mother and Father of my decision when I was officially married and it couldn't be undone. They'd try their best to convince me out of doing this, but moving away with Jeremiah was something I had to do. Every instinct I possessed said this was important. I sat at my small desk for what would be the last time and wrote my farewell to the only remaining friend I had from my old life.

Sleep came fitfully that night. How could one sleep with such change in the air? As I lay staring at the cracked plaster ceiling and peeling pink paint, I couldn't help but imagine what he was doing. Likely he was fast asleep in the comfort of his tavern bed. The memory of our kiss touched my lips over and over until I was hot and writhing in the confines of that small room with a discomfort I couldn't seem to soothe.

With my internal clock set to rise with the sun in order to secure a seat at the poultry house, today was no different. Jeremiah had promised to pick me up at dawn, but I couldn't wait in my stifling room that long. I'd wait on the street so he didn't have to send someone for me. It would be my first kindness paid to him as his betrothed.

Through the buildings, a deep purple and pink stretched across the sky as the first wisps of dawn yawned and stretched. I'd find a dry place for my bag and sit upon it until he came for me. The stairs seemed endless in my haste. What if he'd changed his mind in the night? What if he realized he really didn't want another's cast offs and didn't come for me at all? What if I sat here all day as people passed and sneered at me for my naiveté?

I almost tripped over a large form in the dark and strong hands reached up to steady me. "Jeremiah?" I'd never been talented at seeing in the dark, but a mass so big could only belong to him or the other men in his family. "What are you doing here?"

His voice was deep and full of sleep. "I wanted to make sure you were safe in case your husband came for you."

I crouched down beside him and squinted through the darkness. "Have you been here all night?"

"You running away?" he asked instead of answering.

"No, I was coming out to wait for you."

His deep voice had a smirk in it and he slid a glance to the coming sunrise. "It's five in the morning."

"Well, I was trying to be helpful. That and I couldn't sleep," I admitted.

"Did you get the closure you wanted?"

"I did."

"Good, let's go get some breakfast then." Fluidly, he stood and held a hand out to me.

The crook of his arm provided a safe, warm place for my chilled palm and I didn't cower away from the closeness as I had earlier. Maybe it was because no one would see the gesture here in the dark before dawn, or perhaps I just wasn't as hesitant about his offered touch anymore now that we were engaged. Whatever the reason, it felt right and safe to be physically connected to him somehow. A feeling of naughty rebelliousness washed over me, and I didn't completely hate it.

He gallantly carried my bag like it weighed less than air and here, in the silence between our boot prints through the black slushy piles of snow, a weight lifted from me as a comfortable quiet between us blanketed the crisp morning air. I wanted to drink up every single detail about this mysterious man I'd soon call husband, but for now, I was content to just be with him.

The baker and his wife worked feverishly to bake the foods breakfast goers would soon be demanding, but they opened the door at our soft knock. Jeremiah paid for three giant cinnamon pastries still hot from the oven and we ate two of them as we walked slowly toward the tavern we were to meet Luke and Kristina at.

When we arrived, I balked at the door. Old habits and manners said a lady should never go inside of one of these establishments. In fact, the wooden shingle outside specifically advised I didn't.

"It's okay if you don't want to go in. I can run up and tell them we're ready to head to the train station, and then I'll come back and wait with you out here if you want."

I rocked on my tiptoes and tried my best to peer over the swinging doors. A pair of men with their arms over each other's shoulders stumbled out slurring an old Irish drinking song, giving me a small glimpse into a nearly empty bar area.

"I've never been in one," I admitted.

"Well we don't have to start tonight."

"I want to. It can't be worse than the inn Daniel sent me to the night he denounced me." Something in Jeremiah's face, or maybe it was the air around him, warned to proceed with caution and I stepped back just a little.

"I ain't gonna hurt you, woman," he said. Pulling my hand, he led me to a hallway in the back of the bar. At the third door, he rapped light knuckles across the wood grain, which was answered almost before the knock sounded.

Luke grinned and jerked his head in invitation. "Kristina's getting ready."

"Oh, should we come back later?" I whispered, but Jeremiah had already pulled me inside.

Kristina poked her head around a folding screen while Jeremiah laid on the bed with a giant sigh and pulled his hat over his face.

"Guess what I got back behind this screen?" Kristina asked. "Come here."

A steaming soaking tub had been filled and sat invitingly in the corner. Kristina stood in a thin robe and gestured to the tub. "You want to take her for a spin?"

"I'm sure your husband filled that for you," I said, though I wasn't quite able to take my eyes away from the billowing steam as if it were fingers beckoning me into the dark heat of the water.

Kristina yanked her robe out of the way and revealed the most atrocious injury I'd ever laid eyes on. Morbidly, I stalked closer until I was bending over in front of her burned skin. Bile caught in my throat. Someone had done this to her on purpose and I couldn't even imagine the pain of healing from such a wound.

"It's too hot on my burns. I have to wait a while for it to cool down. It's a long trip home though and if you want a bath, you'd better do it now."

"What about the men?" I whispered.

"Kristina, we got you a pastry for breakfast," Jeremiah's deep voice sounded from the other side of the screen. "I'm setting it on the table. Luke and I are going out while you ladies get ready."

Had he heard my whispered worry?

Kristina poked her head around the screen again. "Give me," she said, twitching her fingers. She pulled the pastry in and groaned as the door to the room shut. "Oooh, it's still fresh and everything." She plopped into a chair and motioned to the tub. "Go for it. I'm savoring this."

Servants had often been present when I bathed before. I shouldn't worry overmuch about bathing in front of my sister-in-law, right?

Kristina pointed to herself. "Whore, remember?" she said around a giant bite of breakfast. "I've seen a hundred girls naked. Don't mind me."

She had a point. Still, I shed my clothes and slipped into the tub as quickly as I could. I tried to imagine that kind of heat on a burn but failed. Such pain was beyond my limited comprehension of such things. The crude lye soap prickled my skin but it could've been because I scrubbed it within an inch of its life. The goal? To rid myself completely of the smell of dead poultry and feathers.

In the midst of scrubbing my hair with lavender wash Kristina kindly offered, she wiped her hands loudly and asked, "So what do you think of Jeremiah?"

The water lapped at my chin but it couldn't hide me completely. "He's a very nice man."

"Fetching too, isn't he? Come on. You can tell me. I have personal experience with a Dawson. Those boys are the handsomest men I've ever laid eyes on. And Jeremiah? Now that's a man a woman can wrap her legs around."

I slunk under the water as long as I could hold my breath and until the soap was completely rinsed out of my hair. Disappointingly, when I emerged Kristina still waited for my answer. "He's very handsome," I allowed.

"I bet he's a demon in the sack," she said. "From what I gather, all were..." She froze, then cleared her throat. "All Dawson's are."

I frowned and took the towel she offered. She disrobed and slipped into the cooling tub and hissed as she lowered into the water. A great pity took me at the pain she must be enduring.

"Does Luke mind your scars?" I asked as I ran the towel soothingly through my hair.

"Not one bit far as I can tell. I got them saving him though. He tells me they're a badge of honor and he's always brushing his fingers across them like he can't help himself, so I don't think it matters overmuch to him." She leveled me with an earnest blue-eyed gaze. "You just have to accept the imperfections in the one you love."

I slipped into my dress and pulled the sleeves over my shoulders.

"Does Jeremiah have imperfections?"

Kristina closed her eyes and leaned back into the tub. "Nobody's perfect. Give him half a chance though and he'll be the best thing that ever happened to you."

Here, in the glowing lantern light of the tavern room, it became clear that her lack of education and proper etiquette didn't make a difference on how intelligent she was. She was wise beyond her years, and maybe it was because of her life experience that I'd judged so harshly. It'd take some getting used to, accepting life advice from a whore, but what she said made a lot of sense. It touched on something I'd always thought was wrong with my marriage.

Daniel had tried to change and mold me until finally, he'd given up and wanted nothing to do with me. In return, I'd wanted him to show me affection. To show me he loved me when he so clearly did not. Our marriage had been one of changing the other to better suit us, when the truth was we'd never been right or healthy for each other in the first place.

This time around, I'd try a different approach and hope for different results.

Chapter Nine
Lorelei

Jeremiah and his brother took their time returning to the room. "Are we going to miss our train?" I asked.

Kristina didn't seem overly worried, but in the excitement of my escape, I fidgeted like an anxious child. My hair was long since dried and in its pins by the time the light knock on the door sounded.

Jeremiah entered with Luke and another man I didn't recognize. "Lorelei, this here's Randall Craig. He's a preacher around here, and if you're willing, he's offered to do our service before we leave for Colorado.

I looked from face to face in shock. Was he serious?

"I'd take him up on that offer if I was you," Kristina said. "You'll likely have to wait until the circuit preacher's baptized all of the spring babies before he makes it our way again. You'll be out on Dawson land with an unmarried man for some time before the wedding is official unless you take care of it now."

"I'd be living with you before we married?"

Jeremiah's eyes were soft but solemn as he nodded. "Ain't much help for that. Living space is limited out where we live."

"Okay," I said as my heart leapt into my throat. "Where will the ceremony take place?"

"Here's as good a place as any," said the preacher from behind a set of thick bifocals.

"But it's a tavern." I wasn't trying to be argumentative but never in my wildest imaginings would I be marrying a stranger in an ale house with the sound of singing whores as my wedding march.

"She's right. This ain't no place for a wedding," Jeremiah said.

Thank goodness he agreed with reason, but that didn't mean I'd given up on the notion of making our arrangement official before we hopped the train. "What about the train station? We can do the ceremony there before we board."

The shift in Jeremiah's stance settled my nerves. If relief had mass, it would've filled the entire room. "Okay, the train station it is. You ready to go?"

I clamped my mouth closed and nodded. He would hear the tremble in my words if I gave them a voice. Today was my wedding day and in a couple of short hours, I'd no longer be a Delaney or McGregor. I'd be a Dawson bride.

Despite my conscious effort to stay in the here and now, everything suddenly seemed terribly surreal. I hefted my floral bag, made much lighter over the month of hard work to strengthen my arms. "I'm ready."

I'd never forget the buggy ride to the train station for as long as I lived. It encompassed my final moments as a lady of Boston, the final moments of living in the only city I'd ever known, and the final moments of my single, wanton life. I'd no longer be around to hear the snickers and crude whispers about delicacies I'd never thought to hear spoken on proper men and women's tongues. This was the final moment before everything changed, and for better or worse was still a gaping mystery.

The late winter air stung my cheeks but the whipping wind had died down as a pleasant surprise send off. The old carriage horse's hooves clomped across ice and cobbled stone. Jeremiah sat so close to me, his warmth swept through my layers and brushed my bare skin. His arm draped across the seat back, but I was leaned forward saying my silent goodbyes to the streets I'd known since childhood.

"We'll pass near the house I grew up in," I said.

He studied me with a clear, dark gaze. "Do you want to see it before we leave?"

"Would it be a terrible inconvenience?"

"Not at all. Driver, could we make a small detour?"

I gave him my parents address and he turned the horse from the main road. As the homes passed, I pointed out which ones had housed childhood friends, first crushes, and now people who had been close to me just a matter of weeks ago. Kristina drank in the gargantuan homes with their sprawling gardens and towering columns with a look of wide-eyed wonder. The driver stopped in front of my home. With a little luck, Mother and Father would still be asleep in their beds and wouldn't wonder outside to see their only daughter in a cart full of common strangers. What a colossal disappointment I must've turned out to be.

The home was large, one of the largest on the street in fact. If only Jeremiah could see it in springtime. The gardens rivaled the most beautiful in the city and the colors were so brilliant, they were almost overwhelming to the senses. An imposing but elegant iron gate surrounded the property and the home stood two stories tall with cascading balconies and cobbled walkways. The main house was even larger than it looked from here because it stretched back to an impressive size.

"You grew up a regular princess, didn't you, Ms. McGregor?" Kristina asked softly, like she would disturb the magic of the place.

"If you're impressed with this view, you should see the ballroom."

"No," she drew out. "You held fancy parties and dances here?"

Jeremiah's eyebrows furrowed. "Are you sure you want to leave this behind?"

Warm air steamed against the cold in front of my face as I sighed. "It isn't my place anymore. Take us to the train station," I told the driver. The horse jerked forward with the snap of the reigns and I fell backward into the cushion of Jeremiah's arm. "Sorry." Awkwardly, I pulled forward again. Unable to shoulder the disappointment I knew would be on his face at my hesitancy to touch him, I watched the houses pass instead.

At the train station, he offered his forearm for me to balance on as I made my way down the rickety steps of the buggy and then pulled away. Was he trying to touch me less because of what Daniel said last night? Or was he already tuning into my cold nature?

The pain at his willing distance was a pin prick. It was nothing less than I deserved though. How many times had I pulled away since he'd met me yesterday? Unable to stomach that I brought the kind stranger pain, I wrung my hands against the chilly morning.

The loading platform was busy with the bustle of farewells and the clutter of luggage and boarders. The preacher led us to the side of the ticket building that boasted a small porch and bench seat. As Jeremiah and I stood in front of him, Kristina took her place beside me and Luke beside Jeremiah. It was strange to stand for a wedding with no parents here, but the ceremony had been unplanned and there hadn't been time to send out formal invites.

The preacher said a few words about the importance of marriage and read a small passage of scripture about the kindness of love. The vows were simple but I still stuttered my way through as heat crept up my cheeks and I mouthed an apology to Jeremiah.

He took my hand in his and the warmth and strength of it settled me a bit. "It's okay," he said.

"Do you, Jeremiah Cade Dawson, take Lorelei Dawn McGregor as your lawfully wedded wife?"

His dark chocolate eyes burned with emotion. "I do." He slid a thin gold band, the width of a cobbler's awl, onto my finger. It glinted in the sun. Had he brought it from home or bought it this morning while he was out?

The preacher turned to me and smiled in encouragement. "And do you, Lorelei Dawn McGregor, take this man, Jeremiah Cade Dawson, as your lawfully wedded husband?"

I opened my mouth but the train blasted an ear shattering whistle from the tracks behind us. Jeremiah and Luke both doubled over and covered their ears. The sound had startled my heart into a gallop and as Jeremiah straightened up again, I couldn't help the giggle that escaped my lips. Inappropriate, yes, but Jeremiah's answering smile made it hard to feel too guilty.

"That was a yes. I do," I said.

"Kiss your bride," the preacher said with a gesture to Jeremiah.

Right. I'd forgotten about this part and suddenly my palms became very clammy. Last night had been easy. He'd kissed me without any warning and took complete control. I didn't have to do much more than exist in the warm stirrings his lips created. Now, I had to be an active participant in our first wedded kiss—and in front of an expectant audience, no less.

Jeremiah, in his strong, calm way, lifted my chin gently and pressed soft lips against my own. This kiss wasn't fierce as it had been last night. This one asked permission and left my entire body warm despite the frigid air of the platform. As he pulled away, the soft pad of his thumb stroked my cheek.

I couldn't take my drunken gaze from the satisfaction that adopted his face as Kristina pulled me in for a lung-squeezing hug. "Welcome to the family," she said.

The preacher congratulated us before taking his leave and Jeremiah leaned forward. I didn't know if my knocking knees could handle another touch of his lips but I sure was ready to give it a try. He leaned against my ear instead and over the noisy bustle around us, he said, "I'll go get the train tickets if you want to wait here."

Leaning helplessly into the delicious scratch of his jaw until it caressed the skin at my neck, I murmured, "okay."

The intensity in his eyes turned my insides molten as he hovered just inches away from my face.

It was Luke who interrupted the most intimate moment of my life to date. "Come on lover-boy. Go get those tickets before we miss the train."

Jeremiah's gaze dropped to my lips, which throbbed with wanting under the intensity of the hunger in his eyes. He spun and disappeared into the crowd as I rocked forward on the scuffed toes of my heeled shoes like a Snapdragon reaching for sunlight.

Luke picked up my bag in a very gentlemanly manner and hoisted it easily with the other three he already carried as he led us to the loading platform. Jeremiah was back shortly, and despite my frightened urge to run from his touch lest he turn me to melted butter again, he helped me onto the train with a tender palm to my lower back. Guiding me past the short bench that nestled Luke and Kristina, we took the seat right behind them.

Luke turned and twitched his head to the door behind us. When I looked I couldn't see anything abnormal about it, but Jeremiah's dark eyes narrowed with a thoughtful expression.

"This train don't have the extra passenger cars for us to escape it," he said, and Luke turned back around.

"What's wrong?" I asked.

"I don't like us being this close to the cargo car is all," he said. "It's nothing to worry about though."

As the train steamed slowly from the station, it became quickly apparent that traveling by rail and carriage for this long would likely be the best way to get to know Jeremiah and my new family. I hadn't even brought a book to read or catalogue to flip through. The views were lovely though as the country surrounding the city became breathtaking wilderness blanketed in a thin coat of sparkling snow. Luncheon was served in a matter of hours, and though it was far from elegant dining, my stomach rejoiced over having been fed so well since I'd met my husband.

Husband. What an odd title for the stranger sitting beside me.

He'd gallantly given me the window seat and now he stared over the seat in front of us and out the windows farther up. He hadn't shaved this morning and the first shadow of dark stubble shaded his jaw. The urge to touch the texture was so acute, I took another bite of my buttered bread and cheese to dissuade myself. His jaw worked and flexed as he chewed his meal and the delicious dark in his eyes seemed to miss nothing, much like his mother's.

He'd shed his long jacket and it lay draped over the back of our seat. He wore a tight fitting cotton shirt and black sleeveless vest over it. His riding boots were worn but cared for and covered most of his calves before his tan fitted pants disappeared into them. An outfit to show off the lean musculature of an able man. The breadth of his shoulders was wide in comparison to his hips, and something about his figure turned my thoughts to a scandalous nature. What would a man like him look like without any clothes on? Surely he wouldn't have the soft look of a city man with no physical duties. It was obvious Jeremiah got his strength from the life he lived because the cut of muscle under his thin shirt was curved steel, not the malleable edges of a one born to an abundance of rich foods.

Kristina turned with a mouth full of food. "The train ain't no place to spend your wedding night, is it?"

"Kristina," Jeremiah warned. "We'll layover in St. Louis for a night before we hop the carriage."

The mention of a break in our trip dried my mouth right up. Would he want to consummate our marriage in some saloon along the way?"

"Hey," he said quietly, like he could hear my racing thoughts. His hand rested steadily on my knee and I jerked. Why did I always do that? Frustration with myself only deepened to some endless chasm when he pulled his hand away from my skirts. "I ain't gonna force you to do anything you ain't comfortable with, you hear?"

I bit my lip and stared out the window. The last thing he needed was to see his new bride falling apart. If I were a braver woman, I'd put my arm in his. I would kiss my new husband on the cheek and assure him everything was all right, but somewhere in the past year, I'd grown cowardly. My insecurities at the beginning of my marriage to Daniel had only grown with his apparent displeasure in my body, and they had exploded over the past month as my mind sifted through all of the things that were likely wrong with me to cause such a reaction from a man I thought I knew.

And now, with my new groom, I hadn't the bravery to touch him without the nagging little voice in my mind saying he'd be disgusted with me and flinch away.

Poor Jeremiah for tethering himself to such a damaged woman.

****

There were stops along the railway that gave us the opportunity to get off and use the washroom. The first break didn't come until the evening of the first day, but it was long enough for us to dine at an eatery for dinner before boarding again for the night. The stretch of the short walk to the restaurant was precisely what my cramped legs required, and Jeremiah's mood seemed to improve as we hit the fresh country air outside. Kristina and Luke walked ahead of us, talking animatedly, and Jeremiah and I followed at a slower pace.

I'd been fileting myself over my earlier insult to him and in desperation to make it up to him, I squeezed my eyes tightly and took his hand. It was the most uncomfortable feeling in the world, climbing to the edge of a redwood branch and leaping with the hope of not hurling to my emotional death. But Jeremiah only looked down at our intertwined fingers with a questioning glance before he squeezed my hand in what I hoped was a silent thank you and not pity.

"The more you touch me, the more you'll get used to it," he said in a deep voice. "It'll always be welcome to me, Lorelei, but I know this is a lot for you. We'll go at your pace."

How had I been so lucky to marry the one understanding man I'd ever met? I wasn't ready to provide him with an explanation on why I was broken, but with an offer like this, the man deserved one.

"I was shy before I was married, and after, well—Daniel didn't like the touch of me. He was very outward with his distaste for me and it has turned me into a frightened woman, I'm afraid."

"That man was a canker sore. It wasn't you he was disgusted by. I could see it in his eyes last night. There're bad people on this earth, Lorelei. Men who need a woman cowed and under their thumb to feel like they have control fall under that category. Unfortunately, you married one of those men. I don't find you disgusting. On the contrary, your touch makes me feel things I haven't felt in a very long time."

I wished I could tell him how grateful I was for his words but the emotion in my throat would surely drown my sentiments and I'd had enough embarrassment for one day. We climbed the steps to the nearby eatery and Luke held the door open for us to follow them inside. In a surprising gesture that sent my insides to fluttering, Jeremiah lifted my fingers to his lips and kissed my knuckles lightly before he pressed his hand on the small of my back and guided me to an empty table.

"Tell me about your childhood," I said as we waited for our meal to be delivered.

Jeremiah's eyes took on a faraway look as he leaned back in his chair. "I loved it. Ma and Da were the best parents a person could ask for, and my brothers and I always seemed to find just enough trouble to keep them on their toes."

"You have more brothers?"

"Just one besides Luke. Gable is the oldest by one year."

Luke chimed in. "He was the worst one of us. He only came up with ideas that would likely end up in us getting hurt or in trouble. Like the time he was convinced we had to follow a bear to find honey. You don't, by the way. You follow the bees. Well, he'd pissed that bear off good and that thing had us treed and kicking at him by the time Da came and rescued us. Ma was fit to take the hide off of all three of us by the time we came in for dinner that night."

"I bet," I said around my own giggles. "Raising three boys? It's no small miracle she isn't completely grayed yet."

"Do you have any brothers or sisters?" Kristina asked.

"No. My parents tried for years, but I was it for them. I'd always wished for a sibling though. You?"

"Single child here too," she said. "I, however, did not wish for a sibling because I liked having my mother's attention all to myself."

"Why," Luke asked, "am I not surprised by that?"

Kristina pelted his arm playfully but his dancing green eyes never left her.

Ingrained in me was the urge to eat slowly and enjoy the meal, but while the others had finished and I was only half way done, the train whistle trilled from the station.

There was no way I could eat it all, but Jeremiah didn't seem bothered in the least. "Eat the fish and we'll bring the rest with us. You can finish it on the train."

It would be atrocious of me to take my dinner on the run and eat it in front of others on the train, but I hadn't even had a bite of the bread yet as I'd been saving the best for last. I shoveled as much as I could into my mouth and my new husband finished the leftover catfish in one fell swoop. We jogged down the street with the weight of the roll beating against my thigh from the pocket of my dress. With legs like a wet noodle, I found our seats again. Jeremiah and his brother acted as if they'd taken a leisurely stroll while Kristina and I chugged breath like we'd nearly drowned. How very intimidating that they were so well conditioned for the life they led and that I would soon be required to take part in it.

My days of gentle living were over.

Chapter Ten
Jeremiah

Little by little, Lorelei seemed to warm up to me. I didn't have a guess at what had happened between her and Daniel to create such a fear of intimacy, but if it was the last thing I did, I'd get her over it.

I needed touch. Most werewolves did. We were an affectionate breed and to secure a strong mated bond, we needed the frequent reminder of devotion. Wolves in the wild were the same and the longer I ran as one, the more similarities I found between us.

She lay against my offered jacket propped on the train window, still and breathing steadily. Sunlight filtered in through the glass and brushed her dark, downcast eyelashes as they rested against her cheek. Luke was trying to teach Kristina how to play poker on the bench seat in front of me, and the other passengers were in different stages of boredom. We'd be to St. Louis by tonight to rest before boarding a carriage in the morning.

Six days of rail and no way to change had my bones singing. The marrow had melted into something molten that belonged in the rivers of hell. The smell of wolf was heavy in the air as Luke and I struggled against the bonds that would force us to change sooner rather than later. We just had to make it to our stop tonight. We'd slip out while the girls were sleeping, and if Lorelei happened to wake and wonder where we'd gone, Kristina would cover for us. She was good like that.

It hurt to move. It hurt to stay still. I shifted my position against the tension in the strips of muscle that gave movement to my back. Every fiber in my body was on fire and I was helpless to ease the pain for another six hours at least.

The train ride had been uneventful and relaxing if not for the wolf and it's want for the hunt. But here, as the pinpointed pain burst with excitement over the nearing sweetness of release, in the wilds between civilizations, a noise pricked at my oversensitive ears.

The galloping of hooves was so faint, it was the vibrations that washed over me first. I flicked my head to the side and frowned, but they'd disappeared. The sound of shuffling cards carried on and Luke gave no inclination that anything was amiss. Maybe it was just my crazy wolf again, creating paranoia where none should exist.

But then, there it was again. Lorelei didn't stir as I leaned over her to look out the window and as soon as I determined no one was there, Luke's head snapped up. His eyes were fever bright on me. I couldn't actually read his mind, but I knew him better than anyone. He'd heard it too and if I wasn't mistaken, his instincts were probably screaming like mine were.

We jumped to an empty seat across the aisle and pressed our faces to the glass. Six horses carrying six armed riders were barreling down on our train from behind.

"What do we do?" he breathed so softly no human ears would hear.

Our options were limited and if my brother and I got involved, there'd be no stopping the storm of the wolf that would burst out of us like hellions come to earth. "We let 'em rob the train."

"You know well as I there's probably a payroll for the track workers in that car behind us, Jeremiah. Hardworkin' men won't get paid."

"Nah," I said as I leaned farther into the window. "Payroll will be insured. Their pay'll be late is all. Lay low and keep them safe."

Luke's green-eyed gaze fell on Kristina, who watched us with a look of curious dread.

"Listen up," I called to the other passengers. Most were women and children, though a few men dotted the other seven groups. "This here train's about to get robbed." I held my hands out to steady the hum of fear. It only got louder when the masses rushed to the windows and saw the fate that was coming for us. "If you want to live, you'll listen! Let them have it. Don't nobody try to be a hero. The faster they get what they want, the faster they'll be on their way so just stay still, stay calm, stay alive."

A man in a top hat cocked his ivory handled pistol. "What if we don't want to be robbed?"

"I recon it's your funeral, sir. Try not to get the rest of us killed though, you hear? It's six trained guns against your pea shooter."

"Sit down," his wife said as she pulled on the tails of his coat.

Lorelei was awake now, and the fear that swam in her eyes pulled at me so deeply I wanted to kill those sons of bitches for what they were about to do. "It'll be all right. I promise."

An explosion quaked the ground beneath us and in the chaos of screeching breaks and terrified screams, the passenger car slid from the tracks and followed the engine through a cloud of smoke at an angle. I launched myself at Lorelei to keep her from rocketing into the seat in front.

"Shut the window," I yelled as black smoke billowed into the car from the front.

The man in the top hat jumped across the aisle and slammed the only open one closed as we skidded to a screeching halt.

"The plan still stays the same," I said over the cries of terror.

Lorelei's breathing was ragged and rushed and the smell of terror wafted off of her in waves. "They just blew up the train."

"No, they blew up the tracks. Train's still mostly intact. We're going to be fine."

The sound of clomping boots and jangling spurs strode across the roof of our car and the woman who held a baby beside us whimpered.

A man with an old, dirty handkerchief covering his face came in through the connected door up front. A long barreled pistol hovered in his steady hand and swung to each passenger in turn. He smelled of whiskey, and if the filth on his skin was any indication, he'd been living rough for a long while.

"Make no mistake," he said. "We don't plan on killing the ones who do what we say, but we will, without hesitation, blast a hole in you if you don't."

Another two men entered the cabin with their peace makers drawn and descended without delay to the back where the cargo was being stored. Another three took their place up front.

"First thing's first," the leader snarled. "We'll be needin' all them weapons you got on you. Don't be shy."

The outlaws behind him scuttled from row to row collecting pistols from the men. Luke gave me a questioning glance but I shrugged. We had more weapons than just guns between my brother and I. The glint of gold in Lorelei's ring brought a slither of unease to my stomach. "Sit on your hands," I whispered as I pulled my guns out of the holsters on my hips and held them up harmlessly by the barrel.

She shoved her palms under her skirts just as one of the gunmen came to relieve me of my pistols.

"Gotta couple of big ones here fellas," he sneered through rotted teeth and rancid breath.

Holding my hands up in surrender, I said, "We don't want no trouble."

His half-cocked glare and narrowed eyes were a temporary discomfort as the train robber behind him announced it was time to relieve us of our valuables.

That's exactly what I'd hoped wouldn't happen. The men behind us had already managed to jimmy the cargo door open and were shoving paper money into a knapsack.

The man standing over me lifted a poisonous glare to Lorelei and said, "Since your man said he don't want no trouble, I think we'll start with you."

A snarl ripped through me before I had the mind to stop it and the cold barrel of my own gun was against my temple.

"Show me your hands, Ms.," he said.

"Please, sir. I have nothing else but my wedding band to my entire name," she pleaded.

Dangerously slowly, he said, "Show me…your hands."

A tear streaked down her face as she lifted them and the man grinned cruelly at his find. "We've got us some well-to-do's here, boys!"

He leaned over me to yank the ring from her, and my eyes rolled back in my head with the loss of myself. His chin made a cracking sound as my palm smashed against it and while he was still shocked I spun my gun around in his hand and pulled the trigger into his neck. Luke was already moving and leapt onto the nearest robber like a jungle cat. He'd have to handle the men up front while I took out the thieves in the cargo room. I ducked as a bullet went flying past my head so close I could feel the breeze from the path of the trajectory grace my cheek. I jumped for the storage above and used the leverage to hurl my booted kick into the gunman. Shots fired from the front of the car and women shrieked in horror.

"Jeremiah!" Lorelei screamed as the man in front of me crashed back into the cargo area.

Her panic was enough to make me hesitate, bringing me within a hair's breath of doom. The man behind the felled robber took his shot as I swung to the side, and the bullet ran a blazing trail across my rip cage. Letting the momentum of my swing carry me, I snapped man's wrist before he could pull the hammer back again, then pulled his body over my shoulder and slammed it downward until his dead weight pummeled the struggling man on the ground. Between the two downed men, only one of them was able to get a good punch in as I wailed on them until they stopped moving.

I was lost, a Berserker, a Bringer-Of-Death on the edge of sanity with the lust of the kill.

"Jeremiah," Lorelei whispered, as a chilling chuckle gurgled forth from the maimed throat of the man on the ground beneath her.

Time stopped. She stood with amber eyes only for me as he lay on his back with my pistol pointed at her head. He watched me with a wicked and bloody smile as his finger squeezed against the trigger.

"No!" I yelled.

And then, Kristina was there. From her own seat she held her intricate little Derringer. The one the men hadn't thought to look for. The one hidden where no one would find it. Her face held such intensity as she pulled that trigger and blasted her one-shot through his head. His laughter stopped and the gun clattered to the floor.

Luke was crouched with an inhuman light in his eyes. He'd been shot if the blood pooling beneath him was any clue.

"Make sure," he said in a raspy voice. I took a pistol from the limp hand of one of the outlaws and emptied bullets into their heads for good measure. We didn't need anyone else coming back from the dead. Luke did the same up front and when we were certain none would hurt any one of these frightened people huddled together on this derailed train, then I gave into my need to see Lorelei safe.

She was huddled into herself in our seat with a wide and vacant look in her eyes. They were rimmed with unshed tears and she rocked gently.

"Jeremiah Cade, you're a mess," she said in a strange tone. She pulled a white handkerchief from her pocket and started wiping smears of red from my face. It wasn't even my blood.

"Are you all right?" I whispered.

She didn't flinch from my touch as I stroked her face and hair. I couldn't have kept my hands from her if I tried. Her frightened eyes landed on the body beside me.

"I'll get them out of here, okay?" I murmured.

Luke's face was buried in Kristina's neck and she rocked him slowly.

"We need to move these bodies," I said. "They can't stay in here with all these good people."

Kristina shook her head. "No, Jeremiah. *You* need to move these bodies. Your brother needs a minute." Her eyes were wide and steady. She was hiding what he was from the bustle of everyone around us. He was injured and on the verge of a change and dragging around bodies wasn't going to keep him human.

I wasn't much better off, but my injury wasn't so bad and I still had some semblance of control. I pulled my hat farther down over my eyes and grabbed the legs of two of the train robbers. When the bodies were piled up near the blast site in the rails, I peeked my head into the engine car up front to find the three workers there all shot through. Damn those wicked men for shooting unarmed rail workers and robbing women and children. How far did a man have to fall to lack any trace of honor?

The dark tendrils of evening stretched across the clearing and I gave the tree line a quick look over to make sure there weren't stragglers waiting to take their revenge in the night.

The woman with the baby squeezed my forearm when I returned. "Thank you for what you and your brother done, sir. That was mighty brave of the both of you."

I gave her a tired smile. My body was a writhing ember and it was all I could muster. I locked my arms against two seat backs and lifted my voice. "We aren't due in St. Louis for some time yet, but they'll figure out something's happened when we don't show up. We aren't close enough to any towns to walk and it would be too dangerous in the dark anyway. We have no choice but to stay here overnight and wait for help. I recon they'll get to us by mid-day tomorrow."

"What if more of those men come back in the night?" a quite woman in a cream colored dress asked.

"I already checked around and it looks like these men were the entirety of their outfit. Just to be sure though, my brother and I will camp outside tonight to keep an eye out for any mischief. I'm sorry for what you folks have been through and I wish it hadn't happened, but we can't change what is. We just have to wait out the storm and move on when help arrives." I made my way back to Lorelei through the chaos of the small, frightened mass.

"I'm coming with you," she whispered.

"You'll be more comfortable in here," I argued.

"But I'll be safer with you."

Well, that was to be determined. If she came outside this train tonight, I wouldn't be changing into a wolf like I so desperately needed but the pleading desperation in her eyes made me not care so much about the pain. I didn't like the idea of not having her with me either.

I sighed. "You." I pointed to the man in the top hat.

"Blake Parker," he said.

"Mr. Parker, would you be so kind as to get these people some dinner from the car in front? Blankets too if you can find any."

He left immediately and I pulled Lorelei behind me. "We'll be camped just inside the tree line. Holler if anyone needs anything and we'll hear you," I said before leaving the car.

Luke and Kristina followed closely behind us, dragging her bag.

Inside of the protective arms of the forest, I sat heavily on a boulder.

"You're hurt," Lorelei said.

The fire across my ribcage was nothing compared to the burning in my marrow. "I'll live."

Luke nodded his head toward the woods. "There's a creek runnin' about fifty yards that way. We could use some water."

"Come on, Lorelei," Kristina said as she pulled a canteen out of her bag.

"Is it safe?" she asked.

"Got my Derringer," she clipped. She took Lorelei's hand and pulled her into the woods.

"How bad is it?" I asked Luke gruffly.

He pulled his jacket aside to show an impressive dark stain soaking the shoulder of his shirt. "I'll live," he said with a wry smile.

Chapter Eleven
Lorelei

It was difficult to appreciate the cold beauty of the woods because most of me was consumed with thoughts bathed in the violence of the robbery. I'd never in my life witnessed something so horridly brutal.

"Where did Jeremiah and Luke learn to kill like that?" I whispered to Kristina. She walked just ahead of me in the direction Luke had pointed us.

"Some men are born with an instinct for it." She pulled the branches of a shrub back for me to pass through. "The difference between our men and those train robbers is that Luke and Jeremiah have a conscious reservation about such things. Don't mistake them killing for us as evil. They saved us and every other innocent on that train, and neither one of them thought about the bodily risk to themselves."

"I'm grateful. It's just I've never seen a more lethal man than the one I'm married to."

"Worried, are you? Well, you never have to worry about him turnin' that violence on you. Jeremiah's a good man. I mean, right down to his core good. He only kills when he has to and part of that is a product of the times, of our situations, of the land we live on. You want a man like Jeremiah to be protectin' you, Ms. Trust me when I say, you don't want a man hesitating to keep you safe."

The bile I'd been holding down ever since I watched all of those men die revolted on me. Doubled over, I wretched over and over again. A warm hand rubbed my back as Kristina crooned nonsensical things until my stomach had emptied itself completely.

"I forget you're used to tender living sometimes," Kristina murmured.

I pressed the back of my hands to my lips. "Don't tell him."

"He won't see it as weak."

"Please."

The blue in her eyes swam with understanding. "I won't. Come on. The creek is just through there. I think I can hear it."

The creek was wide and carried chunks of ice down the currents. She filled the canteen while I rested my quaking knees on the pebble beach. She squatted there a long time by the babbling water before she turned to me again. "We almost died just now, didn't we?" Her cheeks were rosy in the cold wind and the blond hair that had escaped her braid whipped around her face.

I took a long, shaky drag of air and nodded. "Thanks for shooting that horrible man," I said. The image of his laughing, filthy face with blood gurgling freely from his throat as he aimed that pistol at me would haunt my dreams. Kristina had stood for me though. She and those Dawson boys had changed my fate.

"Don't mention it," she said in a shaky voice. Maybe pulling the trigger would haunt her dreams, too.

The canteen sloshed with a satisfying sound as she handed it to me, and I took a healthy swig. I poured the frosty water into my hand and splashed myself in the face. I had to get a grip. Jeremiah was hurt, and even if he thought he was fine, his wound needed tending. I refilled the canteen and followed Kristina out of the quiet of the woods. By the time we arrived back, Jeremiah had a sizable pile of wood stacked and was starting a fire with a small mound of shavings and two pieces of flint. Why was I not surprised that he brought fire making materials with him wherever he went?

Kristina didn't ask permission. She pulled at the buttons on Luke's shirt until the oozing wound on his shoulder was exposed. "It went clear through you," she said, prodding the other side.

She didn't have to ask, but I did. Jeremiah was mine, but only newly so. I wrung my hands. "Will you let me look?"

A fiery turmoil knitted his eyebrows. "I told you it wasn't so bad."

The wave of rejection was heavy, like a tangible weight upon my shoulders. "Okay."

He stood and strode quickly into the trees. "I'm going hunting."

Ridiculous man. Putting me off was one thing, but if he thought he was up for traipsing through the woods to hunt down goodness-knows-what, he'd lost his blasted mind. I ran after him, fueled by my anger. Anger over his rejection, anger over his stubbornness, anger at the danger of this place.

"Jeremiah!" I yelled, spinning. He'd disappeared like some apparition of the forest. I turned and turned until I was dizzy. I couldn't remember the way I'd come and nothing looked familiar. "Jeremiah?" I whispered.

There. He stood like a statue against a giant fir tree. Had he been there all along? Pulling himself to his full height he stalked closer. "It's dangerous to run off into the woods alone." His voice sounded strange—raspier than I'd heard before.

"I wasn't going alone. I was following you to keep you from running off wounded to hunt or whatever it is you think you are supposed to be doing."

He stood so close I could smell the iron of his spilling blood. "I need meat," he murmured. "I can't heal on cheese and bread. Go on back to camp and I'll be back with dinner."

I tipped my chin upward and glared. "I'm not going back without you. Let me see it."

If I wasn't glaring directly up at him, I would've missed the slight turning of the corner of his mouth. Instead of telling me to get lost, however, he pulled his jacket back to expose his bloodied shirt. Well, I'd asked for it. Clenching my hands didn't steady them like I'd hoped, but I untucked his shirt anyway. I lifted and pulled until the cloth separated from the drying blood that held it. Jeremiah's eyes never left me and he never flinched, but as the tautness of his skin and musculature was exposed to the cold breeze, I sucked air through my teeth at the sight of the extent of the injury. I wasn't practiced in medicine but I was pretty sure that was part of his rib peeking through the open skin and muscle. It needed cleaning but I was too chicken to even touch it.

He grabbed my wrist and pushed the palm of my hand against the stone hard flatness of his blood-slicked abdomen. Fear suffocated me as his other hand brushed a strand of hair away from my face. His muscles flexed with every breath he took, and an unfamiliar churning spilled warmth into my center. His eyes, dark and hungry, held me frozen in place, like he held some power over my ability to flee.

The spell was broken when he loosed my gaze and brought his lips to mine. Instinct born of learned fear had me pushing him away despite my wanting. "Don't."

He eased back for a moment, but then his lips crashed onto mine and the earth around me vibrated like another stick of dynamite had been lit under my rails. My back was against a tree before I knew we'd even moved, and his weight was so great against me, I gasped for air as his teeth grazed my neck. His tongue brushed the closed seem of my lips as if he were asking for an invitation. I'd never kissed like this, but instinct told me I wanted to open for him. He invaded my mouth and my knees buckled at how good he tasted, at how good he felt against me. Long, lapping strokes explored my mouth, then trailed down my jaw to my throat. I wanted more. "Jeremiah," I breathed. I didn't know what I meant to say, only that I needed to utter his name.

Hands gripping the back of my neck, hips bucking against me in a slow motion and I gasped when I felt just how riled up I'd got him. That tiny noise from my throat seemed to break the spell Jeremiah had fallen under. His lips pulled away from the tender skin at my throat, leaving the chill of the loss of our connection. We stood there, panting and staring at each other warily. Slowly, I unclenched my fist from the back of his bloodied shirt. When had I clutched onto him like that?

"Camp's that way," he rumbled against the overly sensitive nerve endings by my ear. He pointed and through the woods, the glow of a campfire beckoned me. His weight lifted and like a dream, he was gone into the lengthening shadows of the woods. Like some drunken boozehound I stumbled toward the inviting warmth of the campfire.

"Are you all right?" The look of alarm on Kristina's face would've been comical if I could think straight. Her eyes stayed riveted on my bloody hand.

What must I look like to gain such worry from her? I patted my hair gingerly but really I didn't care. Luke grinned like a cat with a mouse from across the fire.

"Oh, I'd say she's more than all right," he said.

"Luke," she warned.

I cleared my throat once and then again when nothing intelligent came to mind. "Jeremiah went hunting."

Luke's grin grew to an obnoxious size. "Yeah, we got that when he said, *I'm going hunting.*"

"Oh, right." I plopped down on an overturned log while Kristina finished tying a knot in her husband's bandages. The frayed fabric looked suspiciously like the underneath of Kristina's skirts. Clever.

By the time my husband arrived back with four fat hares, the fire had warmed me straight through and I was again in control of my mental facilities.

"How did you get four rabbits so quickly? I thought they were rather hard to catch and I didn't hear a single shot."

Jeremiah balanced the spitted meat over the flames with a system of y-shaped branches. "Hunting's always come natural to me."

Kristina snorted but covered it up with a cough. I caught it though and narrowed my eyes. Obviously I wasn't in on the joke, and the feeling of being the outsider not trusted to get it was a slap to cold skin. My thin jacket enveloped me as I huddled deeply into it. If I was pouting, so be it. He wouldn't let me dress his wounds, he'd kissed me like some rutting animal in the woods, and now he was a jester at my expense.

"Here." He shed his coat and put it over my legs. It was a long, weather-proof duster that went down to his knees which meant it nearly covered me entirely. The air inside was warm and smelled of him.

"Won't you be cold?" I asked, eyeing the ripped shirt and the red gore beneath it.

"No. I can handle the cold better than you."

I scowled. "You can do everything better than me, can't you?"

He turned the spits and sank back against the log beside me. His arms enveloped me with the immoveable strength of an ancient oak tree. "Shh, now. I wasn't trying to offend you, woman. I was just answering your question."

Between the warmth of my jacket, his duster, his body heat and the way he lit my insides on fire, I was likely to burst into flames at any moment, but as time dragged on, each of my muscles relaxed in turn. Just as I was about to shed the heat of his duster, he left me to pull the spits from the fire.

"For you, my lady." A very dead, skinless, headless bunny steamed away on the stick he handed me.

"What do I do with it?"

Kristina grabbed two more from the fire. "You eat it," she suggested.

I took the hot stick by the end and waited until it cooled. Luke and Jeremiah apparently had no sensation of heat in their mouths, since they immediately pulled hot strips of meat from the ribs and legs and ate with the tenacity of starving dogs. Kristina blew dainty puffs of frozen air over hers and my assumption that women were, in fact, the more intelligent gender was encouraged.

The rabbit wasn't half bad if I ignored the imaginings of the poor bunny's ended life and of the babies that were probably waiting for it to come home while I ate their parent. Did rabbits have babies in late winter? I finished most of mine and Jeremiah skillfully plucked anything I'd missed.

The train sat derailed in the clearing in front of us, and lanterns lit it from the inside. Every once in a while one of the passengers would move across a window. They were able to move at all because of Jeremiah and Luke's bravery. A stoic sense of pride filled the parts of me that hadn't been taken with fear. My husband was a ruthless killer, but only when he had to be. He'd tried to cooperate with the robbers and spare everyone's life. Whatever he'd seen in the man who was about to steel my new wedding ring had caused his violent reaction, and despite our new acquaintance, I trusted him. My life had been spared because of his actions, of that I was certain.

Kristina handed me a thin blanket to coat the ground beneath and with Jeremiah's strong body curled around me and the hypnotizing fire in front, I fell asleep easily enough enveloped in a fog of safety.

That night, I dreamt terrible things. Daniel was there but his face was always in shadow and I was running but not fast enough to ever truly escape. As I rounded the corner of my drab room in the city, he was there with eyes shining bright and red as Oklahoma dirt. "The wolves are coming," he hissed in a voice not entirely human.

I startled awake to an urgent shaking. Jeremiah's back was to the fire and he hunched over it with his weight to one side. Though the embers were blocked, Kristina's figure was dim against the lighter sky.

The panic was high in her voice. "We have to go now."

The sound of something cracking was like a canon blast here in the still of the night. A tree branch? My mind was sleep muddled but I scrambled to my feet. A long, low rumble came from somewhere close by and I searched the woods frantically. Kristina was half dragging me and Luke was nowhere to be found.

"Jeremiah?" I asked in a small, frightened voice.

His neck made a strange popping sound as he turned to me, and in the dim radiance of the fading embers his eyes reflected a strange light, like that of a wild animal who waited just outside of a lantern's glow. I blinked hard and when I opened them again, the reflection was gone and Kristina was pulling me behind her. Her fear encouraged mine.

"What's happened?"

Panting, she whispered, "The wolves are coming."

Chapter Twelve
Lorelei

The distance between us and the train and the safety it could provide was too great. I wanted to scream to rid myself of some of the confused terror that came after dreams that directly preceded running for my life. Wolves? What about Jeremiah and Luke? Sure they had proven they could fend off human monsters, but wolves were ravaging predators with fangs. In the dark there was movement running alongside us at a distance. I couldn't see it well, but I knew we were being hunted.

"Faster," Kristina yelled never letting loose my hand.

Brave girl would die along with me and my slow, city legs. I lifted my skirts and pumped my legs harder than I'd ever had need to. They burned and screamed at their treatment but I couldn't stop. Fright drove me.

The snarling reached us just as Kristina pulled on the passenger car door. I stood there in the dark as she tried frantically to wedge it open. "Help us," she screamed. "Let us in!" *Bam, bam, bam* rang her fists as they beat against the window.

I turned as a shriek lodged in my throat. It was coming. A great gray and white beast had come to brutally kill me. I'd repay Kristina's lifesaving kindness by standing between her and the snarling, snapping killer. Just as I lifted my arms to shield my face, hands grabbed my waist from behind and pulled me into the open door. I went limp and let them drag me to safety but not before I saw it.

Another darker wolf came from the shadows of the night, as fast as the wind with white bared teeth glistening to match the snow, and the gray wolf, much closer, turned and catapulted his weight against the other. A fearsome fight raged just outside the windows. Kristina and I and the man in the top hat, Mr. Parker, watched the two wolves try to tear each other apart. Whatever had caused their war, whether it was from encroached territory or the need for an outlet after a failed hunt I hadn't a guess, but the violent efficiency in which they tore into each other was mesmerizing. Kristina stayed plastered to the window with a look of wide-eyed horror until they'd disappeared back into the shadows.

"They'll kill each other," she whispered.

I put my arms around her and squeezed tightly. "At least they aren't focused on Jeremiah and Luke out there."

A tear spilled from her pooling eyes. "Yes," she whispered, though she didn't sound convinced.

The run left me breathless and my arms shook from fear, but Kristina seemed to need more comfort than me. "Come on, we shouldn't wake the others."

The rows of seats were taken with slumbering passengers and the only other one awake besides us and Mr. Parker was the young mother who had her fussy babe at her breast. I didn't bother to lay us down. It was unlikely that either one of us would get sleep with such terrified excitement pumping through our bodies, so instead, I set Kristina onto a bench beside me and pulled her head to my shoulder.

She cried quietly and I understood. I was so worried about Jeremiah I was having trouble swallowing the cotton in my throat. She'd been married much longer and would have a stronger bond with Luke. She must be worried sick with him out there in the cold with those wolves.

****

Jeremiah

The light that filtered through the tree branches and threw blinding rays against my eyelids woke me up. I groaned at the pounding in my head but the tiny noise in my throat only made it much worse. I didn't usually feel this close to death when I changed. Rolling over onto all fours, I took stock of my body. All of it was still here, but most of me was covered in blood. *Blood?*

Come on, Jeremiah. Think. What had happened last night that my wolf had managed to bathe in blood? The teeth wounds on my wrist were what gave it away and in a flurry of bombarding memories, like the pepper of gunfire, painfully jagged pieces came back to me.

"Luke?" I yelled in a voice like my wolf had clawed up my vocal cords on his way out. "Luke!"

Logic didn't return until I'd run a good twenty yards. I had to be a good hunter now, like Da taught me all those years ago. Stilling every shivering muscle, I scented the breeze. The faintest noise drifted on the wind from over the hill and I ran until the numbness in my legs slowed me. I hadn't a clue where I was or where my clothes would be. All I knew was I had to find my brother. Sliding down the side of the hill, dodging snow covered boulders and branches, I found him in a drift of red snow—glaring at me.

"That was too close, Jeremiah."

"Are they all right?"

"Kristina got them into the train before you could get to her."

I sank to my knees. "Good girl," I breathed.

Was I hunting Kristina, as my wolf always did, or had I been hunting Lorelei? Had I been trying to kill my own mate?

Luke stood stiffly. "Stop it."

"Stop what?"

"I can practically hear you planning your own death from here. You aren't mated yet and even if you were, you can't be certain you weren't just going after Kristina again. Maybe Lorelei had nothing to do with this. Let's go before my cock freezes off. Kristina would be pissed."

Blood loss and the cold made our journey back to our waiting clothes painfully slow. I'd never blacked out before, but by the time our trusty noses led us to the long cold campfire and the waiting warmth of the garments my wolf had somehow wiggled out of, it was close. Washing my half frozen, injured body with snow to clean the red away was likely one of the most miserable three minutes of my life. It at least made it to the top five which was impressive by werewolf standards. It was a rare feat that one of us lived life easy.

Lorelei's voice echoed across the clearing. "We're not leaving here until you send another search party out for our husbands!"

"Ma'am," a man I didn't recognize said. "We already sent two parties out this morning and we found not hide nor hair of your men. This here's Indian country. Their scalps are probably bouncin' across the backside of some painted pony by now."

The sharp crack of palm against flesh had me galloping as fast as my weary body could manage.

"How dare you," she spat out. "How dare you talk about my husband like that. Can you not see my friend is at her whit's end and here you are, talking about such horrid things."

"Luke?" Kristina called. Her eyes were red and swollen like she'd been crying for some time. "Luke!" she cried, flying down the curve of the snow drifted glade toward my brother.

"I told you," Lorelei said behind her. "I told you he'd come back."

I was so damned glad to see that woman, my insides threatened to burst on me. The snow slowed her down, but not by much. She didn't look like she'd been crying like Kristina did, but the dark circles under her eyes said she worried all night over my fate and that was good enough for me. She hurtled into me so hard I barely caught her.

"It's okay," I crooned. "I'm here now. You're safe."

Her voice was thick with emotion. "Oh, Jeremiah. The others have all gone already. We've been waiting for you to come back and I was so scared you were lost or hurt out in those woods somewhere." Her arms shook around my waist from cold or fear or maybe both.

"Come on," I said against her hair. "Let's hop this wagon before that fine gentlemen over there feeds us to Mother Nature."

"Fine gentleman, my arse," she grumbled and threw her hands over her mouth like it would take the words back.

I stifled a smile. "You're a feisty little curser when you're mad."

"I'm so sorry," she said. Her amber eyes were open wide and her pupils were dilated, making them look darker.

I pulled her behind me. Maybe if we were moving she wouldn't be able to tell how badly my own hand was shaking. "I don't mind you being defensive over me, Lorelei, and I ain't your keeper. You talk however feels right."

Kristina's bag of tricks had already been hauled to the waiting buggy and as I reached for Lorelei's waist to help her in the back she shook her head. The disappointment that welled up inside of me was sharp like the crack of the whip.

Her words soothed the ache. "It isn't about touch. I just don't want you injuring yourself any further on my behalf."

I'd done a decent job of covering all of my cuts and bites and scrapes with winter clothing so the injury she spoke of must've been my grazed ribcage which, as it happened, was already half healed thanks to the regenerative properties of me changing last night. That wasn't something I could easily explain though so I nodded my thanks and jumped up in the bed of the buggy beside her. One shaggy buffalo blanket was all there was to lend warmth to all four of us on the long ride to St. Louis, and though it was big, Luke and I were bigger. We sat the girls together and covered them between us and whatever was left over was plenty enough because I'd nodded off in two swings of an ax once those two ponies pulling the wagon hit a good pace.

If the weather held, we'd be to town by nightfall, but the weariness down to my very bones said I wouldn't be conscious for most of the trip.

Chapter Thirteen
Lorelei

When I was a child, I'd had this fantasy about living in the wilds somewhere. I'd only just started my courses and was on the cusp of womanhood, and Mother had started daily conversations about who would be appropriate to marry me off to. A marriage was years down the road for me, but at the time it felt just around the corner. I was much too young to be a wife and dreamed of running away to some unknown place no one from the city would ever find me. I'd sit in our lush spring gardens and pretend it was the wilds of the Carolinas and I was living alone and fending for my own independence. I'd hidden books, toys, and food I'd managed to steal from the kitchen and some days, I'd hide out there for hours.

The actual wilds were nothing like I'd imagined. A dangerous beauty shadowed everything. The trees grew close together with barely enough path to walk through them, and the colors were blindingly beautiful. I'd had no idea that many shades of green existed on this earth.

The carriage rocked precariously to the side as the wheel found yet another deep etched divot in the road. The closer to Colorado Springs we drove, the more canyons dotted the road from extensive use. I leaned my cheek against the window. If I lay just so, I could see the side of Jeremiah as he rode up front on top of the coach with the driver. As the days had passed, he'd only grown more agitated and fidgety until finally, he couldn't bear to ride in the small cabin with the rest of us.

What could his distance mean? He stretched his long leg out to the side like it hurt to stay still, and the early morning sunlight glinted off of the spur on his boot. Had I done something to upset him? Maybe he'd tired of me already and couldn't stand to be in such close quarters with someone he could barely stand.

The day was uncommonly warm for early February and the gentle breeze stirred up by the motion of the two horse team in front brushed my cheek in comfort. It was here, laying across the carriage window that I saw Colorado Springs for the first time. This would be my new home and a mass of emotions flooded me. Homesickness, hope, and nervous tension were the front runners. What if I accepted my new home, but my new home didn't accept me back?

A quaint wooden bridge pointed our carriage down a main street of sorts. It was like no town I'd seen. If I blinked, I'd miss the entirety of it. Men in cowboy hats and hide pants loaded wagons and tied up horses. Ladies in plain dress talked in small groups outside of a dressmaker's shop. A wild horse ran down the street and no one even bothered to notice or chase it down. The town's people simply stepped out of the way as it barreled down the main road. Chickens pecked lazily through the muddy snow and a fat sow peeked her head out from under a cabinetry shop. I was no longer in Boston, that was for certain.

The driver pulled the horses to a stop in front of a saloon, and no sooner than the wheels halted, Kristina poured out of the carriage door and onto solid ground.

"Home," she groaned.

I stepped onto the wooden walkway in front of the shops and stretched my back. An older couple waddled past and I waved. "Good day to you."

The woman's face tightened into an unimpressed grimace, and she huffed angrily when her eyes lit on Jeremiah. "The devil's breeding right here in town," she muttered. "Right under our noses."

I frowned up at Jeremiah but he only shrugged. "You need anything from the general store?" His boots made a tremendous thud as he jumped gracefully from the top of the carriage.

"I don't think I do. I don't really know."

"She needs an apron," Kristina said. "Come on. The boys have to get a few supplies and grab our horses and it'll take them a bit. There's someone I want you to meet."

"Trudy?" I asked. I'd heard so many stories about her, I felt I already knew her.

"Yep." She led me to the back door of an eatery named Cotton's and there, for all to see, she snuck up on a freedwoman and threw her arms around the back of her.

The woman laughed and turned, her profile full with child, and hugged her back. I wasn't the only one who looked scandalized. Half the town seemed to be eating in the restaurant and scowled in unison.

Now, Massachusetts had been a huge driving force toward anti-slavery long before the Civil War, and we were more open than most with the Emancipation and I was proud to come from a place that encouraged change and freedom. However, even in Boston freedmen still worked as paid servants for most of the families I knew. They were trained in kitchens, stables, and gardens and as such would tend to work in areas they knew well. The difference now was they were usually compensated for their work. Even in Boston, it was a rare sight to see two different races embrace each other in such a public fashion. I frowned. Really, it was rare to see any women embrace in such a way because it was considered improper manners and common. Kristina wasn't any woman though and I really shouldn't have been shocked that her best friend was a freedwoman. She didn't care about pleasing anyone else outside herself and the Dawson family, and I was starting to realize the benefits to that mindset. Never before had I met a happier person than my sister-in-law.

Kristina's face was lit up like a lantern. "Lorelei, I'd like you to meet Trudy. Trudy, Lorelei."

A polite smile took over Trudy's full lips and her caramel skin glowed around her dancing eyes. She was a striking woman, with thick, dark hair pulled back into pins. Her dress was almost the same charcoal grey color as mine, but hers looked finely made, while mine was frazzled at the seams due to rough use.

She held out her small hand. "Nice to meet you, Mrs. Dawson."

I shook it gently. *Mrs. Dawson.* That was the first time I'd heard my new surname.

Kristina gave a delighted gasp. "We're both Mrs. Dawson now!"

It was hard to stay reserved around her level of excitement all of the time. She made me want to join in on her completely inappropriate jokes or in the very least, laugh. I knew she didn't need the encouragement and that Jeremiah leveled her a disapproving look at minimum ten times a day, but I couldn't help but want to join in on the fun. My husband's subtle disapproval was the only thing keeping me a lady.

"It's very nice to meet you too, Trudy. Do you work here?"

"I do. I run the kitchens here and seeing as how this is the best eatery in town, I'm sure you'll be tasting my recipes at some point."

"It smells delicious."

"You know," Kristina said, "when I come here fresh off the

carriage, I had two hungry men to feed and not a lick of experience in the kitchen. It was Trudy here who taught me how to keep a man from starving."

"Well now, I can't take all that credit. You had to improvise and learn to cook over an open fire."

Kristina shot her a frantic look and shook her head.

"Y'all going to stay for dinner or are you headed on up to your place?" Trudy asked without missing a beat.

"I'm famished," Kristina said. She turned to me and grabbed my hands. "I have enough coin to share a meal if you want."

"Okay," I said uncertainly. "What about the men?"

She waved her hand nonchalantly. "Those boys can fend for themselves better than I've seen anyone do it."

"We're all filled up for lunch but you can eat back here if you want to," Trudy offered as she gestured to a small table away from the prying eyes of the main room.

I should be trying to integrate into my new home but after the long journey, I didn't have a clue how I looked. I wanted to be a proper lady for Jeremiah and make a good impression on his town so I said, "That sounds wonderful."

Kristina went through the foods they served like she'd memorized them. Trout, beef stew, roasted beef, grits, chicken and dumplings, fried chicken, and every savory, buttery side and vegetable wild country was known for.

"I love it all, so you pick," Kristina offered.

"It all sounds lovely but I have to admit, the mention of roasted beef has my stomach smiling."

"Roasted beef it is. Kristina you want your regular sides?"

"No, we have to show off your cookin' to my new sister, Trudy. Give us mashed potatoes with that thick onion gravy you make, and the beans."

The food was as delicious as promised and Trudy had been generous with the portions, so it was plenty of food between the two of us. She stopped by and talked to us whenever she had a second to breathe from the demanding dining room. The private space to eat was a relief. It was quiet and relaxed and the perfect way to come down from the long trip.

That was, until Kristina opened her mouth. "My bum is probably seven shades of purple after that carriage ride."

I wiped my mouth delicately with the corner of a napkin at the lovely mental image. "No doubt it will be nice to sleep in a warm bed tonight and not leaned against that carriage window."

Kristina pursed her lips and just as she was about to say something, someone blocked all of the light seeping in through the open back door. Only a Dawson could cause a shadow that big. Jeremiah's cheeks were pink from the cold outside and his hat gave him an air of mystery. His dark eyes landed on me and the corner of his mouth turned up just enough to cause a swarm of butterflies to erupt from their resting place in my stomach. Sweet blueberry pie, that man was as handsome as they came.

"You ladies about ready?" he asked. Even in his own environment he seemed to fill up the room.

"Trudy, lunch was lovely," I said as she flitted by with an armful of metal clinking plates.

"Glad you enjoyed it. Y'all come back soon."

"Of course." It was the easiest thing in the world to see why Kristina was close to her. She had an easygoing personality and a take-no-grit-from-nobody demeanor in the dining room. Maybe the people of Colorado Springs would learn a thing or two from their friendship in time.

"You should've seen the look on your face when you realized Trudy was a freedwoman," Kristina said through a toothy grin.

"It was a bit of a shock," I admitted. "I'd imagined her differently from your stories. She's really sweet. When's her baby due?"

"Less than three months now and I aim to be there for it."

"What about a midwife?"

"If you find a midwife around these parts that would cater to a freedwoman, you let us know. Her husband and I have asked nearly everyone from here to Denver."

"That's awful. Do you know anything about midwifing?"

"Nope, but I got me a book and Luke's been reading to me when he has the time."

Jeremiah stopped in front of a post of horses. Two were black as night with stockings and one was a beautiful red color with a spotted blanket across her flanks. The fourth one was brown.

"This one's yours," Jeremiah said, tightening the cinch on the horse the color of crop soil. "What's the matter? You look like someone killed your dog. Do you not know how to ride?"

"No, it's not that." I bit my lip and considered telling him yet another thing I was ashamed of. "Just forget it. This one's fine."

He sighed heavily. "Lorelei, if you don't learn to tell me what you want, it's going to be a long life for you out here."

I straightened my spine. "I don't like brown horses."

His face looked almost comical. "It ain't the color of the horse, it's the temperament. You know that, right?"

Kristina was already mounted on the spotted horse. "Jeremiah

Dawson, your woman wants a pretty horse. Get her a pretty horse!"

He ran a giant hand down the entirety of his unshaven face. "Is this a test?"

Luke and Kristina rode on ahead and I leaned forward to avoid the wandering ears of the passersby. "Someone once told me I was boring, like a brown horse. I don't want to be boring anymore."

Jeremiah's eyes went cold as winter, and he spat before he asked, "Daniel?"

I gave a stiff nod.

"Can you ride this one home? I promise we'll set out tomorrow to trade for something flashy but all the blacksmith had for sale were brown horses."

"Okay." The flood of guilt over being so hard to maintain was enough to make me close my eyes against the shame it caused. "I'm sorry."

"Don't apologize for that man. Kristina's right. Luke found her that spotted pony because she'd asked him for one. I should've found out your preference first. It's been a long time since I had a woman to consider."

I mounted the horse and sat sidesaddle while he climbed up on his own.

"Is that how they ride in the city?" he asked.

"It is if you're a lady."

"You sure you aren't going to just slide right out of the saddle?"

"I don't suppose we're traveling at a full out run, are we?"

"No, ma'am, not just now."

We took the less traveled road out of town at a leisurely pace. "Back there, you said it's been a long time since you had a woman? How long is long?"

There were ghosts in the grim set of his mouth. "My first wife, Anna, passed three years ago. Feels like a lot longer some days though."

I wanted to know everything, every single thing about this enigma of a man, but I couldn't gain the courage to ask him how she'd died. It was too personal. The details of something so hard were too intimate, and it felt like a slight to the shade of his past lover to conjure those words from his mouth.

The trees were still bare and the bulk of them so close to the road I could reach out and touch them with my outstretched fingers. The warmer weather had melted much of the snow, but every so often a drift showed up here and there. Fluffed up winter birds called to each other from the branches of giant oaks and a cold weather hare dashed in front of our horses. Gently rolling hills stretched elegantly across the landscape and here, in the quiet of the woods, this wonderland looked like it belonged on some easel under a painters brush. Magical places like this didn't exist in the bustle of the city. It reminded me so much of my garden in the winter but on a much grander scale. A dangerous allure lived here, like the inviting downy pink of a thistle that would prick your finger the moment you mistook it's brilliance for weakness.

Despite my awe with the wild land, the ride to the Dawson homestead seemed to drag on and on. So restless was I to finally lay eyes on my new home that my horse skittered under me, perhaps reacting to my nervous energy. Jeremiah had become so quiet and withdrawn, I'd given up conversation with him and instead concentrated on memorizing everything about the road that would lead me back to civilization on the occasions we traveled to town. Was that a daily thing around here? What exactly did small ranches do to take up all of their time? Surely some socialization was to be expected.

He pulled his horse onto a small gravel road that wound at a slope uphill. At the precipice of that mound of earth, stretched as far as I could see, he told me this was our land. *Our land.* I'd never owned anything. Not really, and all of the sudden this rugged forest that I'd make a home on was partially mine. A stirring deep within me that tasted of pride and hope was my companion as we rode through frozen meadows and thick woods. At long last, we came to the edge of a clearing.

I scanned it in expectation of the grandeur that this place deserved and was rewarded with a barn, tremendous piles of lumber, and the charred remains of something substantial. The waiting smile remained plastered on my face. The house must be in the woods somewhere, though why someone would put it in the woods when there was a perfectly decent cleared area was beyond me.

I slid from my horse at the entrance to the barn while Jeremiah held the reins. "Where's our house?"

He cleared his throat once and then again, though it didn't seem to help him find his words.

Kristina sauntered out of the barn. "I told you, Jeremiah. You should've told her. This ain't the way she should be finding out."

"Finding out what?" I asked through clenched jaw.

He gestured to the burned scrap heap. "That's our house. Welcome home."

Chapter Fourteen
Lorelei

"Welcome home? There is no home! Where do we sleep? Where is our bed?"

Jeremiah removed his hat and ran giant hands through his short, dark hair until it stuck up on all ends. "I sleep in a tent in the woods, and Luke and Kristina sleep in the barn."

Infuriated, I snapped like a dried winter twig. "So my choices are to live in a tent in the woods or in the barn with the pigs?"

"Well, technically the pigs are outside."

"Not the point, Jeremiah!"

"Right. Well, the barn ain't the best option because Luke and Kristina are still newly married, you see."

I didn't see.

"Well, things get pretty loud in there at night when they get to breeding—"

"All right! So I'm supposed to camp out in the woods for eternity like a savage animal? I'm not a mountain man. I'm a lady, born and bred."

"Not for eternity, woman. Just until Luke and I can get our cabins built. We have the lumber, we just haven't had time to build yet."

I gasped. "Is that where Kristina's burns came from? Who burned the house, Jeremiah?"

The sound that escaped his throat said he was trying to decide to lie or not. "Honest is best," I helped him out.

"A band of men came in the night. Called themselves Hell Hunters. They burned the house with Kristina in it and tried to hang my brother and me from that tree over there."

I stared at the ancient gnarled oak in terror. "Why would they do that?"

"The sheriff and Trudy and her husband showed up in time to help Kristina get out and cut us down."

"That's not what I asked you. Why?"

His throat worked to swallow. "They thought we were evil."

Silence stretched between us like a taut rope. "Are you?"

"No, we're just different. People don't understand us, and they fear what they don't understand."

The woman's comments about the devil breeding in her town struck me. I needn't have worried about integrating into the town at lunch today because the Dawson's, despite obvious years in this community, were still feared for reasons I didn't understand.

And I'd married right into this chaos.

I wanted to run away. I wanted to scream and claw at him for bringing me to this place. Where could I hide in this unfamiliar land that he couldn't find me? I'd been ruined and desperate in Boston, and now I wasn't any better off.

As if he could see the running in my eyes, he said, "I'm going to make the camp more comfortable for you. If you need anything, ask Kristina." He turned on his heel and dragged both horses behind him into the barn.

A pile of lumber clunked hollowly as I sat upon it. What was I going to say in the letters I wrote to Mother?

I'm happily living on some forest floor in Colorado. Don't worry about me; my husband was smart enough not to build our tent on a snow drift. If you ever want to visit, you'll have to sleep in a barn, and we'll probably be eating worms for dinner.

I plopped my head into my arms and allowed a tear to fall to the moist earth below. One tear—that's all I'd grant for the trick that had been played on me.

"Lorelei?" Kristina said softly by my elbow. "Come over by the fire before you catch your death."

I followed her like a loyal mule and sank into a rocking chair that was burnt around the edges and smelled of smoke. She'd already conjured a fire like some magician and it billowed and roiled, much like my frayed emotions. She disappeared, but returned with an arm load of onions, potatoes, carrots.

"Where'd you get those?"

"You didn't think we'd be living on leaves and dried honeysuckle did you? The house burned but we dug through the rubble and our root cellar was still intact. This late in the winter, you have to cut off the rotting bits though." She wiped a large knife on the side of her dress and cut a chunk of blackened, squishy spud away, revealing the healthy portion of vegetable underneath. "I do miss our stove somethin' fierce though. Cooking over an open fire takes more time and gets food burned a lot easier. You almost can't take your eyes from it."

Luke came tromping across the clearing. "Bear raided the smokehouse. I'm going hunting."

"Bears?" I asked in a tiny voice.

She waved her knife before running it through an onion. "They only bother the smokehouse. They won't bother you none unless it's a momma with cubs or if you're shooting at it. Something must've woken it up for him to be out of hibernation this early. It's happened a couple of times around here."

I gulped and scanned the woods. "Fantastic."

"We'll get your cabin built first. I'm okay with staying in the barn for now and with Luke and Jeremiah working on one house, it'll get done a lot faster."

"How fast is faster?"

"You mean how long will you be sleeping in the woods? I don't know much about these things, but I do know they are trying to tie up loose ends before they have to plant the crops here in a couple of weeks. They'll be driving a new herd of young cattle up here soon after and things will be too busy to lend too many daylight hours to building." She leaned forward and winked. "I do say there are worse things than being snuggled up all close to your man for warmth at night."

The heat that raced up my neck and into my cheeks was as unavoidable as breathing. "Do you think he'll expect it tonight?"

She stopped peeling potatoes. "Don't you expect it? You've been on a two week journey, newly wedded and not bedded, and Jeremiah— well, Jeremiah's a tasty morsel, now ain't he?"

How did I admit this was the scariest part of being married for me? Just thinking about it made my mouth go dry.

She cocked her head like I was an enigma. "You were married. Didn't your man ever show you how fun it could be?"

"I don't think that is anyone's business but mine."

"Why?" she asked, looking around the empty clearing. "Ain't nobody here but us and I won't utter a word to a soul."

Defensively, I said, "He bedded me."

"But did he show you the fun in it? I was a whore remember? I know the difference. Most men are in it for their own pleasure, but sometimes you get a man who likes pleasing a woman. Which was your man?"

Defeated. I was utterly defeated to the point of tears at what I was about to admit. "He bedded me four times and I don't think we did it right. He liked looking at my back and it hurt so badly I didn't want to walk the next day. He only found pleasure if I screamed out. It was horrible."

Her eyebrows shot to her hairline. "Bollocks. No wonder you don't like to be touched, Lorelei. You married a demon is what you did. It don't feel like a favor now, but that man did you one the day he divorced you. It won't be like that with Jeremiah."

"How do you know?"

"Whore, remember? I can tell how a man beds before he takes his pants off. Jeremiah's a tender man and I've been watching. Every time you touch him he all but melts like butter in a pan. He'll savor you if you let him."

Her words were crude and highly inappropriate but despite all of that, they made me feel a little better. I didn't know if it was just getting that horrible admission off of my chest or if it was the easing of the rampant fear her reassurances brought, but I was grateful either way.

The sun sat low in the sky by the time Luke returned with a limp deer thrown across his shoulders. Jeremiah showed up as he was cleaning it on the other side of the barn. I was learning the intricacies of peeling carrots with a gargantuan knife but I was slow as molasses trying it. I was peppered with visions of chopping my fingers off and I liked my hands just as they were, thank you very much.

"She needs a knife of her own," Kristina said as Jeremiah warmed his hands by the fire.

"Don't be ridiculous," I snorted. "Where would I even put a knife?"

"In your pocket," he said seriously. "You never know when it'll come in handy. We'll pick you up one when we trade your horse in tomorrow."

I'd had venison stew at an inn that served it on one of our many stops. It somehow tasted even better cooked over an open fire. Or maybe it was because Jeremiah sat behind me with his legs alongside of mine that made the dinner seem more magical. I'd tried to stay angry and wiggle away from him as punishment for withholding the truth from me, but he wouldn't have it. Eventually, I had no choice but to relax against him.

He gifted me with an irresistible set of apologetic puppy dog eyes, and I softened even more. Leaned up against the log behind me, he listened to Kristina and Luke tell stories and laughed in the places I did.

It was nice. Daniel never found humor where I had. A short time out of that poisonous marriage, and suddenly all of our differences seemed obvious when I had a man of substance to compare him to.

I'd leaned forward to give Jeremiah room to eat but as soon as he set the empty dishes down, I folded into the warmth of him once again. My skin yearned for the safety of his touch. It was scandalous and I'd never seen a woman so wanton but I couldn't help myself. There in the firelight with conversation and company who so obviously didn't care about my affection toward my husband, my wants went unchecked.

He slipped his arms around me as I drifted into him and the warmth that enveloped me made a jacket on this cold night obsolete. How could a healthy man be so warm? I'd only felt heat like that once when Mother had come down with a fever one autumn when I was younger.

Kristina and Luke said their goodnights and excused themselves to the barn. I reached for our empty plates but Jeremiah tugged me back to him. "No. Just stay here a little while. The dishes will hold."

The scared crevices inside of me wanted to balk against his pull, but the darkness made me braver and I relaxed into him once more.

His voice was a delicious rumble against my neck. "I'm sorry I didn't tell you about all of this earlier. I meant to. I was going to tell you that first night but you were so damned beautiful and I knew I'd lose you if I told you I had no home to give you."

"How do you know I wouldn't have come anyway?"

"Anyone with eyes in their heads could see you were well-bred, Lorelei. I already didn't deserve you."

"Don't say that. Neither one of us is beneath the other. I felt like that in my last marriage and I'd never wish it on you. I think after that night you talked to Daniel, I still would've followed you here. He scared me."

"Mmm," Jeremiah rumbled. "You don't have to be scared again. I won't let nothin' happen to you."

I turned so I could see his eyes when I asked, "Is there anything else I should know?"

His eyes dropped for a moment but were on me again. "I mail-ordered Kristina first. She was supposed to me mine but I couldn't settle with marryin' a whore, so I pushed her off on my brother."

Pursing my lips, I let that little tidbit settle on me before I lashed out. I had no reason to be jealous. She and Luke were a good and loving match, and even though she seemed to have insight into Jeremiah that was downright unsettling at times, she was happy being Luke's wife. It was obvious they loved each other deeply.

"That ain't all," he said.

I tried not to glare.

"Luke ran scared last year and left her in my care for a season. When I was pretty sure he wasn't going to come back and give her a name, I proposed to her."

I scrunched up my face and squeezed my eyes tightly closed. "So, you lived with Kristina for some months, up here all alone, and both of you unmarried?"

"Nothin' happened. We weren't ever physically attracted to each other, Lorelei. My word is good and I give you my word on my honor. I care for her as a sister, but I know you two are friends now and I want this coming from me."

I huffed air and leaned against him none too gently. They were up here all alone with no society to hold them accountable on decorum, and they hadn't been intimate? "Did you kiss her?"

"Never."

I suppose I could understand it, but I sure as hades didn't like it. "I forgive you."

His chuckle reverberated through my dress and caressed my back. "Good. You ready to see where you'll be sleeping?"

"Show me to my castle, good sir." I stood and wiped dirt and dried leaves from the back of my skirts.

He groaned as he tried and failed to stand and a tiny sliver of worry snaked through me. He was hot as fever and sore. He was too strong a man to be this weak while healthy. I offered my hand but he waved me off and used the log for leverage instead.

"Are you all right?"

"Just sore from the carriage ride is all. This way."

He pulled me by the hand down a well-worn path behind the charred remains of the house. The trail snaked and curved through the trees until the half-moon glinted off the shell of a canvas tent, much like the ones I'd seen in shanty towns. There would be room enough for both of us, and he'd built a wood floor to keep us hovered above the moist, bug-riddled ground, so at least that was something. The floor was covered in furs, though what kind I hadn't the experience to identify. They were big and warm looking and that was good enough for me.

Seducing a man was a talent I hadn't mastered, and likely never would, but Kristina's words had me feeling bolder than I ever had with Daniel. While Jeremiah talked about his plans for a cabin and rearranged the furs, I pulled on the back laces of my dress and it billowed into a pool around my feet like the fabric of some great sail. My shift was next and Jeremiah froze with his profile to me. The wind was a soft caress as it lifted the strands of my hair that had escaped their pins. Maybe if I clenched my hands, it would stop them from shaking. My breath, however, quaked on.

"You don't have to do this tonight," he said in deep, husky voice.

I closed my eyes against the embarrassment. "You don't want to?"

Faster than I thought humanly possible, he was here with his arms around me. He captured my mouth with his and some deep instinct had me gripping him closer. I didn't know he'd lifted me or carried me into the tent until I was there, under the furs with him. His touch was fire against my skin—teasing, consuming...mesmerizing."

My body reacted with blooming warmth, and my mind threatened to shut down completely to ride the waves of want. I plucked his buttons open one by one and slid my cold hand against the warm, hard planes of his chest. Good gracious, my hand was meant to be against the steel planes of his silken skin.

So this was what it was like to touch a man—to *feel* a man.

Pulling at his shirt until it gave under my frantic grip, he shrugged out of the confines of the fabric and pressed his bare skin to mine. How could I have lived my entire life without his embrace? How could I have lived another day more without it?

A helpless groan escaped my lips and Jeremiah dipped his head to my neck. "Please," I breathed against his ear. I didn't even know what I was begging for.

A long, low rumbling sound came from the depths of his chest. It vibrated against my skin and called to the warmth deep within me. His arms were stone as he froze and my fingers searched his skin for softness where none could be found. Iron hard muscle twitched under my fingertips.

He turned his face from me and sat up. "I can't tonight," he gritted out.

A stinging ache brushed my skin where his warmth had left it, like a part of me was missing and left the rest of me raw and exposed. Cold air slithered in between us and sang of my failure. "Why?"

"I just can't." His voice sounded off...raspier and deeper. "Use that pistol if anyone comes before I get back."

"I don't understand," I said to his back, but then he was gone. I crossed my arms over my bare chest, exposed to the elements and chilling to the bone. "What did I do wrong?"

The song of breeze against barren tree branches was my only answer.

Biting my lip, I sank into the warm folds of the furs and pressed my hand against my chest until the pounding of my heart slowed to its normal rhythm. Rejection burned like a hot ember against my soul and I squeezed my eyes closed against the pain. An intense desperation washed over me for unconsciousness to free me from my churning thoughts and wonderings.

Unfortunately, sleep came slowly, like the first buds of spring after an eternal winter.

I'd tied the tent opening as tightly closed as I could and stared at the holster of pistols for a long time. Even if I wasn't deathly afraid to touch the things, I wouldn't know how to use them on an intruder. He'd left me alone on my first night in this scary place. I didn't trust myself to make it safely back to the barn or I would've escaped my tiny prison.

Finally, in the wee hours of the morning, I'd found the comforting darkness behind my eyelids.

I only woke once in the night to the shuffling and snuffling of some wild creature outside my tent. Try as I might, I couldn't make out its figure through the tent walls but it sounded big. I lay there in terror, too afraid to move for fear of alerting the animal an easy meal lay just inside the fabric of the camp. And just like he'd appeared, the sound of his feet against the dry forest carpet faded into the night and I slept again.

Chapter Fifteen
Lorelei

I awoke to the gray light of early morning. As I stretched my legs they brushed against something solid and warm.

"It's just me," Jeremiah said in a sleepy voice.

"Aaah!" I squawked. Why on earth hadn't I put my clothes back on last night? I yanked on the covers until I likely resembled a wooly bear with human eyes, then shoved Jeremiah away with the tips of my toes.

"What're you doing?" The tiny remnants of his amusement were obnoxious.

"What are *you* doing? You don't come back all night, you leave me to the animals on my first night home, and then you snuggle my naked body without my permission?" Okay, I was yelling, but so what? The man had clearly lost his mind.

"I thought you gave me permission last night. You were the one takin' all your clothes off if I remember correctly."

"Well...a lot of good that bloody did me! I'm mortified!"

He moved with the grace of a deer with none of the soreness he'd showed last night. He grabbed my kicking ankle and gave me a devilish smile. "Now why are you feelin' mortified?" He pulled my bare foot against his lap. His thick, long erection pressed against his thin pants, and I gasped as he drew the pad of my big toe the length of it. "You got me riled up to an inferno in two seconds flat."

"What? I don't even know what that means. You left me...like that. In the middle of..." I yanked my foot out of his grasp to save what was left of my dignity. "I want my dress!"

How could he be so rampantly happy when I felt like the grit underneath the floorboards? Had he no consideration for me at all? He stood and disappeared from our flimsy shanty, then tossed my dress into the open tent flaps. The unapologetic oaf waited just outside with a baiting grin on his face. He had nothing more than light cotton trousers on and his torso, which I hadn't been able to make out much in the dark last night, was bare and tantalizing for me to glare at. Hard planes of muscle rippled and flexed as he lifted his hands to rest on his hips. Breathtaking, infuriating man! Not an ounce of fat was on the entirety of his body. Jagged little scars ran over the majority of his skin but they looked old and long healed and they only added to his rugged appeal. They didn't make them like this in the city.

"You like what you see?" he asked.

I clacked my gaping mouth closed. "Turn around. I need to get dressed."

He leaned against a tree and scratched his lip with the back of his thumbnail. "If I turn around, how will I see your body?"

I opened then closed my mouth, floundering for words like some landed trout. The fur was warm and soft as I clutched it tighter. "Please, don't look at me."

He frowned and shoved off the tree as I escaped the tent with my furry shield. "Hey," he said, pulling me to him and rubbing a finger down the side of my face. "What happened to the brave woman from last night?"

"You rejected her." With my back to him I slipped into my dress. He could look or he couldn't. My pride hadn't been bruised. It had been annihilated and now, on top of everything else, he was laughing at me.

When I turned around, his back was to me. At least he had some manners.

"I'm taking you to visit some friends. They have a bunch of ponies they'd trade for the horse you have now and you can pick what you want."

"Fine," I growled. I tried to stomp away through the forest but I got lost in about two and a half yards and had to wait for Jeremiah to lead me back to the clearing. And tapping the toe of my high button leather shoe with impatience didn't make him go any faster.

"I'll saddle your horse. Why don't you go get some breakfast?" he offered.

I stomped off toward Kristina without another word. Without turning around, I could feel his eyes upon me as if they bored tiny holes into the back of my neck. I curbed the urge to throw a stick at him, but just barely.

Kristina sat by the fire licking her fingers. "Did you guys have fun last night?" she said, waggling her eyebrows.

"That depends on what you call fun. I thought we would, but obviously I've done something wrong, yet again, and he disappeared for the rest of the night." I squashed the lip tremble. Riding my anger out was better than giving into the sting of my welted pride.

"He didn't bed you? Oooooh," she said with serious eyes gone wide enough to rival a wood sprite's. "Yeah, that wasn't your fault."

"Then whose fault is it? What possible reason could a man have for running out in the middle of—well, you know?"

She shoveled scrambled eggs and thinly sliced venison steak onto a plate and handed it to me. "Now I can't tell you anything about that stuff because it's Jeremiah's place to answer those questions. But trust me when I say, it ain't you. Now, where do you want your house? Luke is starting on the hearth today while you're away."

Well, that was an unexpected turn of conversation. The house was actually much more preferable to talk about than the embarrassing events of my failed seduction. "I can pick anywhere?"

"Anywhere in this clearing. It's safest if we can get to each other easily though. Traipsing through the woods trying to track each other down is a bad idea. Oh, and probably not on that side of the barn unless you want to be downwind of the pigs and chickens and wake up to someone cleaning game meat on the hook every other morning."

"Unsavory. What about…over there?" I pointed to the far end of the clearing on the other side of the old burned house. "I should ask Jeremiah if he's okay with being that far away from the barn though."

Kristina slurped a bite of eggs. "Good wife. Jeremiah," she said at a normal conversational volume.

"What do you need?" he yelled back from the doorway of the barn like he'd heard her.

"If you don't answer he'll eventually come over here and find out what you want," she said, shoveling another bite.

"More marital advice?"

"More Dawson advice. They think its fine and dandy to have a conversation from a mile away."

Jeremiah pulled two horses behind him and left them to graze the half frozen grass near the lumber. "Did you need something?"

"I was thinking the house could go over there."

He pulled his pants over his boots and squinted in the direction I pointed. "We'd have the wind at our backs and if we face it right we could keep the sun out of the bedroom window in the morning so you could sleep in when you feel like it. Let's go take a look at it."

Like I'd never yelled at him at all, he encased my tiny hand in his and walked beside me until I said, "Here."

He took a few giant steps and spun around in a circle. "It's not too far from the barn. I like it. Come here." He wrapped his arms around my waist and my traitorous body leaned back into him. "Imagine," he rumbled into my ear, "we're standing at the front door of our home, the home we built together, and we're lookin' out over the clearing. Is this the view you want, Lorelei?"

The tension left my body as I exhaled. I could imagine it all too well. With children running around and Kristina and Luke waving goodnight from their house across the way. "I want a porch with rocking chairs."

"Naturally."

"And I want a bed to sleep on, Jeremiah. Not just a pile of furs. An actual bed."

"We may have to wait for the money from the next cattle drive, but I'll give you what you need."

I gave a curt nod. "Pretty horse, porch, bed. Those and you, and I'll be happy."

A delicious smile edged his voice. "You've already got one of 'em, now let's go work on that pretty horse for you."

Mounted sidesaddle, I waved to Kristina who was rinsing dishes inside of a small wooden bucket under the water pump. "Tell Kicking Bull hi for me," she called.

"Who's Kicking Bull?" I asked.

Jeremiah nudged his horse with his knees. "You'll see."

Chapter Sixteen
Lorelei

"If the Ute are a nomadic tribe, then how do you intend to find them?" I asked as I ducked under another passing tree branch.

"I can smell them," Jeremiah said.

"Oh, you can smell them," I said lightly. "Well that's good for you. All I can smell is fur and copious amounts of equine fecal matter."

"Equine fecal…you mean horse crap? That's because your horse is working through some serious stomach cramps."

"Will they have any spotted horses like Kristina's?"

"Maybe. My advice, for what it's worth, is to pick a horse you like the temperament on first and the looks second. You don't want a demon with a pretty face. We can pull a few you'll like and you can figure out which one you get along with best."

Three young boys met us at a tree line and pretended to throw toy spears at Jeremiah. He laughed and acted like they'd got him, then they ran off whooping and celebrating. Seven large teepees dotted the land and a rushing river snaked behind the Indian's camp. Dogs and horses roamed freely and children ran around harried mother's legs in play. Women were dressed in rich earth tones and their dark, cascading, parted hair lifted loosely in the breeze. Warriors wore their hair in braids with feathers and carried spears adorned with the tails of animals. Some wore elegant head dresses with hundreds of feathers that draped strings of beads.

"Mahtuhgurch Sahdteech," the men said in slow, lyrical voices as we passed.

"What does that mean?" I asked Jeremiah, who greeted some he obviously knew.

"The translation doesn't work exactly right to English. It's a name they call my brothers and me. It means something like Dog of the Moon."

"Strange nickname," I said, waving to a trio of curious little girls. They waved back and ducked into one of the teepees.

"Not strange to them. It's a term of respect they don't give out lightly." He hopped from his horse and pulled me down from my mount. "It's an honor."

"It does have a better ring to it than Grub Worm."

"Exactly. Kicking Bull," he nodded respectfully to a man in a huge headdress who approached.

He said a string of musical words in his language and I rode the notes with interest, though I couldn't understand a letter of it. His words were like a song—rhythmic, rich, and inviting.

Jeremiah responded in the same language and shocked, I watched his mouth move in the tongue of the tribe. The man's mysteries only seemed to grow the better I thought I knew him.

"Kicking Bull, this is my woman, Lorelei. Lorelei, Kicking Bull, chief of this band of Ute."

The white of his teeth contrasted against the olive tones of his sun leathered skin and his dark eyes danced with easy humor. "Bride of the Wolf, welcome."

"My new wife here took a fancy to that pretty Nez Perce pony you traded with Luke for. She's wanting to trade her new horse in for something with a little more flair."

Kicking Bull twitched his head toward the horse behind me and one of the men ran a hand down its back and studied it with a seemingly experienced eye. He pulled open her mouth to reveal straight, white teeth and nodded to Kicking Bull.

"We also need one of your knives if you have any to spare. Something that'll fit her hand well." Jeremiah patted the hide that was tied to the back of his saddle. "I'll throw in the bear fur for the knife and as a thanks for the warning of the crows."

"It's a good trade. Who killed the bear?"

Jeremiah snorted. "Kristina."

The old Indian's booming laugh was deep and easy on the ears. Kristina killing a bear was news to me, and I'm sure my face showed as much.

A woman gestured for me to follow her. She wore an ankle length dress made of animal hide that was so light in color it competed with the white of the occasional snow drifts that still clung stubbornly to the landscape. The hem was heavily fringed and around her waist was tied a wide strip of leather. The shawl she wore to ward off the chill was intricately beaded in blues and whites.

"I'm going to talk with Kicking Bull for a bit," Jeremiah said. "You'll be safe with his woman, Tauri. I'll come get you soon."

Oh, I heard what he was really saying all right. No girls allowed and all that. Fine, I could entertain myself. I followed the striking woman without a goodbye. Take what he would from that.

"The men," Tauri explained, "they have much to talk about."

Her English was a pleasant surprise. "Like what?"

"Your man defied his fate and survived something most wouldn't. He has strong magic and Kicking Bull respects his friendship. They have known each other for many years, and now that our future is uncertain off the reservation, he will ask Mahtuhgurch Sahdteech for council." She stopped in front of a trio of deer hides stretched across the ground and staked into place. "Do you paint?"

"I'm dreadful at painting. My mother tried to tutor me in fine arts, but I never had the eye for it."

"You can help me tan these hides then. Here, like this." She handed me a blade with a handle across the side for a two handed grip. "Work one section until it is soft and smooth, then move to the next."

On my hands and knees, the work was tedious and my shoulders ached with the strain, but the rhythm of work eased any tension we had as strangers. She talked freely of her children, two grown sons and a daughter, and her grandchildren, two grandsons with another on the way. She thought she'd have a granddaughter by the end of the moon's cycle.

One of her grandsons came and sat quietly propped against a pole that held an unfinished painting of a wolf and a giant tree with flames licking its branches. The young boy looked different than the others running to and fro between the teepees. His skin was lighter and though his hair was dark, his eyes weren't. Instead, they were the gray color of a dove.

Somewhere in this boy's family tree, one of the branches had been white.

He waved shyly when I greeted him and his grandmother looked at him with such a pride, I ached for my own family. His looks didn't make any difference to the woman beside me and I liked her more for it. When the sun reached its highest point in the sky, Tauri wiped her forehead and pulled me off my aching knees.

"Did you paint that?" I asked of the colorful hide.

"I did. We paint things that happen to and around our people.

Pictures and beadwork are a way to preserve stories from our history."

I angled my head and squinted at the picture. Something about the tree seemed so familiar, like I'd seen it in a dream or something. When I turned to ask her more about it, Tauri had disappeared like she'd never existed in the first place. I spun around but all the faces around me were unfamiliar. A flap to the nearest teepee opened and she reappeared with a necklace of white beads. It was adorned with a small pendant of beads the color of Mother's brightest red summer roses from home. She held it up and arched her eyebrows in silent question.

"For me? It's beautiful." I ran a light finger over the medallion.

She tied it in the back and patted my shoulders gently. "You'll be a good woman for Mahtuhgurch Sahdteech. You'll soothe the fire in his animal."

Tauri's way with words didn't make much sense sometimes but I thought I got where she was coming from. If every man had inner demons, the right woman should be able to calm them.

She nodded slightly. "I liked talking to you. Maybe I'll come with Kicking Bull next time he seeks out Mahtuhgurch Sahdteech."

"I'd love that. Please do."

She gestured to a string of four Indian ponies tied to a rope stretched between two teepees. Jeremiah stood to the side and talked softly to two fearsome looking braves.

"That's sure a pretty necklace you got there," he called.

"Thank you. Tauri gave it to me."

He smiled affectionately at the woman beside me, then arched his gaze back to me. "These are your options. These fillies are young and sound, good teeth and any one of these will make you a fine horse."

One was mostly white with a black face and a couple of tar black patches across its body. Her eyes were blue and she blinked slowly behind dark eyelashes. The horse beside her was pure white with a soft pink nose and cream colored hooves. The next was another paint, but she was covered in chestnut spots with very little white. The last one was a color I'd never seen before. It was white as the snow except its legs from the knees down were black as pitch to match her dark tail and mane. All were equally beautiful and most certainly not boring.

I approached the white with black socks first. She tossed her head as I came closer and snorted as I reached for her. The next, the chestnut paint, didn't seem to even notice me there and only moved to shift her weight on relaxed legs. The next wiggled her lips at me and made me giggle but it was the last, the mostly white with the black face and blue eyes that captured my heart. As soon as I was close enough, the mare pulled me to her chest with her chin across my shoulder and gently nibbled at my shirt. When I placed my hands on her neck she pressed her face against mine and waited. Her breath was steady and strong, blowing little tufts of steam across my shoulder. Feathers tied into her black mane fluttered in the wind.

"This one," I said, pulling back to get a look at her delicate face again.

"I had a feeling as much but here's the catch." Jeremiah drew up beside my choice and ran a hand down her back. "You can't be riding this filly sidesaddle, you hear? She's quick and young, and sooner or later you're going to need her to run. It ain't safe to ride a horse like this one sidesaddle."

I pursed my lips. "I've never ridden like man before."

"That's the deal. You take this one, you'll ride split-legged from here on."

Her blue eyes watched me steadily. She was already mine. "Fine." I was trying to contain my excitement but a tiny squeal still managed to escape me. "She's perfect," I gushed.

His smile melted any resolve I had, and I flung my arms around his neck. His surprised tension melted as he chuckled deeply against my hair. "She suits you. Here." He pressed an antler bone handle of a large knife into the palm of my hand.

I pulled it slowly out of its sheath and the blade glistened in the sun.

"There's the second part of your wedding present. Keep it on you at all times and I'll feel a little better about draggin' you all the way out here."

When my pocket was heavy with the weight of it, Jeremiah took the saddle from the brown horse and hefted it over the back of my paint. We said our goodbyes and headed back to the long trail that would lead us home. Sitting split-legged was about the most scandalous thing I'd felt since my fall from society. Holding a saddle in between my thighs and telling my horse where to go with the pressure of my split knees was a new experience, but I had to admit, it was more comfortable not twisting in the saddle to hold the reins.

Jeremiah shot me glance after glance, like he didn't quite know what to make of me on the new horse, but the ease in his speech made me think he didn't mind it.

"What're you going to name her?"

"I have to name her?"

"I don't have a name for mine and I'm pretty sure Luke doesn't either, but Kristina named her spotted pony Rosy."

"A horse this pretty should have a name," I crooned. "When I was a child I rode a stick about between lessons. The horses I learned on were horribly stuck up, you see, but my imaginary horse was wild and did anything I wanted her to. My stick horse's name was Beigha."

"Beigha," he murmured. "I like it. Beigha, the least boring horse I've ever set eyes on."

He bobbed easily in the saddle as his horse trotted slowly beside Beigha's quick pace. He held the reins in one hand and the other rested on his thigh. His back was straight and strong and never before had I seen a man so capable and beautiful in the saddle. "Jeremiah?"

"Hmm?"

"Thank you for understanding about the horse. You paid for another man's mistake, and you did it without complaint. It means a great deal to me."

"I'm glad." A mischievous grin stole his face. "Now, I've been waiting for the chance to get you at more than a slow walk since yesterday. You ready to see what your new horse can do?"

"You mean run her?"

"Hold onto the saddle horn and give her a kick. If she's too fast, slow her down."

"Are you wanting to race, Mr. Dawson?"

"That's what I want."

I shook my head slowly. "I don't think that's such a good idea— hyah!" I yelled, kicking my horse while disappointment still swam in my husband's eyes.

His booming laughter mixed with my own as we dodged trees and brush. My heart raced faster and faster to the beating of Beigha's hooves. Jeremiah was right behind, and it made the race that much more exciting to think he would catch me any moment. The race stretched on forever and as I adjusted to the gait of my horse, my new riding style only became more comfortable.

My instructors had never let me go faster than a trot, and here my husband was, telling me to let my horse loose, trusting me too compete with him as an equal.

When I lost track of the way home, his horse danced with mine in a subtle cadence that told me the way. The race stretched to the stars and back and when we were finally, finally at the edge of our clearing I pulled my tiring horse to a trot and then to a walk. She'd given everything I asked and more. Much like my husband had done today.

His eyes flashed with fever bright excitement as he pulled next to me and here, in the deep afternoon shadows, in the shelter of the Dawson woods, he leaned over and kissed me. His hands cupped my face, and his fingers intertwined in my tresses that had bounced free of their pins. Gently, he urged my mouth open with his own. My breath froze as his tongue brushed softly against mine, and I gripped his forearms to keep him near.

Beigha moved to the side, separating us, and I stared at his cocky smile like I was too drunk on champagne to find my mental facilities again.

"Hup," he said, kicking his horse into a trot. He looked behind him once, and humor danced in his eyes. I don't know what he saw on my face, but a short laugh burst from his lips.

My horse moved to follow, and thank goodness for that. The man had kissed me too thoroughly and now my hands didn't seem to want to work right with the reins.

Kissing while riding—yet another lesson my hoity-toity instructors forgot to teach.

Chapter Seventeen
Lorelei

"Look there," Jeremiah said, leaning his horse into mine and so close, I could almost feel his warmth through my own layers of fabric.

Squinting through the trees, I could just make it out.

"That right there is the start of your house, Mrs. Dawson."

I inhaled sharply as my body tingled with excitement at the sound of our name upon his lips. I gripped the reins and squeezed Beigha with my knees. Luke worked feverishly and, to my open astonishment, had three quarters of the stone hearth already completed. How could a man accomplish so much in a day? His energy seemed endless as he waved and smiled before going straight back to work slathering some kind of sealant between two stones. Kristina hauled the rocks to him one by one, and while they looked to completely weigh her down, he snatched them from her like they were pebbles.

"I want to help."

Jeremiah offered me a slow smile. "The house will mean more if you do."

I liked that he didn't tell me to sit there and look pretty as the gentlemen I was accustomed to had done my entire life.

Kristina propped her fists onto her hips and blew a strand of sandy blond hair out of her face as she spied us. "Hey!" she yelled. Beigha tossed her head as the woman ran for us. "Oh, she's just beautiful!" She held the reins and looked into my horse's dark face. "Such pretty eyes,

and she takes a bit and saddle? What's her name?"
Excitement bubbled out of me as I said, "Beigha."
Kristina beamed. "How dandy, and now we both have flashy Indian ponies."
Another layered sense of belonging drifted over me. My situation wasn't ideal by any standards, but I'd been accepted into this little family. I had a husband, and a horse of my own, a brother-in-law who'd spent the entire day constructing a hearth for a home to house me, and a friend to share this challenging experience with. So I had to camp in the woods, and didn't have modern day comforts. There were still bright spots in my life, and they somehow weighed more than the dark.

Kristina walked beside Beigha with her hand resting on her twitching withers. Jeremiah rode on my other side, strong, constant and with an easy smile at the ready just for me.

"I'm going to go put her up and then help you haul the rocks," I said.

"It's rough work," Kristina warned. "My hands are already torn up." Indeed they looked a little battered. One of her fingers was even bleeding.

Determined, I said, "I'm up for it."

Jeremiah showed me Beigha's stall and where to put her tack. The brushes sat on a rail against the wall and after a quick rub down and a bucket of water, Jeremiah led me outside with a gentle hand resting on my lower back. My, but that man made my insides warm right up.

"I want you wearing these." He handed me an oversized pair of roughed up work gloves.

"Are these yours?"

"Yes, but I'll be fine. If we work quickly, we could get the hearth done and start on the foundation." He pulled a folded piece of paper from his pocket and on it was a drawing of a bunch of squares and numbers I couldn't make heads or tails of. "I thought we could have the kitchen and den as soon as you walk in, our bedroom over here, and two small bedrooms on the other side, right here."

"Three bedrooms?"

"They'll be small but necessary if we're planning on having a family someday." So casual was his tone, I glanced up to make sure he wasn't teasing. His eyes were steady and serious under his cowboy hat. "I mean to have a family with you, Lorelei."

I had to swallow my emotions down before I answered, or he'd see just how much his desire to have children with me affected my feelings for him. Jeremiah didn't need an oversensitive woman. Not out here in this rough land. He needed a level-headed one. "I'd like that, too."

Daniel had wanted an heir, but he'd never talked about wanting to start a family with me. It was just the necessity for a son to pass his wealth and name to that was important. Not whom he put his child in. While I'd accepted this as normal for the society I lived in, now I wasn't so sure it had ever been all right by me—not deep down in the tender bits of me that had feelings and wants. Not the pieces of me that hungered for affection and love.

Kristina had been right that hauling rocks was hard work, but on top of that, we couldn't carry them fast enough to keep up with those tenacious men. Like beavers on some northern dam, they never stopped or even slowed. While Kristina and I struggled to work faster, they never pushed or gave us impatient looks. On the contrary, they joked around, or went over Jeremiah's rough floor plan, or mixed mortar. My excitement grew as the hearth angled in and with the men balanced on tall, crude wooden ladders as they created the final lip.

Awestruck, I stared at the looming fireplace that had been built in a day.

Jeremiah scrambled down the ladder and stood by me while he admired their work. "You build the hearth first so it doesn't pull on your foundation," he explained.

"Have you built many of these?" I asked.

He shrugged. "A few. We moved around a lot when we were little. Built many a home with Pa and my brothers." His nostrils flared delicately. "You're bleeding."

"What?" I searched my arms and low and behold a long, shallow cut graced my forearm. "Oh, it must have been from resting the rocks against my arms when I carried them. Some of them were jagged."

"Hmm," he grunted. "Kristina, we got any clean cloth?"

"Maybe in the barn."

He jogged toward it while Kristina pulled me by the hand to the simmering fire near the old house. "Can't be too careful with injuries out here. Doctors are a rare find this far out, and even small hurts can bring you big troubles."

I plopped into the singed rocking chair while she pumped water into a pan and set it on the fire. I suppose the cut wasn't as shallow as I'd thought because it was starting to drip.

"You ain't scared of blood?" she asked me warily.

"I suppose not. I haven't really seen too much of it bar the occasional scrapes and cuts of childhood."

"Well, good because this probably ain't the last you'll see of it around here."

Jeremiah returned with two strips of white cotton linen. Without a word, he dipped one in the boiling water and cleaned the cut slowly until the bleeding had stopped. My lips were pursed at the sting, but I rather enjoyed the view of my stranger husband bent over my arm in concentration. After bandaging it, he leaned forward and smelled my arm, and with a slight nod of the head, he kissed it lightly and stood. "Luke and I are going to start measuring out lumber but I want you taking it easy."

"I can help Kristina start on dinner."

He hesitated and a flame of worry flickered in his dark eyes.

"Aw, piss off, Jeremiah," Kristina said with a wink. "She's fine. I won't let nothin' happen to your wife, now go on."

After he left, I said, "I can't believe he lets you talk to him like that."

"Who, Jeremiah? A man doesn't *let* me do anything. And besides, deep down he likes when I'm vulgar. He's just too mannerly to admit it."

"I heard about him proposing to you," I blurted out.

"Yeah, that wouldn't have worked. We would've killed each other by the end of the first day. Did he tell you we spent a season up here, without Luke? We worked well together but we bickered like two panthers fightin' over territory." She looked up from a pile of meat she'd been sawing on with a faraway expression behind her distracted smile. "Naw, Luke was always my man. If somethin' ever happened to him, I'd never marry another."

Her heartfelt admission eased a tiny sliver of green jealousy that had been waiting in my heart since Jeremiah told me of his proposal to my sister-in-law. It hadn't worked out between them because it wasn't supposed to. Though they hadn't been able to see it at the time, he was being groomed for me while my troubles were brewing hundreds of miles away.

By the time the venison was finished and the potatoes browned over the fire, the Dawson brothers had managed to secure the main beams that made up the frame of the house and already started nailing the floor boards down around the hearth.

"Is it normal for men to build houses so quickly?"

"They ain't normal men. Here, set this over there." She yanked the cast iron pot from the embers with the handle wrapped in the skirts of her dress.

Gathering my own skirts, I took it and set it beside the rocker to cool. She dug the potatoes out of the fire with a stick and with dancing hands tossed them onto a plate. "I have a pail of milk inside the door of the barn. You want to grab it while I tell the boys supper's on?"

The barn was a short walk and the bucket was just where she said it would be and covered with a cheesecloth. What I hadn't expected was for it to be so blasted heavy. I sloshed it with every step.

"Let me help," Jeremiah said from right behind me.

I nearly jumped right out of my skin. Eying the distance between us and our future house, I glowered. "How in tarnation did you get here so fast? I just saw you all the way over there."

He hauled the milk pail and said over his shoulder, "I ran."

"Oh, he ran?" I grumbled. "Faster than a horse on fire, he ran."

His shoulders shook but I hadn't a guess what he found so humorous. He was much too far away to have heard me.

Dinner was warm and satisfying after a long day. I'd missed lunch somewhere along the line without noticing until my stomach rumbled at the smell of the roasted venison when Luke pulled the lid from the iron pot. "How do you eat these?" I asked, eyeing my ash bathed potato.

"You can peel the skin off real easy," Jeremiah said. He picked his up and took a long strip right off with his fingers.

Easy enough if my potato wasn't still on fire. I'd have to wait for it to cool. Maybe Jeremiah didn't have any feeling in his fingers after working all day in the cold, and the majority of it without gloves. His plate was completely clean before I'd even taken my second bite and without a word, he and Luke slunk into the waning evening light to return to work on the cabin. Relentless, tireless men. I sank back into the rocking chair and watched them work. They didn't seem to say anything to each other, yet they knew exactly where to put every board, where to help hold lumber, when to hand the other more nails. The speed and efficiency with which they worked was downright disconcerting.

"What're you thinking?" Kristina asked as the firelight danced across her face. "I can see you're workin' something out over there."

"I've just never seen men quite like them."

"Nor will you ever again. We got lucky they mail-ordered us if you ask me."

"Are all country men so fast and strong?"

She shoved a giant bite of food into her maw and shrugged.

We talked by the firelight deep into the night. How Luke and Jeremiah could even see where to bang a hammer was beyond me, but then again, it was growing obvious there were a lot of things they could do. I'd have to work on controlling my surprise.

Kristina told me stories of her days before the saloon—of her mother and odd jobs they'd worked in Chicago. I found it comforting to listen to her voice. She looked at life differently than anyone I'd ever met. Where a woman would be bent to breaking, Kristina found humor. Where a lesser woman would drown in sorrow, she found a positive light cast on every situation that had happened in her life. Her happiness was like medicine for my soul. How could I mourn my old life when she'd suffered worse and came out of it with a genuine smile? I'd do well to let her optimism infect me.

I told her of friends and grand parties and the dresses I'd worn, and she listened with the intensity of a child who was hearing about dragons and castles for the first time. If ever we went back to Boston, I'd like to go to a party with her. It would be an experience just watching everything through her eyes.

Somewhere in the wee hours of the night, I nodded off. I woke to the smell of man and pine and jostled gently as Jeremiah carried me through the woods that led to our crude camp.

"I didn't say goodnight to Kristina," I argued half-heartedly.

"She's already asleep in the barn. You can tell her tomorrow."

That defeated the purpose but I didn't tell him that. As I scrambled for the furs inside the tent, Jeremiah snatched a folded towel and small leather bag from the corner.

"Where are you going?" I didn't mean to sound hurt but still, it came out that way.

"I'm going for a swim."

"A swim? But it's freezing out here."

"Woman, I've been working on that house for the better part of the day. I need a bath." The jangle of his spurs was loud in the quiet of the night as he turned and paused. "You wanna come with me?"

He turned his head slowly, and in the moonlight on that cloudless night, I could see the expected answer in his eyes. He didn't think I was brave enough, and that stirred within me an empowering stubbornness I hadn't felt in years.

I'd show him. "Do you have soap?"

Chapter Eighteen
Jeremiah

Very few times had anyone managed to shock me through the years, but Lorelei had just done it in a big way. I'd mostly invited her along to draw a wide-eyed look right out of her. Through the days we'd spent together, I'd latched onto that doe-eyed look she graced me with when I surprised her. Admittedly, I'd been saying and doing little things so I could watch her pretty face transform from reserved and passive to animated. Her eyes were the color of fine whiskey and surrounded by all those dark eyelashes—well, she nearly knocked me over with a look sometimes. Add that to the staggering fact that my wolf hadn't tried to eat her last night, and I'd been floating on a cloud of downright jubilation since the early morning hours.

My wolf had gone straight for her. He could hear her breathing and smell her fear and still, he'd sniffed around the tent and when he was satisfied she was safe, he left. I remembered because I'd been present. He'd let me share his head space for the first time since Anna had passed.

Now, I wasn't a reckless man. I had Luke sittin' in the tree above the tent to make sure she was safe from me, but even he'd relaxed and eventually left for the barn when I'd let her be. There wasn't a better test for my psychotic wolf other than to put her out there in plain sight and see what he did.

I was as close to flying as a man could get.

And then after the best day I'd had in years, Lorelei just said she'd go skinny dippin' with me? I must have fallen into a patch of four leaf clovers without knowing it somewhere along the way.

Listening to her stumble through the dark behind me was a lesson in patience. I wanted to help her, to hold her hand and make sure she didn't fall, but there was a very real risk she'd balk at my touch and change her mind. She'd done it time and time again. I didn't have a guess what her last husband had done to cause her so much fear of affection, but he'd sure done a number on her confidence. I'd gift it back to her if it was the last thing I did, but going would be slow. Damage like that wouldn't be undone in a week, or a few months, or a year even. She'd have to be reconditioned to accept that she was worthy of a love. I didn't know her entire story, but no small piece of me wanted to kill that rat bastard Delaney for giving her one to tell.

The creek was across the clearing and through the woods. As soon as the house was finished, I'd build her a soaking tub so she didn't have to bathe like a mountain man. She deserved better and I was going to give it to her.

The night was much colder without the sun to warm the land, and the chilly breeze rocked the bare tree branches that creaked and groaned in a lullaby only the forest knew the cadence to. An old hoot owl asked who was trespassing in his woods, and the sound of scurrying field mice traveled from the dry leaf blanket of the wilderness floor to my oversensitive ears. Though the night woods likely seemed quiet and unsettling to Lorelei, for me it was vibrant and humming with life. The sound of the babbling brook was soothing and as we approached, I hung my towel on a nearby low-hanging branch.

Her brows were knitted in fierce stubbornness as she passed and without a word, she slowly began to unpin her hair in what was the most seductive dance I'd ever seen. Tendril after tendril of raven-dark hair fell and tickled her hips. She never looked back but she had to have known I was watching. I shed my clothes as she unlaced her dress and by the time it billowed in a pile around her ankles, I was ready to race into that half frozen creek. The sight of her stopped me in my tracks.

I'd seen her body last night, but this was different. The moonlight caressed her skin and made it glow as she dipped her toe into a lapping wave. The wind kicked up and gooseflesh rippled across her back.

"I can't swim in there," she mumbled.

"Oh, no you don't." I catapulted at her before she could step back, and in one fluid motion I scooped her up and jumped into the deepest part of the creek I knew would submerge us.

"Jeremiah!" she gasped as we broke the surface. The cold and shock leeched away any anger from her tone, and the rasping of my name against her lips brought me a chill that had nothing to do with the weather.

The freezing water was needles against every square inch of skin but I'd been prepared for it. Lorelei, on the other hand, panted with the pain and shock of it.

"Not quite as romantic as you'd imagined, huh?" I said.

Her teeth chattered away. "Give me the soap so I can get this over with."

When her feet touched the rocky bottom, I scrambled for the leather pouch I'd dropped on the shore line. As I turned with the lumpy bar of lye soap in my hand, Lorelei sank into water up to her nostrils. Her fixed eyes were as big as fine porcelain tea plates as she raked her gaze over my bare skin. I could no more stop the satisfied grin that commandeered my face than I could the tiny water droplets from freezing in my hair. She could give a man the hungriest looks I'd ever seen on a woman.

We scrambled to scrub our numbing bodies in what had to be the fastest bath in the history of the world. She made little squeaking sounds as she rushed to lather her hair, and stumbling over a slick river rock, I rushed to help. In the springtime, I'd take my time and enjoy her wet hair in my hands, but right now, my instincts were screaming to get her out of the water and warm again. When her hair was rinsed thoroughly, she stumbled for shore.

Lorelei fell on the craggy rocks before she could reach the warmth of the towel, and the little gasp she emitted as her knees hit earth was too much.

To hell with not touching her.

Even a patient hunter had his limits.

****

Lorelei

Jeremiah was there almost before my knees had even scraped the rocks. It should've hurt but I couldn't feel anything but the pricking of cold numbness from my neck down. Then, fast as a lightning strike, he was there lifting me away from the jagged stones that cried for a taste of my tender skin.

"I can't feel my legs very well," I whispered like talking in a normal voice would wake up the forest. Like it would chase away the magic somehow.

"I've got you." He whipped the towel from the tree and dried me off with a rough hand and before I even had a chance to reach for my dress, he'd thrown one of the furs he'd snatched from our bed around my body. "Shhhh," he told my chattering teeth as he rubbed life back into my arms through the blanket.

Maybe it was the enchantment of the woods playing tricks on my eyes or maybe Jeremiah really did just run as hot as a steam engine because under the light of the moon, a thin veil of steam wafted from his bare, moist skin. He wasn't even shivering. Before I could chicken out, I threw my arms, and the fur, around him and hugged him close. He wasn't exactly a campfire, but he was certainly warmer than me and selfishly, I absorbed as much as I could.

A contented sound rumbled from his chest as he pressed my back against a tree. He was the noisiest man I'd ever met. He had a sound for every emotion and though it was strange and new, my body unceasingly reacted to it. This soft noise ran a delicious shiver down my spine. His back was firm and strong under my hands and slowly, I ran my nails down the length of him, raising gooseflesh with my touch.

He pressed his hips against me, and his thick erection pressed into my belly while he looked at me like I was the most beautiful thing he'd ever laid eyes on. I wasn't repulsive or unsavory to him like I had been to Daniel. On the contrary, my touch sped up Jeremiah's breathing until he finally rested his face against my neck and kissed it gently.

How could a man make me feel so much? Every single fiber in my body reached for him, like I could never get close enough to be completely satiated.

"Lorelei," he rumbled against my sensitive ear.

I could hear the question in it, and I lifted my chin. I wanted him to see the truth in my eyes as I told him, "I want you, Jeremiah. I'm ready."

The thick cords of muscle in his throat moved as he swallowed. I thought he'd take me right away, but he didn't. Instead, he lowered his lips to mine and cupped my sex with his warm palm. A soft sound came from my throat unbidden as he ran his finger along my wet seam. This was scandalous. I hadn't the foggiest idea what he was doing, only that it felt good for him to touch me.

My knees grew weak as he slowly slid his long finger inside of me, and his other arm held me tight so I wouldn't go down to the gravelly ground at our feet. His lips trailed down my neck and I lifted my chin and stared at the moon through the tree branches above. He eased out of me, and pressed upward again, and pleasure burst through me as his knuckle rasped against a sensitive spot. The man was going to bring me to my knees.

If I'd had any doubt that what Daniel had done with me was wrong, those were laid to rest under Jeremiah's tender caresses. This was how making love should be.

My new husband wasn't stalling.

He was preparing me.

I should've been embarrassed at how wet I was becoming with

each stroke he pressed his finger into me, but as his erection grew impossibly hard and thick against my belly, it was difficult to hate what excited the man I was falling in love with. He liked me like this. The frantic way he nipped my bottom lip, and the helpless sound that came from his throat as I found the confidence to wrap my hand around his shaft and pull upward said he needed me just like I needed him.

His teeth grazed my sensitive earlobe, and he cupped my neck with his hand as he pressed into me up to his knuckle. "I'm going to find every sensitive place on you, woman," he rumbled softly. "I'm going to make you feel how much I care about you, and when I'm through, you won't be afraid of my affection anymore. You hear me?"

The chill was banished with his words. Between the confidence in his promise, the blanket wrapped around us and his warm body pressed against mine, there was no room for winter. There was no room for doubt.

Something was happening to me. Something amazing and terrifying all at once. I rocked my hips against his hand in order to get closer to…something. Tingling pressure was building and I wanted more. I wanted everything.

"Jeremiah, please…" What was I even begging him for?

He pulled his touch away from me so quickly, it made me gasp at the disappointment. I'd been so close to the edge of something big. Something that I knew in my heart would change me from the bones out.

With a feral sounding growl, he lifted the back of my knee and pressed the head of his cock inside of me. Slow, shallow thrusts had me clawing at his back and stretching up to kiss him.

"Tell me what you like," he said low.

"This," I breathed, "but deeper."

He pressed into me until I was filled and stretched around him. Heavens and stars, he felt so good as he pressed against that sensitive place he'd found earlier. His breath shook now, and his thrusts became slightly faster with each stroke. The muscles in his arms bunched and flexed as he held me tighter. And the pressure…oh, that beautiful, tingling, stomach warming pressure was back and building with the friction of him burrowing deeply inside of me.

I wanted to feel every powerful thrust of his hips against mine, so I dropped my hands to the smooth, hot skin of his lower back. My eyes rolled back in my head as I arched against him time and time again, meeting every stroke he had to give me.

"No, Lorelei. Open your eyes. I want you to see what you do to me."

Jeremiah eased back just enough for me to see his eyes. They were lighter than I remembered, more the color of good scotch, but perhaps it was a trick of the moonlight. His jaws clenched and he wouldn't release my gaze as he took me harder, and faster.

"You're so...damned..." He gritted his teeth as I dug my nails into his back.

I was going to explode.

"You're beautiful," he rasped.

My body clamped around him and I closed my eyes against the rampant pulsing pleasure that took me. His shaft swelled inside, and warm wetness shot into me as he tensed and snarled out something in a language I couldn't understand. Over and over, he bucked into me. The blanket slipped down, exposing my back to the rough tree bark behind me, but I didn't care about that right now. I didn't care about anything other than how stunning my husband was in full rut. He gritted out my name and buried his face against my neck as he filled me one last time.

I was warm and safe here, cradled in my lover's arms. Something opened up inside of me, like flower petals reaching for the sunlight.

Jeremiah was my husband, but in this moment, he was more somehow.

My knees finally gave, and with my arms wrapped around his neck, Jeremiah carried me back through the woods to our temporary home. His footing was sure as if he'd walked this trail a hundred times in the dark and in much less time than it took us to stumble to the creek, we were back in the warmth of our tent and under a pile of furs.

He played distractedly with a curling tendril of hair that always tried to stay in my face. Here, with my husband propped up on one elbow, looking more relaxed and happy than I'd ever seen a man before, I counted my lucky stars. They'd been many since I decided to answer his advertisement those months ago. He'd picked me. This man who was a more beautifully constructed and masculine creature than any person had a right to be had chosen me for his wife. His help-keep. His equal. This man who was a tender lover, gentleman, and loyal brother had chosen me to bring under his fierce protection.

The corner of his mouth turned up. "What're you thinkin' about?"

I traced the outline of his perfect nipple. It drew up under my touch and I smiled to match his. "How lucky I am."

Humor danced in the shadows of his eyes and he looked around with arched eyebrows. "This ain't exactly a castle, Lorelei."

I giggled. "No, you ridiculous man. I mean I'm lucky to have you."

The grin dipped from his face, and he looked so serious as he said, "Not as lucky as me. You don't even know what you've done for me yet, Mrs. Dawson, but someday you will." He sank down beside me and wrapped his strong arms around my waist. He drew me against him until his warmth enveloped me. "Sleep now, wife. I'll be building you a house in the morning."

I sighed happily. Sleep should've come easily but I kept replaying the beauty of tonight over and over in my mind. The way he'd looked at me, the way he touched me, the way he made me laugh while we bathed when my nerves threatened to overwhelm me. He'd made it possible to lose myself with him.

Jeremiah didn't know what he'd done for me either, and he probably never would.

****

The morning sunlight was red against my closed eyelids. The corner of the tent flapped noisily in the wind and with lazy fingertips, I reached behind me to find Jeremiah's side of the furs empty. My leg brushed the space but it was already cold.

What time was it? I stumbled sleepily into my dress, which Jeremiah must have retrieved at some point early this morning. It had mud stains and had seen better days. Honestly, it needed a good wash. I pulled my stockings and shoes on and when my new knife was safely in the pocket of my dress, I headed out, careful to follow the thin trail until I made it back to the edge of the clearing. Before I even emerged from the tree line, Jeremiah's steady gaze watched me from his position perched atop the high framed structure of our house. His eyes followed me, as if he'd known I'd be coming out of the woods at just this moment.

My smile was shy. How would he act after such an intimate night?

He jumped down and landed with the grace of a panther before jogging toward me with long strides. A surprised giggle rippled out of me when he picked me up and spun me in a circle. And right here, with Kristina and Luke watching, he kissed me square on the mouth.

"Jeremiah!" I chided as I playfully thumped his arm. "They can see us."

"So what? You'll see much worse from them on any given day, I'll guarantee you that."

Fair enough because I had seen worse, actually. It was impossible to hate the outward display of affection. On the contrary, pride swelled inside of me at the idea that he was claiming me in front of other people. And not just any other people, but the people who meant the most to him.

"Come on," he said. "We've been waiting on you to eat breakfast."

"Why didn't you wake me then?"

"Because," Kristina said with a wink. "Jeremiah assured us you needed your rest."

My face was likely red as the streaks across the morning sky but there was no help for it. No one seemed uncomfortable with the subject but me. Oh, if Mother could see me now, she'd have a conniption.

Directly following fresh scrambled eggs and venison jerky that had been smoking since Luke brought it home yesterday, the boys showed me the work they'd accomplished on the house. Astonishing. The flooring was done and the frame in place and today they would be working on the walls.

"We should whitewash it like those fancy houses in Boston," Jeremiah said. "A lady should have a whitewashed house if she's makin' the sacrifice to live out here."

"That sounds like an awful waste of money," I said with a denying shake of my head. "Let's get a stove first and then talk about that later."

"I want a whitewashed house!" Kristina said with eyes that shone like rare, blue gems.

Luke stood straighter. "What? Woman, what do you need a whitewashed house for?"

She crossed her arms and jutted out her chin stubbornly. "Jeremiah said a lady deserves one, and I'm a lady."

"You weren't a lady last night," Luke said in a low voice as he wrapped his arms around her waist.

"Stop that, you brute! I'm serious. Lorelei, can't you just imagine our two whitewashed houses with porches and white rocking chairs to match?"

I grinned at Luke. "It actually does sound lovely."

"You too? Jeremiah, this is all your fault. Now I'm gonna be livin' in some high fallutin' city house."

Kristina argued, "The sheriff whitewashed their house for Daisy, and she loves it. She don't live in the city. She lives on the outskirts of town."

"Oh, yeah?" Luke griped. "And where do you propose we get this magical money to be waistin' on paint, Kristina?"

"I suggest you better get to trapping," she said flippantly.

Jeremiah winked at me and his happy demeanor said he'd enjoyed stirring the pot.

"Guess what we get to do today?" Kristina asked, completely ignoring Luke's glower. "We get to go into town and pick up more nails, and we get to order roof shingles and window glass from the general store."

"By ourselves?" A mixture of fear, excitement, and uncertainty at the prospect of being separated from Jeremiah took me.

"All by ourselves. We'll be stopping by Trudy's today, too, so don't worry about us if we're an hour late, boys."

"An hour," Luke snorted.

"You need help saddling Beigha?" Jeremiah offered.

"No, I'll do it. I'll come say goodbye before we leave."

As the boys returned to work, Kristina said, "Bring your dresses and any of Jeremiah's soiled clothes you can find. Trudy does laundry on her days off and we can do ours with her while we're in town. It'll be much better than doing it down in the creek."

The mention of the creek brought more heat to my cheeks, but she was already headed for the barn and didn't see. "What do I put the clothes in?"

"I have an extra flour sack in here if you want to use it," she called over her shoulder.

Perfect. I scrambled behind but by the time I reached the barn, Kristina was sitting on a one legged stool milking a bellowing cow with udders so swollen they stuck out to the sides. Her half grown calf chewed away on a pile of straw and offered his momma absolutely no relief.

She gestured to a corner without breaking stride in the *pat pat pat* of milk hitting the bottom of the pail. "Sacks are over there."

I saddled Beigha and then hustled off to snatch my other dress, which I hadn't worn since Boston on account of the dead chicken smell, and the small pile of Jeremiah's clothes that sat in the corner of our tent. I hadn't ever laundered clothes before, but surely it couldn't be that hard. Kristina showed me how to tie the full sack onto the saddle bags, then I pointed my horse toward the steady song of nails on wood.

Jeremiah whistled long and low. "Damn woman, you look good ridin' that horse." As I leaned across the creaking saddle, he kissed me soundly. "You be safe today. Stay close to Kristina and you girls head back this-away before nightfall. Oh," he said turning back to me. "And have fun."

Chapter Nineteen
Lorelei

I had to admit, despite my qualms about leaving Jeremiah for the day, the prospect of an adventure was quite exciting. Kristina's infectious enthusiasm only served to heighten the anticipation and by the time we trotted into town on our splashy Indian ponies, we couldn't seem to stop laughing at everything the other said.

After tying the horses to the post in front of her modest house at the end of the main street, Trudy met us at the door with an inviting smile. "I was hoping you'd find a way to stop by today." As an aside to me she said, "It's my only day off, you see."

The front entryway led to a small kitchen with a four chair table. "Come on out back," she said. "I just got the water heated where I want it for laundry and you girls are welcome to it."

Laundry would have been a boring and laborious affair if not for the boisterous conversation between the three of us. Trudy, just like Kristina, was an easy talker who could likely get along with anyone given half the chance. I didn't have to talk much, but it was as I preferred. I was perfectly content to work and listen and laugh along with their whiplash wit.

We scrubbed and scrubbed our clothes onto a ridged washboard and then lathered them up with a horsehair brush and rinsed and plunged until the water was filthy. Then we started over again. When all of the clothes were on the line to dry, the three of us made our way to the general store to put our order for housing materials in and buy more nails with a small purse of coins Kristina brought. The stares and mutterings of some of the town's people were easy enough to ignore. I didn't know why they had a prejudice against the Dawsons and frankly, I didn't care anymore. They just didn't know them like Kristina and I did.

A woman with blonde hair, fair skin, and eyes as blue as a clear spring sky bustled into the general store as we were looking at swaths of fabric. Kristina hailed her over. "Daisy, this is my sister-in-law, Lorelei. Lorelei, this is Sheriff Hawkins's wife."

I politely offered my hand. "Mrs. Hawkins, how do you do?"

"Very well thank you. Sister-in-law you said, Kristina? So does that mean you're married to Jeremiah Dawson?"

"I am. I've only just arrived a few days ago."

A short shout sounded from outside, and two men ducked into the general store. Townspeople in the street were scrambling like panicked ants.

"What in tarnation is going on out there?" Trudy breathed.

We followed her out to the front porch, and from here we had a good vantage point of the seven rough looking men riding through town on finicky horses. The leader had a red beard and his bright eyes landed on me. The squinted look he gave shifted something cold inside of me. Something wasn't right with that one. He tipped his hat and gave me a smile that failed to reach his eyes.

"Who are they?" Daisy asked with a delicately gloved hand over her chest.

"Don't you recognize them?" Trudy asked as she kicked the bottom of the door with the toe of her shoe. Posted on the wall just behind it were four rows of wanted posters. One of them looked suspiciously like the red-bearded man.

A blond-haired man came running up to our small group. "You okay?" he asked Trudy.

"I'm fine, but I can feel trouble comin'."

"Mrs. Daisy," he said. "Where's your husband?"

Daisy's voice had a tremor in it. "He's been out of town all week. No lawmen here except the deputy."

The man cursed under his breath and gathered us inside. "The deputy has Bill Burton locked up and waiting on lawmen from Denver to come get him tonight. Burton's supposed to hang by morning."

"As in Dirty Bill Burton?" Kristina asked. "He's the leader of those men out there. They've been robbing trains and pillaging good folks for years."

He checked his pistols. "That's the one. Go back to the storage room, all of you."

Trudy grabbed his wrists. "I forbid it," she said. Her dark eyes were wide and desperate.

"Nobody else is going to help him, Trudy."

"He's a lawman. You ain't. You have a baby on the way Elias and I'll be damned if I'm losing you today. Put your guns away and come with us."

"Trudy—"

"I forbid it," she repeated.

Trudy was married to a white man? That beat just about all I'd seen. We crouched down in the store room just as the first shots rang out. It was impossible to hear the pepper of ammunition and not think about the people who were dying from it. My stomach grew queasy as the fight raged on outside. A ricocheted bullet hit a sack of flour right above Daisy's head and she whimpered. I held her hand and pulled her closer. "We'll be all right."

Trudy's husband covered her body with his until the blasts disappeared. Five minutes more and he said, "Stay here and stay low." He returned shortly with the sadness of a hundred ghosts in his eyes.

"Deputy's dead and Dirty Bill is free. Best you ladies get on home. It ain't safe here."

Trudy reacted immediately. She pulled us outside into the chaos. Men, women and children were running to help injured townspeople who had been caught in the crossfire. Three men lay dead in front of the jail house and another was bleeding all over the front steps. I wretched at the smell of blood and gunpowder.

"No time for that, Lorelei," Kristina said, tugging on my arm. She snatched the still sopping garments from Trudy's clothesline and shoved handfuls into the empty flour sacks. I helped when my dizzy spell had passed.

Trudy kissed us both on the cheeks and said, "You girls get on back to them Dawson boys. You'll be safe with them."

Up on Beigha and Rosy, we kicked our mounts hard and raced out of town with our laundry sacks making wet thunking sounds against the hind ends of our horses to the rhythm of their gaits. This race wasn't exhilarating like the one with Jeremiah had been. This one was full of fear that those outlaws had gone this way and were hiding in the woods somewhere. I screamed from fright when two men came galloping around a blind corner and almost barreled into us.

"Lorelei!" Jeremiah yelled as his horse reared and screamed. "It's me. It's just me."

Beigha fidgeted to the side under me and tossed her head. "How'd you know to come for us?"

"We heard the shots. Come on, woman. You can tell us what

happened at home."

Beigha bucked to the side once and then tore off after them. "Wait," I yelled. "How'd you hear the shots from miles away?"

He didn't answer, which was highly suspicious because if he'd heard gunfire from that distance, he should've had no problem in the world hearing me from right behind. Or maybe he only heard what he wanted to. Something was going on, and I was just about tired of being the only one out of the loop.

Our furious pace had us back to the homestead well before the sun was at its midway point in the sky. We slowed the horses the second we crossed over to Dawson land.

"What happened out there?" Jeremiah demanded.

Puffing up against his stern tone, I exclaimed, "It wasn't us shooting all willy-nilly!"

"Who?" Luke asked in a voice dripping with quiet ice.

"That young deputy had Dirty Bill Burton in his jailhouse with no back up," Kristina explained. "Elias said he was waiting on lawmen from Denver and his gang rode right through town, shot the place up and freed that black-hearted old buzzard."

Jeremiah threw his hat and cursed. "That was too close!" He sighed and rubbed his hands over his face like he hadn't slept in a long time. "It was too close," he said in a softer tone.

Luke wouldn't look at me but even with his head turned, his eyes were glowing with something more than fury. A sudden unease filled me. There was a charge in the air that lifted the hairs on my arms. It had nothing to do with the cold wind and everything to do with some long sleeping instinct I couldn't put my finger on.

"Luke," Jeremiah warned.

He pulled his horse toward the barn without another word and Kristina followed suit.

"Let them go," Jeremiah told me. He led me to the house, which now boasted two completed exterior walls, and tied our horses to a post he'd constructed in front of the porch. As soon as my feet hit the first stair he caught me and crushed my body to his.

His words rumbled against my hair. "I'm sorry I yelled at you. I was just scared something happened to you."

"A bullet hit right above Daisy's head." The admission was a tiny weight from my chest. I'd been replaying it over and over, but the fear eased once I gave the words to Jeremiah to share.

His lips pressed against the top of my head for a long time before he released me.

"Can I ask you something?"

"Shoot," he said.

"I know there's something big you're hiding from me. I can feel it and you and Luke do curious things. I know we're newly married and don't know much about each other yet, but it's big. I can feel its weight, Jeremiah. What's happening?"

His eyes tightened ever so slightly. The dark brown color was flecked with indecision and as the silence stretched on and on, I lowered my gaze. I'd lost.

"You'll know everything about me in time. It's what I want, but for reasons you're going to have to trust me on, I can't give you all the answers right now. The timing has to be right. I'd never hurt you though. *Never.* And I know it ain't fair of me to say it and not show it, but you can trust me."

His denial was like a slap to the face. Never before had I felt a sting quite like this. I loved him. Lord help me, I loved that man so much it should be against the law, but that depth of emotion wasn't returned. If it were, he'd trust me with his secrets the way Luke trusted Kristina with his.

I was suddenly cold and lonely. "I'm going to hang our clothes to dry. Your nails are in Kristina's saddle bags."

If ever I'd seen a tortured soul, it was there in the churning shadows of Jeremiah's face. I wanted to touch the deep lines of it and ease the tension there, but it wasn't my place. He'd made the decision to shut me out and it would be up to him to pay the consequences of that guilt. It wouldn't be fair to absolve him of the wrong he'd done me. Instead, I pulled the heavy sack from Beigha's saddle bags and hauled them toward the barn. He didn't insult my pride and offer to help. Within a minute, the echoing *crack-crack-crack* of the hammer clattered across the clearing, filling it like an ocean until the waves of his frustration threatened to drown me.

Kristina met me at the clothesline with another bag of wet clothes. "You'll be needing to sleep in the barn with me tonight," she whispered.

"Why?"

"It'll be safer that way."

"That didn't answer my question at all. Is this part of the big secret no one trusts me with?"

She snatched my hand, her eyes wide. "I'd tell you that I could, but it ain't my place. I had to wait a long time too and I know it's frustrating, but when the time comes, you'll understand we kept it from you to make you safe."

Yelling at Kristina wouldn't solve anything so instead, I dug my nails into the palm of my hands and lowered my disappointed gaze. "Fine."

I didn't talk to Jeremiah for the rest of the day but my silence was his penance. Dinner around the campfire was a quiet affair and short lived as the men went straight back to work. By the time darkness had fallen, all four exterior walls were up, the interior separating walls were finished, and the roof was framed. It was starting to look like a house.

When I left off for bed, Jeremiah was sanding two newly sawed doors by the firelight. I hadn't a guess on why it was important I not sleep beside my husband tonight. Maybe he didn't want me to, or maybe he planned on working until dawn. Either way my pride stung.

Kristina had all of the excitement of a school girl at the prospect of me sleeping over. Luke stayed near the hearth, cleaning his pistols while she led me up a sturdy ladder to a loft. It was set up like a bedroom with a bed and crude table housing a lantern. The hay had been pushed to the side and sequestered off with a make shift wall curtain, and the warmth of the hearth below wafted into our sleeping quarters above. A window with wavy glass panes sat just above the bed, and the moon and stars winked through it like they knew something I didn't.

We lay on a bearskin fur across the floor and dangled our arms over the side of the loft. Luke sat below us, seemingly perfectly content to relax out of our way for the night.

The flicker of flames from the crackling hearth danced across the planes of Kristina's face as she swung her arms lazily over the opening. "The boys built the hearth and strengthened the walls when the house burned. We needed somewhere safe to sleep."

My mouth moved in strange ways with my chin resting on the wooden ledge. "What was it like when they burned you?"

"Awful. Not because I was going to die, but because I would die with a broken heart. I couldn't get out of the house. They'd barred the doors with something, and the windows were too small to escape through. I could see just fine from them though. I saw Luke and Jeremiah with those hanging ropes around their necks and I was helpless to do anything. It was Trudy and Elias who cut through that back door. I was already aflame but she pushed me into the snow and then I didn't feel anything. Maybe it was shock or numbness from the cold, but all I could think about was cutting those damned ropes before Luke and Jeremiah were taken from me forever." She turned her face to me and her eyes swam with unshed tears. "I'm glad you weren't here for that. I'll never be able to get the sight of Luke hanging from that tree out of my head for as long as I live."

My heart cried at her story. I couldn't imagine holding that memory for a moment, much less a lifetime. A warm tear streaked down the corner of my eye. "You're the bravest person I've ever met."

The howl of a wolf cut through the air like a knife. Luke threw a cold look at the closed barn door before he went back to cleaning his Peace Makers again.

The sound of sharp claws rasping at the wooden wall sent a shiver through my body. "What is that?"

"Some kind of animal trying to get in. Don't worry, it's probably after the horses. The walls are sturdy and will hold though."

I gave the clawing wall a frightened look and leaned my face toward Kristina again. "Tell me anything to take my mind from it. Tell me about your childhood."

She grinned in the dim firelight. "I had the best childhood a kid could wish for. My mother was devoted, attentive, overprotective, and so full of love I thought I'd burst from it some days. She worked as a maid for some of the rich families in Chicago and I grew up in the kitchens with some of the funniest personalities in the entirety of the city. I'm telling you, if ever you need a laugh, cooks have a mean streak sense of humor that'll just cut right through you. And then when I was old enough to earn a wage, my mother got me a job where she worked and I loved it. We made a good team."

"What happened to your mother?"

"She's still alive, far as I know. Like you, I was part of a big scandal that involved a self-absorbed rich man. His mother set out to ruin me and made me work in the whore house and cut off contact between me and my mother. I obeyed in order to save her from ruin, but then Luke hunted that horrid woman down and now that threat is gone. I'm getting Luke to pen a letter for me when he has time. You want to read what we have so far?"

I answered, "Yes," but Kristina was already up and rifling through a small drawer in her nightstand.

She handed me the paper proudly and I read the few sentences already scrawled across the aged paper. "Can't you write?"

"Oh, no, not me. I don't have much education in me. I used to be real ashamed of it but Luke doesn't mind and since he's the one who matters, it's hard to keep giving myself grief over it."

"Do you want to learn to read and write?" I asked after I'd handed the paper back.

The transformation in her face went from wariness to reluctant hope. "Are you offering to teach me?"

"Of course I'll teach you, Kristina. If you want to read and write, you should learn. If you're okay without that skill, then we don't have to. It won't matter with me and the boys around to read and write for you anyhow, but if it's something that bothers you, we'll fix it."

She dropped her voice to a hushed whisper. "It's just that I was so scared to ask the boys to teach me on account of they do so much for me already and work so hard all day. I just wanted them to be able to relax at night. When can you start teaching me?"

"Right after we finish the letter to your mother. She should know you're safe and happy. I'll write it for you and then we'll learn the first letter of the alphabet tonight before we go to bed."

I nearly jumped clean out of my skin at the squeal of sheer joy that belched forth from her vocal chords as she gripped me close in a bear hug. I could've been imagining it but from up here, it looked like Luke was smiling.

To the serenade of the scratching animal outside, we wrote to Kristina's mother of her marriage, of her husband, and of her new home. She told of her friends in town and her new sister-in-law. I smiled a lot at that part because it was so endearing to hear her thoughts on me as a person.

At the bottom we wrote of the surprising happiness she'd found in an unexpected place and when it came time for her signature, I had her practice her name over and over on a scrap piece of paper until she felt comfortable copying it to the bottom of her letter.

And when her note was folded into an envelope and addressed, we practiced the letter A until we were too tired to see straight.

Somewhere in the wee hours of the night, buried in warm blankets beside Kristina, the clawing animal gave up and I finally found sleep.

Chapter Twenty
Lorelei

Shingle by shingle, the roof had been completed. In a matter of days, two determined men built a house from nothing but piles of disorganized lumber and stone. Luke had blown into town to pick up the cut shingles from the blacksmith, who had a supposed natural talent for cutting them. We would still have to wait some time for the glass window panes to be delivered to the general store, but until then, nailed down canvas to staunch the cold wind would do fine enough.

Today was moving day. The home wasn't completely finished but it was shelter enough to get us out of the woods.

Jeremiah said we'd have to wait for the first rain to see where the leaks were and he'd patch the wooden shingles accordingly. The rails on the front porch were up and the rickety, charred rocking chair from the old house sat invitingly beside the front door. We'd still have to cook over an open fire in the hearth until we could afford a wood burning stove, but at least we'd be cooking out of the wind and from the comfort of an actual shelter.

With our home mostly finished, Jeremiah and Luke started right away on the hearth for the second house across the clearing. Kristina wanted a smaller house with just two small bedrooms off the living room. The second room, Luke said, was for their oldest brother, Gable, when he returned from wherever he'd disappeared to after the war.

My heart sank at the mention of their lost family member. The War Between the States had been over for some time now, and if Gable had survived, he should've already made it back. The Dawson's were loyal though and until someone told them otherwise, they'd keep waiting for his return and Kristina and I would wait right along with them. I was learning an important lesson about family by watching their unerring devotion to each other and their wives. No matter what, you waited for the ones you loved to come home.

It was this lesson that convinced me to finally write to my own parents and tell them of my fate. I'd read it aloud to Jeremiah and then Kristina before I folded it and put it with her letter to send out with the post next time we were in town.

As we packed our small camp in the early morning light, Jeremiah waggled his eyebrows and suggested one last romp in our first marriage bed for old time's sake. I happily obliged. Even with all of his secrets, I found myself as thirsty for his skin as he was for mine. I always thought I couldn't love him any more than I did, I couldn't feel any closer to him than I already was, but then he would touch me and give me exactly what I was thirsting for before I even knew I needed it. And suddenly, somehow, I loved him more deeply with a bond that was nearing unbreakable. He never said he loved me, but he showed me, which was more important for my continued healing. My confidence soared with his compliments and the way he always had a hungry look in his eye when he looked over at me through the firelight. The days of Daniel were released from my heart as it moved onto someone more deserving in every way.

With the manners of the city far away, I relaxed into my place on the homestead. I was still more reserved than the others, but I'd loosened up considerably and was happier for it. I found the humor in Kristina's inappropriate jokes and remarks and in return for reading lessons, I'd taken lessons from her in her area of expertise. Kristina, former whore and proudly so, would have made an excellent madam. With my growing confidence with intimacy, Jeremiah only seemed to melt more deeply into me.

I was highly suspicious that he actually tried to say things to shock me now and again, and I let them affect me. There was no point in hiding my emotions and reactions if it was something he was working for. I don't know what he found appealing about my good humored disapproval but he had qualities that I'd never tell him I loved, so he could keep his secrets too. The rumbling noise he made in his chest when he was angry or content or when he was trying not to laugh at a joke I'd told was something that warmed me from my toes up, every time. If I told him that, I ran the risk of him becoming self-conscious about it and censoring himself. It would be a tragic loss to me so I admired his raw, masculine, animalistic habits quietly. In secret, I'd tried to make sounds like him when I was alone bathing in the creek, but alas, I couldn't come anywhere close.

Jeremiah folded the tent until it was smaller than I'd even imagined it could be while I untied the laundry line from the trees in back of our camp. I could feel his eyes on me as they were most of the time these days, so I turned with a knowing grin to catch him. His head was down but the smirk on his face said he was busted well enough.

His quickness had become normal to me in the days I'd watched him climb all over the house like some surefooted animal. I'd come to accept that he could be across the clearing in no time and I startled less and less at his speed.

"You ready to go home?" he asked.

"It'll be strange sleeping in a house after so long on the road and then in this camp," I admitted.

"If you want, I can set up the tent in the living room," he said with a wink.

"Jeremiah Dawson, you aren't cluttering up my living space with this dirty old thing, now lace me up in back so we can get going."

He pulled and tied before he ran a light finger over my exposed collar bone. He'd shaved by the creek this morning, and the smooth softness of his face against the tender skin of my neck was almost enough to buckle my knees.

"We aren't going to get anything done today if you keep seducing me," I said.

His chuckle vibrated against my skin and he dipped and scooped up most of the camp in his capable arms. I gathered the rest and followed him back to the clearing. Up the porch stairs and to the front door, the house gave a welcome *creak* as Jeremiah hefted me over the threshold, then kissed me soundly.

"Can you organize this while I get to work on Luke's house?" he asked. "Anything you can't lift, leave it there and I'll get it after lunch."

"Okay," I said, but just then he jerked his head to the door.

His eyes looked somewhere beyond the walls of our home and his boots made clomping sounds as he bolted out the door. Luke stood beside his own house across the clearing in an eerily similar stance that my husband had adopted. They were both frozen statues, staring expectantly toward the road. My skin crawled. Simultaneously, they pulled their pistols and Jeremiah shot me a warning look. "Get on back inside."

My heart thundered away in my chest as I slid into the house and pulled the make-shift curtain away from the window. Minutes later, a flatbed buggy pulled into the clearing and Jeremiah holstered his weapons. "Come on out, Lorelei. It's the sheriff and his wife come to visit."

The relief in my chest was almost tangible. I waved to Daisy as her husband helped her out of the buggy. She wore a pale, yellow floral dress that matched her hair and her smile was genuine when she saw Kristina and me.

"That's a mighty fine looking house you've built there," she said.

I waited for her approach with relaxed hands on my hips. "You want the grand tour?"

Kristina had already looped an arm in hers and they chatted in happy animation as we made our way back to the nearly finished building.

The men ambled toward the barn, with a conversation too low for me to hear on their lips. The smallest wave of worry lapped at my toes, but it was such a bare brush it was easily ignored in light of Daisy's questions.

"Sure is a big house for just you and Jeremiah. You planning on starting a family soon?" she asked.

"Uhh," I said, frowning. "We haven't talked about it overmuch, but he's expressed his want for a family and I wouldn't mind little babies who looked like him. He and Luke built it with three bedrooms so there would be room for little ones."

"Oh!" Daisy exclaimed clapping her hands in fast succession. "I bet your boys will be tall and strapping like him."

The vision of a fifteen pound newborn made my mouth go as dry as sand, but surely that wouldn't happen. Jeremiah's ma had delivered them just fine and she was a slight woman like me. "Hopefully our girls aren't as tall as them. We'll like to never marry them off," I said with a laugh.

Something so sad pooled in Kristina's expression. "You won't be having any girls, Lorelei. Dawson's only have sons. I hope you weren't wishing for any."

Surely she couldn't be serious. "What do they do with their daughters?"

"The Dawson family tree is filled with only sons. Not a single daughter has been added, and they know their lineage for centuries. They are a very old name, you see, but boys are the only ones born to them."

My forehead strained under my frown. "I wouldn't mind boys. I'd just want healthy children."

Daisy scrunched up her face and climbed the porch stairs. "So peculiar that there are no daughters born to them. No wonder they've evolved into such great brutes. They have no competition from the farer sex."

Huh. That made sense to me. "Not to mention they are conditioned to live in rough country. I bet that helps them to grow so big."

Daisy's expression looked downright conspiring. "Are they really as muscular as they look under all those clothes?"

"Yes," Kristina and I answered in unison before we burst into snickering.

"We were going to break in the new hearth by making lunch in the big house today. Would you like to stay for a meal?" I asked.

"Oh, we'd love to! I was dreading turning right back around and traveling all that way back to town. Eugene said he needed to talk to your husbands, you see. He's very busy lately so I was just sure he'd turn right back around, but now I'll just tell him I've already accepted your lunch invitation."

I liked the way she thought. "Do you know what he's talking to them about?"

Her blue eyes grew wide and serious. "No. I've been trying to get it out of him all morning. He just keeps telling me he needs to talk to the Dawson boys first. This whole thing has left me very curious indeed."

Kristina shot a worried look to the barn the men had disappeared into. "Luke will tell me tonight. He tells me everything."

I snorted. "Jeremiah probably won't be telling me because he tells me nothing."

Daisy huffed a puff of air and nodded. "He reminds me of Eugene. That man thinks he's keeping me safe by keeping me in the dark, but sometimes I just don't know."

Kristina said, "I'll tell you then, ladies. When I know, you'll know."

We made our way to the charred root cellar and in a basket, gathered everything we needed for an oversized meal.

"Jeremiah said we could fry up chicken for a celebration lunch," Kristina explained. "We'll pick two fat hens and I'll teach you how to pluck them."

"Oh," I said. "I know how to pluck chickens."

"No you don't," she gasped with an open mouthed stare. "But you're a high-born lady. When would you have picked up that little talent?"

At least my days in the poultry house after my denouncement left me with some sort of talent. I smirked. "I bet I could pluck a chicken faster than you."

"You want to race?"

"You're on."

Daisy hefted the basket of vegetables to her hip. "Thank goodness.

I thought you were going to try and teach me how to pluck one. No thank you. I just buy mine from the butcher at the edge of town."

After we'd dropped the fixings off in the big house we snuck as best we could to the barn where we caught the men talking about absolutely nothing of importance. They stood near Rosy and Beigha's stalls and Eugene was telling a riveting story about a horse he'd once seen with a completely rotted hoof. Unpleasant.

My eyes nearly popped out of my head when, as we were walking by to get to the chicken coop on the other side of the barn, Jeremiah slapped my backside like I was a horse. While the others laughed, my husband graced me with a devilish grin.

"I swear," I grumbled, rubbing my bum gingerly and trying desperately to hold onto a stern expression. I was failing but that man didn't need the encouragement.

"Where're you ladies headed?" he asked.

"Chicken plucking contest," Kristina said nonchalantly.

He leaned against the wooden railing of Beigha's stall and scratched his lip with the back of his thumb. "You got your work cut out for you, Kristina. Lorelei's quick with her fingers."

"Jeremiah Cade Dawson! Quit it." My pursed lips probably weren't doing a good job of hiding my amusement so I spun and stomped for the coop to the music of mixed-company chuckles.

Kristina and I hefted two dead chickens out to the big house and after dunking them in boiling water and then briefly in cold, we sat comfortably in two large, carved out tree stumps that Jeremiah had dragged up to the side of the building.

Daisy said, "Looks like you and Jeremiah made a love match. I'm glad for it. I knew about the advertisement he put out and I was afraid it would end badly."

"How did you know about the ad?" Kristina asked as she slid a wide bucket in between us with the toe of her shoe.

"Nobody spits in this town without everyone knowing. Jeremiah's advertisement was the talk of Colorado Springs for some time. Some of the men were even taking bets on how long it would take for an answer and how hideous the new wife would be. You lost a lot of men a lot of money showing up here sophisticated and with a pretty face and figure like you did."

"Idiots," Kristina grumbled.

"Ready," Daisy said with a delicate white handkerchief clutched in the air. "Steady. Go!"

We plucked furiously, and by the time we were using our knives against our thumbs to remove any stragglers, we were neck and neck. I won, but only because when Daisy checked for leftover feathers,

Kristina's chicken had a few she'd missed while mine was smooth.

"Victory!" I whooped.

"Rematch," Kristina declared.

As I squatted nearest the fire to toss breaded chicken over the hot oil sizzling away in the iron pot, a strong hand ran the length of my back and Jeremiah kissed me lightly on the cheek. Grease popped onto the skin of my forearm again and I yanked it back as the burning subsided.

"You want me to do this?" he asked, trailing kisses down my neck.

"Do you know how?"

Amusement hummed in his voice. "Who do you think gave Kristina this recipe?"

"Trudy."

"Not on this one." He pulled me back with a gentle hand. "This one's all mine, passed down from Da to me and my brothers."

I stared at him, dumbfounded. Never in my life had I seen a man who held any interest in cooking. He set the chicken in the pan and pulled back before the oil hit him. He was so fast it was like watching a snake strike. I sat back into the chair against the wall beside him and ran my fingertips lightly over his knee. Luke and Sheriff Hawkins spoke easily from the front porch while Daisy and Kristina fussed happily over a finished pan of warm yeast rolls across the room.

"Is there nothing you can't do?" I asked.

His face was serious in the flickering light of the fire and he slid those burning, coffee colored eyes to me. "I can't lose you."

I pulled my legs up under me and touched the side of his face. "You won't." The smoothness of his jaw was too irresistible not to caress. The angles of his face were sharp and hard like the crags of a mountain and his eyes slanted ever so slightly, which made them look as much animal as man. His dark eyebrows made the perfect ceiling for such consuming windows into his secret self.

"You're so damned beautiful, woman," he said low.

Had he been reading my mind while I sat there trapped in his gaze? I closed my eyes against the loss when he released me. I'd have stayed happily there for the rest of my days, lost in the reflected flames of his eyes. He forked the chicken from the skillet and onto a cloth covered plate to soak up the excess grease.

"Dinner's on," he called out.

He hadn't had an extra moment to make a table or chairs yet, so dinner was served buffet style, then consumed in companionable silence as we dangled our legs from the porch. I leaned against Jeremiah contentedly and when he was finished eating, he draped his arm over my shoulders with a sigh. "We need to talk to you ladies about somethin'."

Why did those words make me go cold inside? My flare of earlier worry came back with a vengeance.

It was Sheriff Hawkins who spoke up. "Deputy McDowell is dead. Dirty Bill's gang of men shot him through, as you likely know, and I aim to go after the sons of bitches who done him like that. McDowell was young and green but his heart was in the right place when he brought that outlaw into the jailhouse. His death can't be for nothing." His stormy eyes were serious over his thick mustache.

"Eugene!" Daisy cried. "They'll kill you if you try to bring him in."

"Stop," he said with a warning look. "You knew I was a lawman the day you married me. This is part of the job. I can't just pick and choose who to enforce justice on, Daisy."

Her lip trembled and she looked away with a pained expression, but held her tongue.

Luke hung his hat on his knee and looked at Kristina. "I'm going with him."

"What? But why? You ain't no lawman, Luke, and this ain't your fight."

"It is," he argued. "In exchange for the sheriff's help when those Hell Hunters came to hang and burn us, I promised him a favor. I swore I'd help him someday when he needed someone with my talents, and that day has come."

Kristina's eyes rimmed with moisture. "Why didn't you tell me that?"

"So you could worry yourself to death every time the sheriff walked our way?"

"I'd be right to worry, now wouldn't I?" She was nearly yelling and he jerked his head like it hurt him. "You didn't see those monsters riding through town, tippin' their hats at the ladies they passed before they put bullets into the deputy and half the damned town to boot!" She jabbed a finger at the sheriff. "You are one man," she jabbed a finger at Luke, "and you are one man. They have at least four of them left, if not more, and at the head of that lot of murderers and rapists is Dirty Bill himself. He's probably killed more people than the entire population of Colorado Springs. He's a professional at pain, Luke, and you're riding off to track that rattlesnake down." She wiped her eyes with the backs of furiously shaking hands. "You'll go anyway. It doesn't matter what I say. Honor above everything, right? Even above me? Jeremiah, go with him."

My heart was already breaking for Kristina and now it crumbled. There was nothing worse than what was being asked of them.

"You two are stronger together," she beseeched my husband. "I know he'll come back if you're there. I saw you in the woods the day I was tortured at the hands of those vile men Evelynn French sent after me. You stood in the shadows, holding the horses, but don't pretend you didn't keep him sane and able to track me. Don't pretend you didn't help every step of the way for a woman you hardly knew. You did it for *him*. You risked your life for *him*." She turned a bright-eyed gaze to Luke. "Avenge the deputy, keep your promise to the sheriff, keep your honor, but Jeremiah goes with you."

The silence in the clearing was heavy, like some weighted stone upon my chest.

"She's right," Jeremiah said softly.

"No," I breathed. I bit my trembling lip and lowered my tear-filled eyes.

"He's my brother," he said. "And we both owe the sheriff a debt. If he wasn't there that night, we wouldn't be sitting here having this conversation." He stroked my downturned cheek. "I wouldn't have met you."

I understood and that was the worst part. A desperate anger churned at him for leaving, for the situation, for that damned Dirty Bill Burton, for the risk he and his gang posed to the one thing on earth I couldn't live without. Daisy sniffled quietly in the corner and her crying made it harder to control the tremor in my voice, so I nodded my understanding instead.

"Where are they?" Jeremiah asked.

"An informant told me they're hiding out up in the mountains not too far from here. Got witnesses saying they've seen them all along the trail they would've taken."

Luke's voice sounded odd and distant. "One week. We can't leave Kristina and Lorelei unprotected for more than a week."

"That should be enough time," Hawkins said. "Kristina, I watched you shoot Luke's hanging rope with your Derringer. Can you shoot a pistol as well?"

She nodded miserably and her voice cracked like she hadn't used it in a long time. "Almost as well."

"Good. Daisy I want you staying here until we get back. Everyone knows where we live and if something goes south, that's the first place they'll go. Don't go back to town. Don't let anyone know where you are and if anyone visits here, don't tell anyone what we're doing."

Daisy refused to look at him but nodded.

"All three of you need to be staying together," Luke said. "In the big house or the barn, either one, but stay together."

Jeremiah stood. "The faster we go, the faster we can get back here."

"Wait." I shielded my eyes from the bright sunlight to better see his face. "You don't mean to go now, do you?"

Sheriff stood and dusted off his pants. "We need to go now before they move again."

Kristina stormed from the porch, followed by Luke, and Sheriff Hawkins pulled Daisy into his arms and whispered into her ear. I left them to their tender goodbye and escaped into the house.

The flames in the hearth licked at the stones. Red, yellow, blue—their roiling colors matched what was happening in my heart. Jeremiah would leave and it wouldn't end well. Everything in my gut told me so.

His hands were feather soft against the tops of my shoulders and he leaned into my back. "I'm sorry, Lorelei. It just don't feel right letting him go alone."

I spun and threw my arms around his neck. "I know. I *know* you have to go. I'm just so scared for what's going to happen out there."

I closed my eyes against the pain of the coming separation as he kissed me with the violence of a tornado. I gasped as his teeth grazed my neck and with barely any effort, he carried me into the back room and slammed the door with his boot.

He set me down on a crude chest of drawers.

"Lorelei," he growled against the paper thin skin of my throat. "I'll come back to you. I swear it."

I groaned at the sensation of his mouth against my neck and he pulled my hair until it stretched farther for him. Pain and pleasure collided as he slid my skirts to my hips and gripped onto my thighs with rough hands. His warmth disappeared as he dropped to his knees and pushed my skirts up farther.

"What are you doing?" I asked, panic flaring in my chest.

"I'm not leaving without knowing how you taste."

I opened my mouth to protest whatever he had in mind that would bring his face so close to my tender bits, but he yanked my knees forward, spread them wide, and then kissed my sex.

I'd never been a part of something so scandalous in all my life, but oh! His tongue dipped inside of me and my legs went soft as dough. About three strokes in, and I didn't care how wanton this made me. I liked this. I needed this. The oncoming separation had me scared and desperate for a connection, and apparently Jeremiah felt the same. And he was so, so good at this. He circled the sensitive spot he was always careful to pay attention to with his tongue, and I groaned and arched back.

I shouldn't like this, but I did. And Kristina had been telling me to own my body more and be proud of the physical relationship I'd been growing with Jeremiah, so hang it all. I ran my hands through his hair and a vibrating growl rumbled against the wetness between my legs. His strokes became faster, and Jeremiah's hands disappeared from my legs. The jangling sound of his holster being removed filled the room. The first waves of my release crashed through me and I cried out as my toes curled. He sucked on my sensitive nub one more time, bowing me forward, then stood and slid his cock into me in one fluid motion.

He wasn't reserved or tender, but I didn't want him to be. He didn't ask permission or take his time. He took me like he owned the deed to my soul. My second round of pleasure became a consuming wave that lapped at the shores of the deepest pieces of me. When his seed spilled into me in hot, throbbing streams, he closed his eyes tightly and rested his forehead against mine.

"One week," he whispered.

And then there was nothing left but the creaking leather of his holster in his hand and his fading boot steps across the home he'd built for us.

I slid to the floor as if I were boneless, then curled up like a child and wept.

For one week, I would cease to exist.

Chapter Twenty-One
Jeremiah

Easily, that had been the hardest thing I'd ever had to do, next to burying Anna. Nothing in me wanted to leave Lorelei. It was our moving day into the big house, a day we'd been looking forward to for the better part of a week. And instead of helping her set up, I was off on some suicide mission.

There was no point in giving Luke hell about it. He'd been stuck between a rock and a hard place and if it were me, I'd have done the same thing. His shoulders drooped on the back of his mount and he'd pulled the brim of his hat low over his shadowed eyes. If utter misery had a smell, Luke would've been bathed in it.

"Kristina rough you up pretty good?" I asked with sympathy.

"She's pissed."

"No, she's scared. Same way we felt when we heard those gunshots in town and couldn't get to the girls soon enough. She doesn't have any control over your fate now. She won't be there with her little pea shooter to help you this time. It doesn't matter that you are werewolf and plenty capable. She just wants to make sure you're safe."

He gave a noncommittal grunt. "What about Lorelei. Was she mad?"

I thought about her hands in my hair as I tasted her and all the needy noises she'd made for me. Through a private grin, I said, "Not after I got done with her."

My brother leveled me with a green-eyed glare. "You know, you used to be all mannerly and boring. What happened to the Jeremiah who wouldn't rub shit like that in my face?"

I shrugged. "Lost him I guess. Cheer up, Luke. We're going hunting."

"We ain't huntin' for bunnies, Jeremiah. This prey has weapons and logic and itchy trigger fingers."

"And we have the element of surprise. They aren't expecting anyone comin' after 'em this quick, and they sure as hell aren't expecting wolves."

"We aren't bulletproof. We can still die, remember?"

I whistled. "Being married has made you soft! What happened to the Luke who was always itching for a saloon fight? You ain't exactly a novice at gun fights, little brother. Get your head in the right place or you *will* be going home in a casket." I kicked my horse into a slow gallop. "Let's get this done with so we can get back to 'em."

We stopped in Colorado Springs to chat up Elias on the way out about what was happening. Other than that, we steered clear of the small towns and homesteads on the way into the mountains for fear they'd send a rider out to warn Dirty Bill we were coming for him. Instead, we rode through the brush when we could and avoided contact with people as much as we were able. By the second day, we were low on smoked deer meat and the canteens needed a refill. We'd be on them tomorrow if they hadn't fled the area already, and a good night's sleep wouldn't hurt before going into what promised to be a dangerous situation.

Luke had stalked off into the wilderness and come back with a fat spring pig that had escaped someone's farm along the way. While it roasted on a spit over the fire, I packed everyone's sloshing canteens back into their horses' saddle bags. Sheriff Hawkins sat with his elbow propped on his knee staring off into the fire like it held the answers to the world's secrets, and Luke squatted near the flames with his hands against the warmth of them. He flipped the collar of his duster up to shield his ears from the cold. The higher we went up into the mountains, the more snow and bitterly cold wind we met.

"When do you plan on telling your wife what you are?" he asked as I walked by.

Hawkins looked up from the fire briefly but he already knew the big secret. He wouldn't have recruited our special talents if we didn't have any.

"When the time is right."

Luke poked at the fire with a long stick. "You know there isn't a right time to tell her something like that. It's best if you do it quick."

I snorted. "Like you did?"

"Yeah, well you could stand to learn from my mistakes."

I sat beside him with a sigh of resignation. I really tried my best not to think about telling her, so talking about it in detail sounded about as much fun as the roasting pig was having at the moment. "I have to make sure she won't run away first. I can't lose her."

"She ain't running, Jeremiah," he said quietly. "Any man with eyes can see she loves you somethin' fierce. You're stalling is all."

The stick between my fingers bent and made a popping sound as I broke it in half. He was right. The time had been ideal for a while now but I'd chickened out time and time again. Every time I'd opened my mouth to tell her I wasn't human, this whining voice, like the buzz of a mosquito said, *you'll lose her if she finds out what a monster you are.* Even if the risk was small, it was still a risk.

"My wolf lets me in now," I admitted quietly. "He ain't so crazy anymore. I forgot what it feels like to hunt as an animal. To enjoy the woods like only an animal can, where my oversensitive hearing and smell make sense. It's a scary thing to feel like someday soon I could be whole again, and that could be taken away before it happens."

Luke inhaled and nodded slowly. "I'd probably be stallin' too if I had that much to lose."

****

Lorelei

Things were downright gloomy around the big house. We'd unanimously decided to live in there until our men came home because it was farther from the entrance to the property and we could each have our own rooms. And it didn't smell like horse poop, as Daisy pointed out.

Three sets of waiting eyes never strayed far from the road, and even though we knew it would be five days yet until they were due home, we continued to hope just the same. An apparent guilt consumed Kristina by the second day.

"I should've sent him off with a good memory of me. I should've been understanding and given him a proper goodbye." It was no secret she agonized over their parting moments together.

She milked the cow while Daisy sewed away at a hole in the hem of her dress with a needle and thread she'd borrowed, and I hauled feed to the horse's stalls.

I dropped the bucket and wiped moisture from my forehead with the back of my hand. "Look at us, wallowing here like they've died," I said. "They aren't dead. They are out for some noble cause to rid the world of evil and we've already given up on them. They survived a hanging and a hail of bullets. They survived a train robbery and killed every last outlaw that boarded us, basically with their bare hands. And then they survived a night in the woods with a pack of wild wolves running around trying to eat people. And lord knows what the sheriff has survived." I arched my eyebrows at Daisy.

"An awful lot," she admitted.

"These aren't normal men we've sent out there. Five more days until they come back. Until then, let's keep busy and enjoy each other's company."

"Hello," a man's voice hailed.

"Aaaaack!" I screeched.

Trudy's husband stuck his head in the barn door. "Sorry, didn't mean to startle you. You ladies decent?"

It was so much easier when Jeremiah and Luke were around to hear every little leaf fall from the trees.

"Yes, yes, come on in," Daisy waved him over.

"I don't believe we've been formally introduced," he said as he held out his hand. "Elias Jones."

"Lorelei Dawson," I said, shaking it gently.

He took off his hat and fidgeted.

"Take a seat," Kristina said between pats into the milk pail. "We were just trying to motivate ourselves to be more optimistic about our gallant husbands and their chivalrous missions."

"Ah, I see. Well, those husbands are the reason I'm here. They stopped in town on their way into the mountains and asked me to check on you every few days. You ladies need anything?"

"Have there been any telegrams for any of us at the post office?" Daisy asked hopefully.

"No ma'am, not unless one's come in from this morning until now. I checked on it earlier, but nothing."

"Who else knows we're out here alone?" I asked.

"Just me and Trudy. Trudy wanted to come today but her ankles are all swollen and tender and I told her she needs to take it easy today. She sent me along with dinner though. It's in the back of the buggy."

The boys hadn't had a chance to hunt before they left and the chicken coop was getting low. The prospect of a dinner we didn't have to cook and of Trudy's caliber of expertise was enough to make my stomach think it was completely hollow. I felt better already. "Have you eaten, Mr. Jones?"

"Please, call me Elias."

Kristina chirped up with a scrunched face. "Seriously do. Mr. Jones sounds mighty strange."

He had a kind smile and laughing eyes and it was easy to see why Trudy had fallen for him. "I have not. I was hoping you'd ask me to stay for a visit."

"Let us finish up in here and then we'll head to the house," I said with a kind smile. Bless that man and his golden heart for checking on us. The least we could do was offer him the warmth of the fire before he had to make that long trip back into town.

With the animals taken care of and the barn locked up for the night, we unloaded bound cloth sacks full of panned food and walked back to the house together. Dinner took time to reheat over the fire, so I gave Elias the tour of the house. It still smelled like newness and sawdust and was mostly bare of furniture, but the walls kept the wind at bay and the fire warmed the living area in no time.

Elias gulped his last bite of seasoned ham and said, "Trudy told me to tell y'all to put the leftovers in a sack and tie them up in a tree to keep them safe from bears. She packed enough for a couple of meals and its cold enough outside that it'll keep. I can do that before I leave if you want."

Kristina clapped him on the back. "Much obliged, Elias."

He stood and stretched. "I'd better get on the road. I want to get back to Trudy before nightfall. Before I leave, Lorelei, can I talk to you in private?"

I frowned and set my fork down. "Of course." I shut the front door gently behind me and waited patiently for Elias to track down whatever it was he was looking for.

From the pocket of his vest he pulled a folded piece of paper. "Jeremiah said to give this to you."

I unfolded the letter carefully.

I love you. Always will.
- Jeremiah

The letter shook in my hands and I fought the stinging tears that threatened to spill over. "What is this?" I asked through clenched teeth. "He's never told me he loves me, so why would he give it to me in a letter unless this was his way of saying goodbye? Is he giving me closure in case something happens to him? Elias, is this his goodbye?"

His fair eyebrows lifted and he looked nothing short of frightened. "No, ma'am. I think he was just thinking of you and didn't want to leave without telling you how he felt."

Sniffing, I wiped my eyes with the back of my hand and tried to smile. My heart hurt that I was reading these words and not hearing them from his lips. "Thank you for bringing me this and for checking in on us today. It was mighty kind of you to think of us." My voice was thick with emotion but it couldn't be helped.

"Are you all right?" he asked in a low voice.

"I'm fine. I'm so sorry. It's just hard not knowing what is going on out there."

His smile was small and understanding. "My wife would be worrying just the same as you are. They're strong and able though, Mrs. Dawson. They'll be fine."

Everything in me hoped he was right.

Chapter Twenty-Two
Jeremiah

The snow hadn't quit the late winter up in the mountains. Here, amongst the crags and cliffs, it was a different world from our home in the valley. The air was thinner and harder to breathe and muscles fatigued faster, requiring Sheriff Hawkins to rest often. We'd left the horses down the hill at the first sounds of a camp up ahead. Someone was up here in the frigid country where no one would willingly inhabit unless they were the occasional mountain man tracking and trapping winter game, or outlaws slipping their nooses.

I'd heard what Dirty Bill Burton had done to the families he robbed. He'd tortured them until every hard-earned penny was squeezed from them. He'd stolen gold fillings from their mouths with a dirty knife, and then he and his men had raped the women in front of their husbands before he killed them all. He'd murdered countless families who lived on the outskirts of small towns, and all far enough away from civilization where no one would hear the screaming.

Just the thought of those children in his evil clutches was enough to run my blood hotter than hell fire. The noose was too kind a death for a man like him. It was too kind for any of them.

With our senses on the camp, we traveled in a circle around them and came out of the scraggly trees that braved yearlong snow above them. They'd been clever about their campsite. There were no trees or places to hide anywhere. Just piles of snow. It meant no relief from the relentless snow and wind for them but it also made it possible to see every mouse move within fifty yards. Unfortunate for human hunters, but not such a problem for a wolf.

"Dammit," Luke breathed between me and the sheriff. "Where's Gable when we need him?"

Luke was right. We worked well hunting as a pack, and two wolves did not a pack make.

We were lying on our stomachs, overlooking a small cliff some ways above them when Hawkins said, "I can't see a damned thing. How many?"

I ticked the bodies off in my head. "Looks like Burton's grown his crew by two men. There's six plus Burton." I'd never seen him in person before, but I had a wanted poster of him in my pocket and he looked spot on. The long scraggly black hair and gold front tooth gave him away. "Wait," I said as a man emerged from the tree line some distance off, zipping up his pants. "Seven and Burton. Eight altogether."

Hawkins cursed and rolled to his back. "Eight to three. What're they doing?"

Luke squinted toward the firelight. "Looks like they're getting ready to eat supper. Their getaway horses are about fifty yards down the hill from them, tied to a line."

Their laughter and conversation whipped around on the frantic wind, allowing only bits and pieces to be heard and none that made any sense. I gauged the setting sun through the clouds. If they kept passing around that rotgut whiskey, we'd be all right but either way, we were going to have to settle into the snowcapped hill and wait for them to fall asleep or pass out drunk.

I turned to Hawkins. "How good are you with a long shot rifle?"

"Good enough to save your carcasses from a hanging."

Fair enough.

By the time we'd stalked slowly back down the mountain and retrieved the proper weapons, dark had fallen over Colorado. The moon glowed as a pale orb through the cascading clouds, and the sounds from camp were starting to slowly die down. For hours we sat there, waiting for that instinct that would tell Luke and me the moment was right. When the moon shone right above us and after we hadn't heard any noise from camp bar the movements of two guards and the occasional snoring of the others, Luke headed a hundred yards down the mountain to change. I'd be worthless as a wolf. A half-crazy werewolf completely unreliable. We needed an animal with human logic, and Luke was the monster for the job.

His fur shone silver, black, and cream in the dim cloud-saturated moonlight.

I crouched down and spoke low. "We can't use guns on the sentries or it'll ruin the element of surprise for the others. Pull one of them into the woods. When they're taken care of we'll attack the camp and Sheriff Deadeye over there can pick off any bodies he can get a good shot on." I turned to Hawkins with as much seriousness as I could muster. "Don't shoot me or my brother please."

He snorted. "You two bickered the whole way here. If I haven't shot you by now, you're good."

I crept as close as I dared to the camp. Inhuman speed was good and well, but we had to be delicate about this if we wanted to survive it. And thinking of Lorelei standing naked in the moonlight that night by the creek, I definitely wanted to survive it.

Two lookouts leaned on trees some twenty-five yards apart. The one nearest me yawned and shifted his weight like he was stretching out sore legs. A flash of gray to my left had him jerk his head up with the movement. He cocked his pistol and straightened his spine.

Another flash.

"Hey, Duggard," he whisper-screamed. "I think there's a wolf out here."

"So shoot it," came the harried reply.

"Ain't there only, say, three hundred or so left in these here parts?" he asked.

And explosive sigh came from Duggard. "Just shoot the damned thing before it brings its friends." He pushed off from the tree and tramped over to where the first sentry was wading into the woods.

Luke ran out from a tree further down the mountain and disappeared behind a snow bank.

"I gotcha, you little bastard," the man said with a grin in his voice.

I stilled my breathing as he passed the tree I hid behind. It was Duggard who was my target. He was quieter than the first and if I had to bet, smarter too. His boots crunching through the snow were as loud to me as someone talking in my face. I yanked the gun out of his grasp and wrapped my hand around his throat so tightly he couldn't utter a sound before I snapped his neck.

Luke's prey hadn't died so quietly. He'd lunged on his back and as the man fell, his gun went off harmlessly in front of him before Luke's teeth sank into his spine. The crack of the shot echoed from the cliffs and there wasn't any time to think. We had to do this now or never and the men in the camp were starting to sit up with questions on their lips.

"Duggard? Campbell?" One of the men called.

I drew my pistols. There was no point in being quiet about it now. The first man fell as my Peace Maker found its mark, but the others were already drawing their weapons, and the sparse trees hid me poorly. I fired and missed but a shot rang out behind me and the Sheriff's aim had been better. Another dropped like a sack of flour, and that's where things went south for us.

A flying bullet ripped through my shoulder and rocked me back into the snow and the firing, running outlaws were almost to their horses. I righted myself and bolted to cut them off.

Burton. I have to find Burton.

He and his men scattered as soon as they were mounted but I'd seen his horse just before he disappeared into the trees. Luke ran at a graceful lope beside me as shots sailed through the quiet forest. Another stiffened body fell with a thud to the frozen earth, and I hoped to God it wasn't Hawkins. Trees whooshed by as I gained speed and the sound of another horse's hooves thundered nearby. Someone from his gang was loyal enough to offer Burton help.

My shoulder screamed with every pump of my arms and liquid warmth oozed down my ribcage, soaking my shirt, but still, I couldn't stop. I was so close.

The other horse was catching up and fast on our other side, and its rider peppered shot after zinging shot at us. Luke cut off and ran for him and just as I launched myself at Burton the other rider found a solid mark.

A bullet made a different sound when it hit something than when it missed. A miss echoed on and on as the bullet sailed through air and space. A hit made a solid *thunk*.

A whine escaped Luke's throat as his body hurdled into a snow bank.

"No!" I shouted as I wrapped my arms around Burton's waist and flung him from the fleeing horse. A tree broke my fall and pain shot through me. Burton rolled several yards before sliding to a stop at the base of a huge pine. Luke's body lay crumpled in the snow and a bone chilling chuckle came from Burton's parted lips.

His pistol was pointed steadily and directly at my face.

"We killed your dog," he gritted out, right before he pulled the trigger.

Chapter Twenty-Three
Lorelei

A week had come and gone. I knew what it meant but none of us dared to breathe life into our fears with words. The musty, gray haze of denial was the only course for my continued existence. I worked from sun up to sun down and as the week went on, Kristina, Daisy, and I stopped talking altogether. Our voices had started to shake, and the cracks in our once strong foundation had become deep and rotted.

We'd all suffered the same fate but wouldn't admit it. Not yet.

Elias came every couple of days with food and a constant borage of hope-filled words, but even those echoed with emptiness now. Even eternally optimistic Elias knew something had gone wrong up there in those mountains. Kristina and Daisy were strong in the daylight, but when nighttime brought the dark, no one was safe from slow realization. Their heartbreak echoed through the empty rooms of the house and at some point, I gave up on sleep altogether. Our sleep brought screams conjured by nightmares.

Swaying to the rhythm of both my pain and the rocking chair I'd dragged in from outside, I lost myself in staring at the flames of the hearth. It's warmth and the sound of the crackling wood it fed upon was a soothing balm on a burn I couldn't seem to escape.

"Lorelei?" Daisy asked in a frail voice. It was raspy, as if she'd been crying her whole life.

I didn't have to say anything. She was looking for comfort, not words. Instead I held my hand out to her and she sank to the wooden floorboards beside me.

Her face crumpled, all semblance of strength gone under the horrible reality we couldn't deny any longer. Clutching onto my leg, she whispered, "They aren't coming back, are they?"

I shook my head slowly as a tear ran down my cheek. I'd have given anything for my answer to be different.

She clutched onto my skin and cried out, "Damn those men and damn their pride."

Her nails dug deeply into me but I didn't mind. At least I still felt something other than the inescapable ache in my heart. Kristina appeared out of the darkness of her room in nothing but a thin nightdress. She looked pale and her skin was covered in gooseflesh. Her eyes had the hollow, sunken look of phantoms and her cheeks were red and adorned with tears.

"Come by the fire," I said.

She sank down and laid her head in Daisy's lap and while she gently stroked Kristina's soft curls with her fingertips, I rocked and hummed a lullaby Mother sang to me when I was a child in need of comfort.

Over and over I hummed it until my throat was dry, and Kristina and Daisy were curled up sleeping near the hearth. And here, in the darkest hours of the blackest night of my life, I heard the scratching again. It was the scratching of my nightmares where I imagined some terrible creature coming to devour me. *Scritch, scratch, scritch, scratch,* it went relentlessly on as I watched the front door and imagined a hundred evil creatures that could be on the other side of it.

As if in a trance, I stood and padded slowly to the door. Crouching down, I placed my hand against the inside of it until I could feel the vibrations of the monster outside. It stopped. I removed my hand and pulled it to my chest to steady my trembling.

The pitiful whine of a dog cut through the night air.

Kristina and Daisy slept soundly behind me, but I shouldn't wake them. Straightening my skirts in determination, I moved to open the latch. Maybe my instincts had burned up with my loss, or maybe I just didn't care as much about living or dying anymore, but I opened that door and stepped out before the dog could come in.

A pile of crumpled fur lay across the porch, and try as I might to make heads or tails of him, the cloudy night sky selfishly lapped up any light I needed. Its fur was dark and its stomach rose and fell raggedly, as if it had difficulty drawing breath.

The dog was dying.

Another whine sealed my fate. Saving it would be my burden. I'd lost too much today and a dog dying on my front porch was just one unfairness too many. I scooped it up before I could chicken out and struggled under its great weight as I carried him carefully to the barn. The horses flared their noses and stomped their feet in the first signs of panic, but I brushed right past them until I was to the hearth. It took two matches for my shaking hands to ignite the dry tender in the fireplace, but when the flames were finally lapping at the stone walls of the fireplace, I turned and stifled a scream.

It wasn't a dog.

The creature I'd carried in my arms was a wolf.

Chest heaving, I backed into the corner and sank down against the wall with a pathetic whimper on my lips. He looked like the wolf who'd tried to kill us outside the train. His icy blue eyes opened slowly and watched me crouched there like a coward who'd accepted her fate.

Another long whine escaped him and something about it pulled so gently at my heartstrings. No way would a wild wolf come to a home for help. He'd let me carry him with no fight, and he'd known to scratch at the door like some tame pet. He belonged to someone, of that I was sure. He'd likely been raised gently to trust humans so much. Wolf or dog, it didn't matter what kind of creature he was. I couldn't just sit here in a cloud of fear and watch him die.

Slowly, I patted my pocket and was comforted by the weight of my knife. At least I had a weapon. I wasn't just blunt claws and teeth and helplessly human. Still crouched, I sidled slowly closer, and he closed his eyes as if he trusted me to touch him.

"Where's your master?" I crooned. The wolf was beautiful. Whomever lost him was likely looking for him. Unless something terrible had happened to them. My heart ached. Perhaps he'd lost the most important person to him, like I'd just lost mine. Perhaps we were the same, he and I.

I closed my eyes and reached out until course, thick fur touched my fingertips. He didn't move or even growl. Eventually I found the courage to stroke him gently, and then to run my hand over his side. Despite being able to feel every rib poking out, the problem was pretty obvious. Even now, I didn't know if I could change his fate. A half-healed puncture wound disappeared into the dark fur of his shoulder and under thin skin, something hard and knotted was burrowed, poisoning him slowly.

Someone had shot him and the bullet was still there. Perhaps he'd taken it trying to protect his master.

My voice shook fiercely as I reached for my knife. A low rumble in his throat held me frozen in place. So familiar was that sound, it stirred in me…something. Confused, I pulled the knife out of frustration.

"You have a bullet in you. It needs to come out." No, I didn't believe dogs could understand humans, but it sure as anything made me feel better to talk to him. I leaned toward his shoulder, blade gleaming in the firelight, but pulled back. "If you bite me, I'm going to kill you the rest of the way."

He turned his head away from me and closed his striking blue eyes.

"All right then." The skin had to be reopened because a knot that size would never fit through a semi-healed opening that small. I made the cut quickly and then flinched while I waited for the wolf to eat me. Nothing happened and I opened one eye to find him still in the same position. "This is going to hurt," I warned.

He was stoic as I pried the seeping wound open and shoved my finger through the hole. I hooked it around the bullet as quickly as I could, and pulled. Out plopped a disfigured chunk of metal. I held it up against the light in my bloodied hand. He must've been in a great deal of pain. A shuffling noise drew my attention. The wolf crept closer on his belly, head and tail down and a soft whine in his throat. He lay his head in my lap and heaved a great sigh, as if touching me brought him relief from the heartache he no doubt felt at losing his master.

Well, if that didn't beat all.

I debated stitching the wound closed but my shaking hands wouldn't give him any advantage. If the wolf lived, he'd just have to be scarred. Perhaps I could keep him. I would be a poor substitute for the master he'd lost, but maybe we could shoulder our losses together.

I cried then as I stroked the soft fur on his face. I let the tide of anguish wash over me as I accepted that I'd lost Jeremiah in those mountains. My shoulders shook with my sobs, and I clutched the fabric of my dress over my heart where it felt like it would burst. I loved him, and now I understood why Kristina had said she'd never marry another.

No one else would compare to my Jeremiah.

Maybe I cried for hours, I didn't know. All I knew was that I'd never be the same. I'd always be sad and broken. My husband had become a part of me, and now the bits of me I'd grown to care for were gone. As my tears had dried, the wolf had laid his head against my stomach as if he knew precisely the pain I endured.

Spent and exhausted, I lay down in the hay beside the dark beast. He nuzzled my face and licked my hand as I petted his ear, and down his protruding ribcage. My eyelids grew heavier with the gentle motion of my hand against him. It was easy falling asleep next to him. Maybe it was because he'd been there for me. Or because he was going through the same heartbreak. He'd never shown any aggression, only devotion to the hands that had saved his life.

I felt safe here in the firelight by my wolf.

He was wild and brave like my Jeremiah had been.

****

"Lorelei." A voice echoed through my dreams. "Lorelei," it repeated. "Where are you?" The voice was getting closer.

I stretched and opened my bleary eyes. Beigha stared at me from the safety of her stall and blasted a snort. Last night came back to me like a thundering avalanche, and with a combination of fear and hope, I felt for the wolf until my fingers found the rough fur of his coat.

I sat up and picked cascading stems of hay from my wild hair under the intense scrutiny of the wolf's blue-eyed gaze. "You aren't going to eat me now that you are feeling better, are you?"

He shook his head with a sneeze.

"Great." My voice was scratchy and raw from crying so much, but the animal didn't seem to mind. "Come on, boy." I stood and hailed Kristina, who had a panicked look to her eyes as she ran for the barn. "I'm in here." The wolf followed me, limping badly.

"There you are!" Kristina said in a tone that all but dripped relief. "I thought you'd gone off and done something stupid."

The wolf growled behind me at the sight of Kristina, and her eyes went round. She screamed and lunged for the ladder as the wolf attacked.

"No!" I yelled as I jumped in between them. It gave her enough time to scurry up a few ladder rungs.

"Where's Luke?" she cried over his snarls.

I backed slowly to the ladder, careful to stay in between them. This was a side of the wolf I hadn't seen. He was terrifying. "What?" My voice shook like a flame. "How should I know?"

"I'm not asking you, Lorelei. I'm asking...Aaah!"

The wolf lunged again and I maneuvered my body closer to the ladder. Kristina scrambled straight up to the loft above me, and the wolf watched her the entire way.

"Don't you feel some kind of connection to the wolf? Anything?" Her tone was getting frantic as the wolf approached me.

Terror snaked through me and I stumbled up the first rung with my back to the ladder. I just had to get far enough up it to escape those gleaming teeth he was baring at Kristina.

Wolves couldn't climb ladders. Could they?

"Lorelei, he'll still be able to get up here. Do you feel a connection?" Kristina asked from above.

"He—he let me clean his wound last night," I stuttered. I crawled up the next rung, never taking my eyes from the hatred on the wolf's face.

"Not what I'm talking about. Think. Why would a wolf let you do that?"

"Because he was tame. He was someone's pet."

"No, Lorelei. That wolf doesn't belong to anyone but you," she said softly. "He's Jeremiah."

I shook my head back and forth as I climbed higher. She'd lost it. She'd snapped with the loss of her husband and now she was crazy. Jeremiah was dead and as far as I knew, dead people didn't reincarnate into black-furred, blue-eyed wolves.

"That's the secret, Lorelei. He's a werewolf."

A hundred things that hadn't made sense clattered into place. His inhuman speed, his shifting eye color and the soft growls in his throat when I pleased him. His heightened sense of hearing, the Hell Hunters, and the reasons the townspeople all seemed wary of the Dawson brothers.

The devil's breeding right here in town...

But Jeremiah was a man. I'd felt his skin and kissed his lips. He didn't match the beast below me.

"You're his mate," Kristina whispered.

Tears made warm streams on my cheeks and it was hard to breathe. "Stop it."

"Lorelei—"

"I said stop it!" I screamed. "What you're telling me isn't real. It's not real, Kristina! Werewolves don't exist. This is just a way for you to hold onto the idea that Luke and Jeremiah are still alive."

My roiling anger did something terrifying to the wolf. He pulled black lips over gleaming white teeth and looked at Kristina with such hatred. Then he hooked his paw on the first rung of the ladder, as if he knew exactly how to get up to her.

He wasn't going to let her escape the loft.

"Save me," she whispered from above me. "He'll listen to you."

I sobbed and wiped moisture from my damp lashes with the back of my hand. I would try anything. She was my sister-in-law. She was the sister I'd always wished for in every way. She was different from me in ways that challenged me and made me better. Kristina always made me laugh when I was sad or confused. She never teased me or abandoned me like all of my friends in Boston had.

I gripped the ladder and lowered myself down.

"Wait," I said as my feet hit the ground. I held my hands out as he backed away. I crouched down slowly until I was eye level with the snarling wolf. "Please. If you're my Jeremiah, you love me. I'm your wife and I'm begging you to let Kristina be. She's my best friend. If you took her from me, you'd hurt me." I sounded so silly to my own ears.

His lips fell and his brilliant eyes danced between us. His face softened and he paced in a tight circle. His lips drew up in a snarl once more before he whined and nuzzled his face against my outstretched hands. A familiar rumble played on some of my favorite memories of Jeremiah, and a tiny sliver of hope snaked its way through me.

Kristina stepped gingerly from the bottom rung of the ladder and shook like the last leaf in winter as she waited. He sniffed her outstretched fist, then licked my chin as I ran my nails through his fur.

It couldn't be possible, could it? Was my Jeremiah in this animal somewhere? "Can he change back whenever he wants?" I asked. If it was really him I wanted him to hold me. I wanted to know what was real and imagined.

"Luke can. Jeremiah's wolf has been broken ever since Anna passed away though. I don't know how it works for him."

"Can you change back?" I pleaded. "If it's you—if you're Jeremiah, I need you."

He whined and shifted his weight back and forth on two humongous front paws before he trotted off for the hay we'd slept in last night.

I wrung my hands. "What should I do?"

"In my experience, its best for both of you if you watch," she said. "Don't scream or look disgusted. It's brutal and it hurts them like hell. Accept him. Accept his wolf. They're both yours for as long as you walk this earth."

My heart pounded like the wings of a falcon but still, I approached him. The wolf's bones fractured and crunched, but never once did he cry out in pain. I tried my best to keep my face neutral as his muscles snapped in two and reformed into something completely new. He had to know I was here because he watched me, and when the fur disappeared and took the smoothness of a man's skin, I knew without a doubt he'd kept his promise and come back to me.

In light of his assumed death, him being a werewolf just didn't seem so bad. I'd rather have him like this than not at all.

He sat up gasping in pain but I couldn't hold myself back a minute longer. He was alive. He'd come back to grow old with me and keep me safe. Jeremiah didn't even lift his arms to catch my flying frame as I wrapped my body around him and cried. Even when he groaned like my touch burned his flesh, I didn't care. I wanted him to feel me against his sensitive skin. I wanted him to feel the agony I'd gone through in his absence. It was minutes before his hands brushed my back and I rocked as I sobbed into the side of his neck.

"Don't ever do that to me again. Don't you ever leave me like that again," I chanted brokenly.

"Shhh," he said as he pulled his strong hand to the back of my neck. "I'm here."

The clunk of a pair of pants hit the hay beside us and Kristina stood in the early morning light, openly sobbing. "I want to know how it happened."

"Stop your cryin', woman. Luke's alive and well. He went with Sheriff Hawkins to take Burton to Denver. He hung from a noose yesterday morning if all went to plan. Your man will be back in a few days."

"Hells bells," she said through a tear stained grin. "I have to tell Daisy!"

She spun and bolted for the barn door, and when she was through, Jeremiah dislodged me from his lap and pulled on his pants. The bullet wound on his shoulder was weeping red.

"I need to dress your wound," I said, suddenly feeling shy. I was finally in on the secret. I finally knew him. *Really* knew him.

He twitched his gaze to his shoulder and shook his head. "It'll be no more than a scratch by nightfall. I heal quickly."

"Will I catch it?"

Buttoning his pants, he lifted a somber gaze to me. "You have to be born with it."

"Is Luke the same as you?"

Jeremiah tugged my hand until I was nestled against his chest.

"And my brother Gable, and my da. Every man in our family is a werewolf."

"Is that why Kristina said your lineage can be traced back so far?"

"That's exactly right. We have so much to talk about with this. I want to share everything with you, woman. I want to show you every part of me, and then I'm going to ask you to accept all of it."

"Is this why you mail-ordered me? Because no one around here would trust their daughters with you?"

"Yes."

I dropped my gaze to the straw at our feet. How scary must it have been to live in this rough land and be *other*? To be tracked down by Hell Hunters for what he was. I was suddenly grateful for Luke and Kristina, so that he hadn't been alone with this before I came along. The werewolf blood running through his veins made him stronger and faster. It was the reason he was still here with me, holding me in his arms. "I'm glad you're like this. You're mine, Jeremiah Cade Dawson. Wolf or man, you belong to me."

The ghost of a smile curved his lips, only to fall as if he were uncertain I was telling the truth. "You mean it?"

My eyes were burning with tears again, and my throat was closing with emotion, so I nodded.

He lifted me up so fast I gasped. I laughed thickly and laced my fingers behind his neck as I gazed down at him. "You're bleeding on my best dress."

"We'll go into town right now and buy you a new one. I'll buy you ten. We'll drop Daisy off at her home, and then we'll go to the general store and put in an order for a stove as well. Whatever you want, Lorelei. You'll have it."

"And with what money are you planning on doing all of this with?" I asked lightly.

"Didn't you know? We're rich now, Mrs. Dawson. Did you look at the rewards posted at the bottom of all them wanted posters in town? Sheriff is vouching for the outlaws we offed and caught. The only one that was specified they wanted alive was Dirty Bill Burton. That's why Luke escorted him all the way to Denver. The others all said *Dead or Alive* and we brought 'em all in."

"Huh," I said, feet dangled far above the ground with my husband's inhumanly strong arms wrapped around me like he'd never let me go. "Well, I just don't think I'm going to be shocked by anything else that comes our way, Jeremiah."

His face dropped just a little. "Now you know my secret. I couldn't tell you until I was sure you wouldn't run away screaming from me."

I kissed the tip of his nose and rested my arms across his broad shoulders. "Do you see me running and screaming? I meant it when I said you're mine." I rested my forehead upon his. "All of you."

"Mmm, well there's still things we need to talk about but they'll hold for now."

"I just watched all of your bones break while you turned from a wolf into a man. You can't scare me away. Kristina said I'm your mate, am I not?"

He closed his eyes and his nostrils flared slightly. With a contented growl, he said, "You're my mate."

Chapter Twenty-Four
Lorelei

Daisy was a mess by the time I'd gone back to the house. Kristina gave me a wide-eyed, frightened look as the woman sobbed into her shoulder and mouthed, *what do I do?*

I cleared my throat. "We're headed to town to celebrate and take you back home, Daisy. The danger's over and your husband will be home in a couple of days."

She gave a delicate sniffle. "It will be nice to sleep in my own bed for a change. In any bed, actually."

Kristina clapped her on the back. "Yep, country livin' ain't for everyone."

"Jeremiah said he'll treat us all to lunch at Cotton's." I'd already chosen my entire meal on the way from the barn and now my mouth watered just thinking about Trudy's pot roast. After days of no appetite and a queasy stomach, I was so hungry I could eat a horse—if it tasted like Trudy's pot roast.

Kristina didn't mind sitting in the bed of the buggy, and Daisy sitting up front with a white handkerchief over her nose meant I was happily squished into Jeremiah's side. He handed me the reins and directed me as he relaxed and draped his arm across the back of my seat.

"What happened up there in the mountains?" I asked.

He told the story as if it were meant to be heard over a campfire. It was a riveting adventure that had my heart racing despite knowing the ending.

"And then Burton said, *we killed your dog*, and pulled the trigger. Except he'd already spent his last shot, and the second my shock wore off that I was still alive, I jumped him and knocked him out with the butt of his own empty pistol."

Kristina's tone was tainted with worry. "Luke's hurt?"

"Shot through once. Bullet went straight in and out the side of his neck. He bled like a stuck pig, but I bet by the time he gets back it'll just be another scar to decorate his noose mark."

"Can the man leave his neck alone?" she grumbled.

"My dadburned horse ran off on me by the time I stumbled back down the mountain and rather than track him down I changed, thinking it would make the pain in my shoulder a little easier to bear and speed up my healing. It didn't. That bullet made me sick as all get-out and by the time I made it back to our house I thought surely I was dyin'. I didn't even have the strength to change back and low and behold, Lorelei is all right with hauling an injured wolf out to the barn and coming at him with a knife." He ducked his head toward me. "We need to have a serious talk about what is and isn't safe out here."

"I thought you were dead and I wasn't thinking straight. Besides I thought you were a dying dog until I saw you in the firelight. Then I thought you were someone's pet. And I think a part of me knew you wouldn't hurt me. I felt safe with you."

Kristina snorted. "That's disturbing."

"Hey, he isn't trying to kill you anymore, now is he?"

Daisy was frowning grumpily like she had become completely lost in the tide of our conversation.

"True," Kristina said. "I always knew deep down you liked me, Jeremiah."

Jeremiah shook his head and pulled his hat over his eyes, then leaned into the seat again.

"Who all knows about you and Luke?" I asked.

"You, Kristina, Trudy, Elias, Sheriff Hawkins, and Daisy." He frowned at the confused looking woman sitting beside me. "Kind of. Needless to say, you can't be talking to anyone else about us. The men who tried to hang us were Hell Hunters who'd got wind of what we are, and they ain't the only ones out there. It's best if this secret stays just that—a secret."

"I'll keep it safe," I promised, and I would. I'd do anything to keep him and my new family from harm.

When we pulled into town, Jeremiah dropped us off at Trudy's house to see if she was up to eating with us. Daisy scurried off to slip into a new dress and redo her hair before she was seen in public.

"I'm going to put in our order for the stove." Jeremiah jerked his head toward the general store. "Holler if you need me. I'll hear you," he said with a devastating smile.

He kissed me softly, and a soft rumble left him as I nibbled his bottom lip. That sound was important to what made him my Jeremiah, and I rested a palm on his chest just to feel the vibration of his wolf. He eased back with a grin, and with a quick glance around, he leaned against my neck and grazed his teeth against the tender skin there. The man knew all of the right places with me, and I swayed toward him.

"Hurry back," I whispered.

Tipping his hat, he turned and strode away with those long, lean legs. His spurs jangled with every step, and I watched as he gracefully loped across the street. That fine man had finally let me in. Now, he felt like he was mine in every way.

The time it took for Trudy to answer the door plastered a worried look directly onto Kristina's face. When Trudy saw who'd come callin' she looked happy but still exhausted, and she was waddling when she walked back to her small bedroom.

"I know I have well over a month left but this baby is taking everything I have. I can't seem to get enough sleep and I'm bigger than the broad side of a barn," Trudy fussed. "I had to quit working at Cotton's until I'm delivered because my feet swell up like watermelons if I'm on them too long." She relaxed onto her bed and propped her legs up on a pillow.

"Ugh, maybe I'm glad Luke doesn't want young 'uns after all," Kristina said while she fluffed Trudy's pillow. "I'm guessing a lunch date with three lovely ladies and a werewolf is off the table then?"

Trudy shot me a wry smile. "He finally told you?"

"Kind of. He didn't really have much choice about it."

"And what do you think?"

"I guess it makes a lot of things make sense, so I'm okay with it. It makes him able to survive all he's been through so I don't mind the wolf if he gives him those capabilities."

"Good girl. He's a good one and I should know. Werewolves ran wild where I'm from and some of them ain't such good men. The Dawson's are a different breed though. It helps that they were brought up in a strong family."

Kristina stopped biting her thumbnail and put her hand over the undulating swell of Trudy's belly. "He's moving today."

"Mmm hmmm. All day and all night. I'm starting to think he doesn't sleep." Trudy cast her gaze to me. "You want to feel?"

"You wouldn't mind?" I asked.

"Not at all."

I lay my palm gently on her stomach, but Kristina pulled it over to the side.

"Right here," she said. "He's got a knee or foot or something right here."

This was magic. It had to be. Trudy was creating a tiny human in her belly and he was moving and rolling contentedly inside of her. She cushioned and nurtured a piece of the man she loved the most. "Does it hurt?"

"No, it just feels like someone's poking me from my insides. I think I'll miss that feeling after I deliver."

A knock sounded at the door. "That'll be Daisy," I said. "We'd better get over to Cotton's to meet Jeremiah."

"I'm glad your men got back safe. I was mighty worried about them out there hunting those outlaws, and you girls out in the wilderness all alone."

I pulled my hand away from her stomach, and clasped them in my lap so she wouldn't see how badly I wanted to keep it there. "Between you and Elias, we're all plum spoiled on home-cooking we didn't have to make ourselves."

"It was the least we could do," Trudy said with a tired smile. "The world is short on good people, and we have to take care of the ones we can."

We said our goodbyes and walked with Daisy to the eatery. It was early for lunch still so we were able to find a nice big table to ourselves. By the time our food was ordered, Jeremiah strode in with his hat in his hand and a contented look upon his face.

He'd gone unshaven for the better part of two weeks now, and I couldn't help my want to touch the dark scruff on his face. "You look like a mountaineer."

"I feel like one right about now," he said with a glint in his eye. "We'll have to go down to the creek when we get back and fix that."

My easy blushes used to be a source of constant embarrassment at parties, but here in this country eatery, surrounded by dear friends and under the loving gaze of a husband who so obviously enjoyed bringing heat to my cheeks, I couldn't say I hated the fire that crept up my neck anymore. The things that used to humiliate me didn't seem important anymore. I'd changed during my short time in Colorado Springs. I'd found myself.

Before we left town, Kristina and I mailed off our letters to our mothers. I'd read and reread mine on the way here, but though so much had changed since I'd written it, it was all information I couldn't share with Mother and Father.

My husband's supernatural family tree was my secret to keep now.

If Mother and Father ever decided to visit, they'd see a drastic change in my mannerisms, my speech, and even the way I carried myself, looked and dressed. I honestly didn't know what they would think of these changes, but I liked them and it was high time I was comfortable in the skin I was given.

The coming days were a trial of Kristina's thinning patience. Jeremiah worked tirelessly on her house and had it very nearly finished by the time he froze in that uncanny way of his. He balanced on the frame of the roof and watched the road like a predator. And then slowly, a sly smile came over his lips and he called out to Kristina.

She flew out of the barn like her shoes had been lit on fire and was half way up the road when Luke finally appeared. There was no hesitation. He jumped from his horse and scooped her up. "Need the barn for a bit," he said with a green-eyed wink at Jeremiah as they disappeared inside.

I laughed and shook my head, then turned to my husband, my mate. We were finally whole again.

Jeremiah jumped from the roof and landed lightly in front of me. No longer did he try to hide his nature. I never wanted him to again.

"It'll be best if we give them some room. Trust me."

"I do trust you."

"Mmm, didn't your mother ever tell you not to trust a werewolf?"

"She skipped over the scary legends, I'm afraid."

He growled and pulled me against him. "So, now I'm scary, huh?"

I tugged his hand gently in the direction of our house, determined to show him how very un-scary I found him.

Our home now had glass paned windows, and the old rocker on the front porch. Jeremiah had offered to paint the chair, but I liked it the way it was. The scorch marks up the legs were a testament to what they'd been through; to what we were still working through. He planned on whitewashing the house with some of the money that was tucked into Luke's saddlebags and if I was a betting woman, I'd wager Kristina's house would get the same treatment with little argument from her husband. Our house lacked furniture but it didn't bother me like it would've the old me—the Boston me. I knew we'd build it up the way we liked someday. For now, I was content to have a roof over my head and warm furs to lay in with my husband at nights.

It was those very furs I was leading Jeremiah to now. It was hard to deny our wanting skin after the separation we'd been through. Whenever we could, we found time to enjoy the intimacy that a strong marriage could create. And there, tangled up in furs and skin was where Jeremiah relieved himself of all of his secrets.

He told me of the daughters who would die at my breast within of few hours of life. He told me of the sons who would survive and turn into wolves near their sixteenth birthdays. He told me of his mother's struggles and the loss she'd endured to raise three healthy boys, and he told me it would be my burden to bear if I chose to give him children.

I was sad and scared at the chasm of loss I faced, but looking into the depths of roiling emotion that swam in Jeremiah's eyes, I couldn't help but want to give him the family he desired. He'd never ask it of me, but it was the greatest gift I could give him. I kissed him gently until we both felt whole and strong again.

My life wouldn't ever be mistaken for an easy one.

There would be ups and downs, and great hardships along the way. We would have to fight to be safe, and keep our family together, but it would all be worth it.

We'd be happy, my wolf and I.

Epilogue
Jeremiah

"Hup!" I called to the mule we'd borrowed from Elias to plant the crops. He was a stubborn beast, but strong as an ox and he liked to move. Even from the front acreage I could hear Lorelei and Kristina talking and laughing as they prepared the vegetable garden for planting, and from the smirk on Luke's face, he likely could too. Kristina was giving Lorelei more pointers to keep me happy under the furs, and I couldn't say I hated the ideas that were being thrown around. It seemed Delaney had been wrong when he'd claimed I'd never get my cock sucked by Lorelei.

The weather had warmed considerably in the first month of spring. The ground was soft enough to plow and between two werewolves with strong backs and work ethics, we'd get the wheat fields done by tomorrow. We'd put the seeds down in a few more days when Luke and his sense for weather decided the clouds weren't going to open up on us and plop down a late season blizzard.

The big house now boasted actual furniture thanks to the money we'd made from the bounties. To my surprise, my proper lady had expressed her like for my hand carved furniture over most of the items she could order in a catalogue, so I'd keep obliging and surprising her with new pieces until our home was fully decorated. Our homestead now contained exactly two whitewashed homes with their own front porches for us to enjoy the cool evenings wrapped in a blanket. Luke and Kristina ate with us most evenings but we tended to switch back and forth between houses based on who had the foods they were craving at the time.

Lorelei had had some strange cravings as of late.

Luke heard it first and jerked his head toward the road that bordered the field we were working. Elias drove his buggy like he was racing some invisible team and a thin trail of dust followed him.

"Whoa," I said with a frown. I waved as he slowed his horses. "You come to collect your mule back already?"

Barely checked excitement drenched his voice. "Trudy's having the baby. She says she's certain this time."

Luke was already unhitching his horse from the plow. "Let us get the animals back to the barn. Go tell the girls it's time. They're up in the garden near the little house."

Elias drove away without another word and as soon as I had the harness free, I hopped up on the balking mule's back and kicked him in the direction of the barn.

Thanks to the still extreme prejudice that seemed to befall freedmen and women, not a single midwife around these parts was willing to deliver her baby. In light of that disturbing fact, Kristina and Lorelei had been pouring over a laboring book for the better part of a month. I swore they had it memorized between the two of them.

The house was a bustle of activity. When the mule was safe in the corral, I took the last bundle of clean clothes from Lorelei's hand and helped her into the back of the buggy with Kristina. She kissed me lightly gave me an excited look before Elias pulled out.

"We'll follow right behind with your horses," I called as Lorelei waved.

With our horses saddled and dragging the painted and spotted Indian ponies behind, we caught up to the flying buggy as it neared town.

The quite of the front room of Elias's house was a stark contrast to the chaos of the past two hours. Blood still pumped rapidly through my body and I fidgeted right along with him. Luke sat still and cool in the chair across the table with his hands clasped in front of his mouth.

"Does it make you nervous?" Luke asked me with a steady gaze.

"A little," I admitted. Try as I might not to, I could hear every single thing in that room. Someday, it would be me waiting on my own children's birth.

"Read it to me again," Trudy said through clenched teeth. Her voice was muffled by the door in between us, but it was plenty clear enough.

"Again?" Lorelei asked.

"Do it!"

Paper crumpled and Lorelei gathered a breath before she read.

Dearest Lorelei,
We were so worried when we couldn't find you anywhere in Boston. Your letter found us with great relief that you are alive and well. Your new husband sounds like a wonderful, honorable man and though your life sounds drastically different from the standards you were raised to appreciate here, you sound happy. We'd like to come visit someday and meet Jeremiah for ourselves and thank him for giving you such unexpected joy. Someday, I pray you learn for yourself that it's the most important thing a parent could wish for their child.
I have news of Daniel Delaney I thought you'd appreciate. He's married now and much returned to his old habits. He flaunts his mistresses in front of his young wife and her parents, very powerful people if you remember, are furious. The scandal he thought he would easily escape has indeed haunted him and affected his social invitations. He has taken to drinking and gambling and is quickly falling to ruin. Now, for the best part. Upon your letter, I went directly to the newspaper and had your wedding announcement printed that very week, and not two days after it ran did Daniel call on us. He asked how you were and if you were truly happy, all to which we said yes, and the poor dufus looked absolutely wretched about the whole thing.
I'm so proud of the way you handled that awful scandal. I knew we raised a proper and intelligent daughter and you've exceeded our expectations. You were right in choosing your own path and leaving Boston, and though your father and I miss you terribly, your life would have been limited here. I think you saw that and I commend your bravery for making a new name for yourself where you can lead a full and happy life with the love you deserve.
I don't even know him and already I'm proud to call Jeremiah my son-in-law.
We love you, we love you, our baby, our little wren.
-Mother and Father

The labor was long and Trudy was exhausted after hours of pushing but finally, finally, in the wee early hours of the morning, a tiny baby's cry rang out through the small house.

Elias jumped up and waited impatiently by the door. "Boy or girl?" he asked.

Kristina opened the door and held the crying bundle to Elias. "Healthy baby girl."

He inhaled deeply and stared in wide-eyed wonderment at his child. "Daddy's little girl," he whispered.

The child was beautiful. She had the rich caramel skin of her mother and steely blue eyes. Her hair had Trudy's texture but was lighter in color. Above the smells of blood and medicine and exhaustion, the child told of new life. Her mixed blood would limit her opportunities if she let it, just like my children didn't have much chance in the world if they didn't create it. They'd be all right because of the love of family though. I knew that with certainty. I'd seen it with my own parent's strength of will to give us a good life despite the challenges Luke and I were born with.

"Jeremiah!" Kristina yelled right before a loud thump sounded.

I bolted through the door to Trudy's bedroom. Lorelei lay beside the bed and Kristina was shaking her shoulders. In a rush of frantic movement, I was beside her. "What happened?" I asked, cradling Lorelei's head in my hands.

"I think it was all the blood that made her woozy," Kristina said with a significant look. "She fainted on us. Take her into the den and lay her on the sofa while I finish up with Trudy."

It took her a while, but eventually Lorelei came to. Her amber eyes fluttered and she winced as she lifted a hand to her forehead. "Bollocks, what did I do?"

Luke stood to my right and Kristina tapped her toe in a very *if-you-don't-tell-her-I-will* kind of fashion.

"You're going to have a baby," I said softly.

She gave a short laugh and waited, as if she thought I was teasing her. "I'm fairly sure I'll know I'm with child before you do."

I rubbed my hand over my face. "You've smelled different for weeks. Have you had your courses since you moved out here?"

Her eyes went wide. "I haven't bled but that's nothing new. I've always been irregular and I just always assumed it would be hard to get pregnant because Mother struggled with it for years and years. And her doctors always looked at me with pitied pouts and said I was built just like her." She sucked in a breath and said, "I'm rambling, aren't I?"

"It's okay." It was hard to control my smile at finally being able to say it out loud. "We're going to have a baby." I was already so protective over that little life growing inside of her.

"Why didn't you tell me?"

"I wanted you to figure it out and tell me however you liked."

"So you'd what...pretend to be surprised when I announced it?"

I frowned and grasped her cold hands in mine to warm them. "When you put it like that, it seems I may have played my hand all wrong."

She searched each of our faces. "Does everyone know but me?"

Kristina sat on the sofa next to her. "Luke picked up your scent when Jeremiah did and he tells me everything, so I've known too."

A slow smile stretched between them, and Lorelei's gaze collided with mine. "Are you sure?"

"I can hear the heartbeat." I strained my ears. "Bum-bum-bum-bum-bum," I said in a quick rhythm. It was much faster than the sound of hers.

Kristina kissed her on the cheek with a tearful smile, then swished back into the other room to tend to Trudy. Luke gripped my shoulder and shook it slowly before letting himself out the front door.

"Oh, Jeremiah." Every emotion surged into the depths of Lorelei's eyes. "What if it's a girl?"

I ran the pad of my thumb over her silken cheek. "Then we'll deal with that together." I leaned down and kissed her until I could taste the sweetness of her lips.

"Jeremiah," Luke said quietly from the doorway. He twitched his head and left the door ajar.

I squeezed Lorelei's hand. I didn't want to leave her right now, but something in Luke's tone said it was important. "I'll be right back."

We stood side by side on the porch, my brother and me, as the first purple streaks of the coming day brushed the horizon of our sleepy little town.

"Do you smell it?" he asked.

I took a long draw of air and filtered through a hundred scents until only one that meant anything remained. I'd known that scent since the day I was born and for as long as I lived, I'd never forget it. Luke's slow smile was contagious.

Gable was back—and he wasn't alone.

Want more Wolf Brides?

Read on for a sneak peek of the next book in the Wolf Brides series.

Dawson Bride

(Wolf Brides Series, Book 3)

By T. S. Joyce

DAWSON BRIDE
(Wolf Brides, Book 3)

Chapter One
Gable

Of all the smells on earth, blood was the most interesting, complicated, delicious scent in existence. It was trapped inside of every living mammal by paper thin skin. While it was probably the most prominent of all smells, such richness and bulk certainly didn't belong in the English countryside. It wasn't the genocide of bunnies or deer, or the slaughter of livestock. Each animal had a different signature in the sensitive lining of my nose. No, this type of richness only belonged to humans.

A lot of humans.

A fog had fallen over the woods, and while it wasn't uncommon where I roamed, it was uncomfortable. Mist dulled the senses. It shortened sight and dampened smells. Even forest sounds were muffled under the blanketing cloud cover. For all of its dimming qualities, still, it did nothing to mask all that blood.

The dark had come, and with it brought no stars or moon to illuminate the wooded land. Animals skittered to their burrows and nests, afraid of the preternatural silence that cloaked the trees. Even the wind had died down to nothing, stirring not a leaf and rattling not a branch. The air filled with tiny, frightened heart beats and they weren't from fear of myself. I was a part of these woods now.

A whine escaped my throat as I slunk toward the intoxicating smell. I wasn't a curious creature by nature but something was off, and some deep instinct pushed me further and further out of my territory.

My ears twitched and filled with the screams of women and the gunfire of men. Whatever was happening here in my woods was of hell's making. I couldn't untuck my tail from between my legs if I tried. The stench of gunpowder, fear, and violence hung in the air, and I paced frantically back and forth as a looming shape appeared through the mist.

Still, I was drawn closer.

I'd been a wolf for a long time but the man in me was still inside there somewhere. The shape was a castle, or as close to one as I'd ever come. Complete with sprawling trout pond in the middle of the entrance and acres of gardens, statues, and elaborate fountains. The road was cobbled for fine carriages, and the mansion boasted stonework from the finest architects. I sniffed again. I'd been mistaken. It wasn't a castle—it was a tomb.

I growled and shifted my weight from side to side. It was time to leave. I'd seen it. I knew what was happening inside. This wasn't my fight. I turned and froze at the soft whimper of a child. If I'd had a chance of escape at all, it had been stolen from me with the fear-filled sigh of that little boy.

Moments came and went in a life where decisions affected the path of destiny. No matter what happened next, my fate had been cemented with that cry here in the woods—the cry I couldn't turn away from and live with myself. I guess I'd die with myself instead.

Shrubs, roots, and night air rushed past as I raced for the side of the gargantuan manor.

My change from wolf to man wasn't agonizing like it was for my brothers. I'd mastered it long ago when I became more animal than human. In a burst of light and pain and cracking bones, my blood was encased in fragile human skin again. I didn't cry out or hunch over in pain. None of those things eased the burst of agony that rippled through my insides. Avoidance was a pointless waste of time and if the boy was going to live, time was a commodity I didn't have.

Front doors were for receiving guests and making a first impression. Back doors led to gardens and quiet getaways where barons and counts snuck kisses to their wives and mistresses. Side doors were for servants.

The knuckles and muscles of my fingers were frozen with disuse and the effort to grip the edge of the cracked door was staggering. I'd been an animal too long. If I was to be of any help to the boy, I'd have to loosen up and quick.

Inside, I was met by the servant's quarters and body after lifeless body decorated the floor. Women. The monsters shot unarmed women. A series of crashes upstairs let me know the hunters hadn't found their prey yet. I slid into a pair of servant's pants I found folded neatly on one of the small, lumpy beds. A large knife shone in the dancing candlelight of the kitchen and I gripped the handle. It wouldn't be much match for the loaded pistols of the men upstairs, but I had other advantages over them.

They were human, and I was not.

Plates of food and half-made pastries dotted the kitchen counters. Shards of fine porcelain lay shattered against the wooden floor boards. Through the door, a dining room lay in disrepair. I listened carefully for any signs of life from the bodies, but there were none. Their hunters had been thorough.

At the sound of a man's voice, muffled through the ceiling between us, I froze. "I think I've found our little chicken, boys," he said.

My heart sank and I bolted for the stairs. I'd made it up the first landing when the pepper of gunfire blasted through the house.

I was too late but it didn't matter. I'd already made up my mind. I'd kill them for what they'd done here tonight.

I'd kill them all.

About the Author

T.S. Joyce is devoted to bringing hot shifter romances to readers. Hungry alpha males are her calling card, and the wilder the men, the more she'll make them pour their hearts out. She werebear swears there'll be no swooning heroines in her books. It takes tough-as-nails women to handle her shifters.

Experienced at handling an alpha male of her own, she lives in a tiny town, outside of a tiny city, and devotes her life to writing big stories. Foodie, wolf whisperer, ninja, thief of tiny bottles of awesome smelling hotel shampoo, nap connoisseur, movie fanatic, and zombie slayer, and most of this bio is true.

Bear Shifters? Check
Smoldering Alpha Hotness? Double Check
Sexy Scenes? Fasten up your girdles, ladies and gents, it's gonna to be a wild ride.

For more information on T. S. Joyce's work, visit her website at www.tsjoycewrites.wordpress.com

Made in the USA
Lexington, KY
13 September 2017